Y

THE MIRACULOUS SWEETMAKERS:

THE FROST FAIR

THE MIRACULOUS SWEETMAKERS

THE FROST FAIR

NATASHA HASTINGS

HARPER

An Imprint of HarperCollinsPublishers

Library of Congress Control Number: 2022933378
ISBN 978-0-06-316127-6
Typography by Catherine Lee
22 23 24 25 26   PC/LSCH   10 9 8 7 6 5 4 3 2 1
❖
Originally published in Great Britain in 2022 by HarperCollins
Children's Books, a division of HarperCollins Publishers Ltd.

First US edition, 2022

For my mother, Alison

Contents

Voices in the Mist

"Thomasina!"

Arthur's voice whirled in the mist, calling her name from the street behind her. As always, she felt irritation flicker deep inside her chest.

"Stop running!" he yelled.

Thomasina sighed, her teeth tasting metallic against the cold. "You're too slow," she said, and she stopped to watch her twin stumble to find her. Snow had quilted the London landscape and fell around them now, catching the candlelight in the windows of Montgomery Street so the flecks sparkled. The apothecary's sign swung in the night wind, creaking above her head in the darkness. Laughter trickled from inns and taverns lining the backstreets beyond them. She wondered how late it was, and how cross their parents would be when they realized she and Arthur had sneaked out to play with the butcher's boys again.

"You need to keep up," she said as Arthur staggered toward her, his teeth chattering.

"I—I *can*," he panted.

Despite being an inch taller and a whole eight minutes older than Thomasina, Arthur was slighter than she was, with sloping shoulders just beginning to broaden. Now his red-robin cheeks were puffing, his dark hair was plastered against his porcelain forehead with sweat, and he was breathing in short, sharp gasps.

"Prove it," she said. "Race me home."

"Just—Just wait."

The wheeze they'd both been born with, which had always been much more severe for Thomasina, was hissing and groaning in his chest, which made her crosser for a reason she couldn't understand. She started walking up a side street.

"Come on," she called, her echoes bouncing off the bolted shops around them. "I'm not even running now. You scared of losing?"

Losing, the buildings taunted.

"N-No."

"Mother and Father will be wondering where we are," she moaned. "Come *on*, Arthur."

She started walking slightly faster again, gritting her teeth against the bitter chill.

"Please," Arthur wheezed behind her.

"Hurry up! I don't want us to get into trouble."

Something dangerous was stirring itself awake inside her: something she'd found increasingly difficult to suppress for months. Arthur was really puffing now. Despite this, she plunged on. The words inside her had been burning to be heard for years.

"Just try," she said. "I know I'm faster than you—I'm better at pretty much everything—but I'll let you win, just this once."

"I can't—"

The dangerous feeling within her yawned, flexing its claws.

"Even Father knows I'm better than you. I should be his apprentice instead of you."

Immediately, she regretted her words. Whipping around so the wind blistered her cheeks, she said, "I'm really sorry, Arthur. That was horrible. I was just trying to get you to— Arthur?"

Her brother was standing stock-still in the middle of the street. His face had drained of color except for the crimson of his open mouth, and his chest was working up and down like a sparrow's.

"Arthur?" she repeated, her voice faltering against the wind.

He slumped forward, and her world crashed apart.

Thomasina ran over to him and crouched down. She saw his hands glow pink with exertion in the cold as he panted on all fours. Arthur, her brother, his chest heaving. Arthur, her rival, unable to breathe. Arthur, her second self, his lips turning blue.

"What's happening?" she cried.

He couldn't speak but coughed instead. The tears that leaked from his eyes were swallowed by the snow beneath him.

"I'm—I'm going to get help," Thomasina said, stumbling to stand.

She didn't want to leave his side, but what else could she do? She scanned the silent street. The sprawling lanes making up this tiny corner of London weren't dominated by night trades, unlike other areas of the city or the streets they'd left behind, but there was a sleepy candle sputtering in the upstairs window of the apothecary's they'd just passed. She ran over, splinters piercing her skin as she banged on the door.

"Help!" she screamed.

The candle in the window was blown out. No footsteps

came. The inhabitants of these streets were used to late-night scuffles. In this neighborhood, it was common for people to look the other way when they heard strange noises at night.

Behind Thomasina, Arthur was wheezing even more than he'd been when she'd left his side, and she ran to him, feeling ice slice through her skirts as she rubbed his back.

"Arthur, I'm here." She gulped. "I'm here, and I'm going to get help—"

"Q-Quick," he whispered.

"Help!" she screamed again, her voice splitting itself apart.

Silence greeted her. She knew what she had to do.

"I need to find someone, Arthur," she whispered. "I'll be back soon."

She couldn't look at him. Her heart was beating so frantically she felt sick. Quickly turning, she ran to the streets beyond, her boots slicked in slush as she skidded around a corner, chest straining, and saw a lit window. Several people were laughing inside a tavern.

"My brother can't breathe!" Thomasina shouted. But in their drunken haze, the people inside were slow to stir, and most of them just sat, unmoving, in their seats. She couldn't wait for them; she was worried that if she did, it would be too late to reach Arthur in time. She ran as fast as she could back to him, tears nearly blinding her as she hurtled through the snow.

When she dropped to her knees in front of him, she saw her brother's face had turned blue.

A couple of men hurried to catch her up. She heard them gasp when they saw Arthur.

"The boy—"

"Good grief—"

"The Burgess kid—"

"Arthur," she whispered, so harshly she heard her voice tear in pieces. "Talk to me."

Hands shaking, she ripped apart the layers surrounding him—the cloak from around his neck and the collar from his shirt—but she knew this wasn't enough as he shuddered.

"Arthur." Thomasina gulped. "Arthur!"

She looked at the person she loved most in the world as his cold fingers trembled on her own, and she knew her brother was beyond words now.

"Just hold on a bit longer—you'll be all right, Arthur, I know it . . ." she said, but the rest of her words died in her throat.

Arthur collapsed onto the snow, where he lay still, his face turned toward her. Motionless, his closed eyes glimmered out their final tears as the wind sang and danced around them.

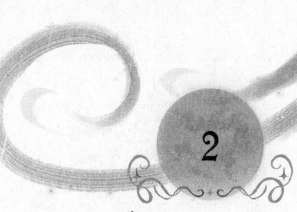

The Frozen River

FOUR YEARS LATER

The Great Frost! It snaked down necks, sliced through bones, and made all the knees in London quiver. Ice and snow crept into every inch of the city it could find, transforming the colors of its brickwork from tawny brown and faded red to startling silver and piercing white. Every night, a hush would descend upon London as fresh snow fell, muffling squeaking mice, forcing thin foxes underground, and freezing birds to the trees they sheltered in. People grew used to waking up each morning with frost cobwebbing their cheeks, and they stopped being shocked that, even indoors, white mist would gush from their mouths every time they spoke, as if the cold had changed them all into different creatures entirely.

South of the Thames, in Southwark, the Great Frost clenched everyone in its ice-scaled grip. The streets were crammed with ice-bitten workers who couldn't afford to cross the river and live in the heart of the capital, and there were more shops and street sellers here than anywhere else. Butchers, bakers, and candlestick makers carried on with business as usual, cursing the fierce winter winds. Weavers, palm readers, hatters, and needle makers sat hunched in pain, and numb-fingered musicians played on as people hurried past them to get out of the cold.

In Raven Lane, a shabby street, nestled a ramshackle shop bearing a faded name:

BURGESS & SON'S, SWEETMAKERS

This street looked different from how it had appeared four years ago when Arthur died and Thomasina's world changed forever. A fire had destroyed parts of Southwark some years before, and new buildings kept rising from its dove-gray ashes. However, that was nothing compared to the transformation that had taken place in the Burgess household.

In a narrow workroom behind the shop, Thomasina was busy making gingerbread with hands so callused and coarse they looked strange belonging to someone aged only thirteen. Ever since Arthur's death, she, instead of Mother and Father, had become responsible for making the sweets, running the household, and keeping everything spick-and-span. This room was where she spent most of her time.

Swirling sugar flecks sparkled in the pale morning light,

and the fragrance of cinnamon and warm, flaked almonds sweetened the air. Thomasina never grew tired of this smell, despite making gingerbread day in and day out during the dark winter months. It reminded her so much of Arthur: they both used to spend hours every day making gingerbread side by side when he'd been alive.

As always, though he was gone, his voice whispered in her mind, a high, sweet sound that always made it seem like he was holding back a giggle.

You're making the gingerbread wrong.

"No I'm not," she muttered.

You are. Father says to put the almonds in before the cinnamon.

"Why do you always have to be right?" she said, turning with a grin to flick flour at her twin, before remembering he wasn't there. She turned back again, feeling a tiny clench in her heart.

A stamp of boots sounded on the stairs, and Thomasina tensed as Father strode in. Short and broad-shouldered, with a sandy complexion like Thomasina, his impatient gray eyes roved around the room. Lips pursing when he saw his daughter, he walked toward the shop in the next room without saying hello. He'd been like this ever since losing his son.

"Good morning to you, too," Thomasina huffed under her breath.

With a sigh, she put down the gingerbread she was

making, washed her hands, then grabbed a hunk of bread and carried it upstairs on a plate. The floorboards creaked as she hesitated outside the room at the top of the house. Then she opened the door with her foot.

"Mmph."

She interpreted this as a greeting from the figure on the bed. Although weak sunlight tried to peer through the cracks in the shutters of her and Mother's tiny bedroom, it was even dimmer up here than in the workroom. The shutters themselves were strapped together with knotted twine and faded ribbons, protecting Mother from the howling winter wind, the curling ivy creeping up the front of Burgess & Son's, and the hustle and bustle of the world outside. A sputtering candle was balanced on a small trunk at the end of the bed they shared, illuminating the delicate stitching of the patterned patchwork quilt Mother had made before she'd withdrawn to her room four years ago because of grief.

Mother was buried in a mess of blankets as usual, her eyes closed to the world. The gray hair that escaped from her nightcap trickled down her long pink neck in rivulets.

"I've brought you some breakfast," Thomasina said. She tried to sound encouraging, but there wasn't much to feel optimistic about. Mother seemed to feel the same and didn't reply.

Thomasina helped her mother sit up and broke the bread

into smaller pieces. Sitting on the edge of the bed, she watched the older woman's eyelids trembling in the half-light, and she knew that thoughts were flitting in and out of her mind like butterflies.

"Do you feel like speaking today?" she asked, already knowing the answer. "Or opening your eyes?"

Mother chewed the bread that Thomasina handed her. The girl's insides churned as she wiped crumbs and spit from Mother's mouth and chin. After a few minutes, it was done, and when Thomasina closed the door, there was no sound from the room she'd left.

Is she still unwell? came Arthur's voice again.

"Yes," Thomasina muttered.

As she trod downstairs, she heard Father call her name. Frowning, she walked through from the workroom and was astounded to find a small crowd of people in the Burgess & Son's shop. Cheap tallow candles soured the dingy room, illuminating the faces of some of their neighbors. Thomasina recognized the thin face of the local undertaker, saw an errand boy, cap in hand, his eyes shining, and noticed the tired gaze of a washerwoman, her hands red-raw from scrubbing. There was such a clamor as they all spoke over each other that at first it was difficult to understand what was being said.

"I've heard it's frozen over completely—"

"Several inches deep—some are going to try and walk on it."

"And I saw a magical goat!"

"No you didn't, Ethel."

Father beckoned Thomasina over.

"There are rumors the River Thames iced over last night," he said with a shiver. "Enough for people to stand on this time, because of the Great Frost—not like in other winters. Go and see it for yourself, then come back and tell me if the gossip is true. I'm too busy here." He gestured toward the people around him.

Excitement fluttering in her stomach, Thomasina grabbed her cloak and opened the door to the street, hearing the bell clang above. Could what the people were saying be true?

A gust of cold air smacked her around the face as she stepped outside. Frost encrusted all the shop signs so completely it was impossible to make out what was drawn on them, and long icicles stretched down from them like spears. Every surface appeared to be covered in snow, several inches thick, and icy sludge congealed on the cobblestones where people had already trodden that day.

As Thomasina made her way down the street, smoke spiraled from the baker's opposite Burgess & Son's, where plump loaves were waiting to be scooped into baskets. Picking her way across, she avoided the scraps of cast-off hides and guts that had spilled out of the nearby tannery and were strewn across the cobblestones, slimed in muck and snow. Bedraggled dogs chained outside various establishments sniffed at bones and empty tankards as she passed.

"Thomasina!"

Heart sinking, she saw a well-known figure in the neighborhood hurrying toward her: a red-faced old woman carrying a basket, hands trembling in the cold.

"Need any parsnips, dear?" said Miss Maplethorpe.

"Sorry, Miss Maplethorpe," Thomasina said, backing away from her. "We haven't finished the sack I bought from you last week."

"Oh, go on, have a little parsnip—"

Thomasina scanned her surroundings and saw a crowd of well-dressed people she didn't recognize walking in the direction of the river.

"Fresh, beautiful parsnips, lovely and big—nice and firm—"

"Good," Thomasina said distractedly. "Maybe another time?"

Crossing the street to escape Miss Maplethorpe, she glimpsed two of the butcher's sons, their aprons stained with blood, and walked behind them to catch scraps of conversation.

"It's all iced up now, that's what I've heard."

"I don't believe it—"

"The best parsnips in all the land—"

Thomasina looked over her shoulder to see Miss Maplethorpe hurrying after her with what she thought was surprising speed for someone her age. Thomasina ducked into a side street.

Shouts echoed nearby, accompanied by the sound of people stamping their feet in the cold. Straining to hear where the noise was coming from, Thomasina turned a corner and saw the street ahead filling with shivering people all walking in the same direction, toward the Thames. She pushed in among them, rubbing her hands, which were already starting to sting. Being smaller than most of the crowd, she couldn't see much over their heads, so she allowed herself to be swept down a lane as everyone crunched forward on the snow, a mass of blue and mud-brown cloaks.

"God's bones!"

"It's a miracle."

"PARSNIPS!"

The shouts came from the folk up ahead. Thomasina squeezed her way through the throng, working her way up to the front, where the city met open space—and she gasped.

The monstrous bulk that glistened black at night, gray in winter, and brown in summer—the beast that had always forced itself through London—was an expanse of crystallized white, glinting in the sunshine.

The River Thames had frozen to death in its sleep.

3

A Curious Stranger

People around Thomasina pushed and shoved, jostling to glimpse the best view. Through the surging crowd, Thomasina took in the frozen river.

Scanning the scene before her, her breath caught in her throat as she spied a fleet of merchant ships in the distance, trapped in the frozen river like insects in white amber. The masts of the vessels stretched out along the ice glinted silver in the morning sun.

"Look!" a little girl beside her cried, jabbing a finger to her right. "Someone's going to stand on it!"

At the edge of the Thames, a group of people were egging each other on. One man blustered forward as his friends cheered, his rosy face shining with excitement. He held up a foot for all to see and placed it onto the frosted surface. Thomasina held her breath as the crowd whispered around her.

"The ice is holding!"

"Well, I never . . ."

After a few moments, the man's foot still hadn't pierced the river's crust. He positioned another foot on the ice, so it was taking his entire weight. It didn't crack. He placed one foot forward, then the other, then the first again, the ice squeaking in protest but never breaking. Everyone around Thomasina broke into cheers, and the man grinned, his face growing ruddier than ever.

"It looks amazing," Thomasina whispered to Arthur.

I wish I could see it, she imagined him murmuring back. Her heart ached when she pictured him alive again, red-robin cheeks stretching as he smiled at the scene. She felt an enormous guilt that she was witnessing this event instead of him, when *she'd* been the one who'd told him to keep running, not noticing his wheezing until it was too late.

She took a deep, steadying breath, trying to suppress her memories. In that moment, she realized she had no one to share her excitement with—not Mother, who hadn't spoken since Arthur died, nor Father, who wouldn't care to hear how magical the view before her was.

Now that the rosy-faced man had proven that they could

all walk on the river's surface, it was as if a spell had been broken. Emboldened bystanders elbowed each other to get closer to the ice, transfixed by the scene.

"It looks so magical," she heard someone whisper nearby.

Thomasina turned and caught the eye of a dark-eyed girl in a crimson cloak. The girl grinned at her, then looked away.

Someone stood on Thomasina's foot, and an argument erupted between two well-dressed gentlemen over who was taking up the other's space on the ice.

"I think you'll find, good sir, that *I* had the prior claim."

"And I think *you'll* find, good sir, that your nose looks like a turnip."

As onlookers surrounded the gentlemen, yelling "Fight! Fight! Fight!," Thomasina turned and hurried back to Raven Lane as quickly as she could without slipping in the slush around her, her mind buzzing with excitement. The streets were unnaturally bare now, with ghostly echoes of footprints in the snow.

When she arrived, she found the sweet shop was deserted—apart from Father, who was counting out the week's measly takings.

"Well?" he said, without looking up as the bell above the door clanged.

"It's true." She wheezed, loosening her cloak from

around her neck. "The river's frozen over completely. People are walking on it."

Father strode to the workroom, coming out moments later with his cloak, which he swung around his shoulders while walking to the door. He opened it and turned back to Thomasina.

"Mind the shop," he grunted. When he slammed the door shut behind him, the bell above was nearly wrenched off its hinges.

Father hadn't always been a man of few words. When Arthur was alive, Thomasina could remember Father talking to him endlessly about stocks and supplies while she, learning to darn clothes at Mother's knee, had strained her ears to listen. Father had treated Thomasina's interest in trade with amusement when she'd been younger. *You'll whip your husband into shape one day*, he'd tell her sometimes, ruffling her hair.

But as the years had crept on following Arthur's death, every time she'd asked to learn more about the shop, a frown had appeared on his face. It created a permanent groove in the center of his forehead, which deepened whenever he saw her. Any hopes Thomasina had fostered about taking over one day had been extinguished. Whenever she was asked to mind the shop for a precious hour or two, like now, she couldn't even pretend to herself that Burgess & Son's would one day be hers. It felt like an impossible dream.

There had been one other person she could talk to about her ambition, apart from Arthur, who'd always seemed to understand her at once—her mother. But now Mother had changed in every possible way, too, since Arthur's death.

Thomasina went to the workroom, bent down to the cupboard where their pots, plates, and knives were kept, and withdrew a battered, leather-bound book. It contained loose leaves and scraps of paper, and she had to clutch it to her chest to keep everything inside. She returned to the shop and opened the book on the counter.

She'd never seen anyone else's household book, so she couldn't make any comparison with certainty, yet she doubted that any other volume was as beautiful and as chaotic as Mother's. Her mother's book was crammed full of dark scrawls of handwriting that Thomasina couldn't decipher, but she knew they contained centuries of knowledge whispered among the women in her family. There were recipes for medicines and meals, as well as doodles Mother had drawn of fantastical creatures, rising from the depths of the hand-drawn seas around the place she'd grown up—*Ayrshire, Scotland.* Thomasina tasted Mother's vowels on her tongue.

"Remember when Mother used to read us stories from here?" she whispered to Arthur. "Before you—"

She broke off, twisting her mouth shut in a frown.

Although she'd been taught the basics of reading and writing, Thomasina had never been given the time to improve, so she stroked the curlicues that formed Mother's Ys and Gs, and looked at the monsters Mother had illustrated. On one page, there were six-legged sea cows and a hideous octopus. Here, fire-breathing birds with cruel, long beaks narrowed their eyes, while fish the size of the boats drawn next to them gaped at her. There, a kelpie, a horse of the sea with powerful hooves and wide, staring eyes, rose from inky waves. The person who'd scribbled and doodled away her time in this book was a force of nature, a world away from the woman upstairs. Whenever Thomasina felt upset or lonely, she'd turn to Mother's household book and try to conjure up in her mind the woman who'd once existed.

"Good day, miss."

Thomasina's head jerked up. She hadn't even heard the bell.

Standing in front of her was a man she'd never seen before. Middle-aged and slim, with ghostly white skin, he wore such peculiar clothing she deduced he must be very rich, as even the wealthiest traders didn't look like him. He wasn't wearing a wig, like other gentlemen she sometimes saw around London, but sported a blue hat, from which dangled a sweeping silver feather. His breeches were enormous, making his feet stick outward. A spindly white moustache curled above his mouth. His doublet was the most glorious thing about him: blue velvet and embroidered with silver stars.

"Morning," she said. "Can I help you, sir?"

"Yes—I mean, er, no. No. I was merely inspecting your charming shop. Delightful. Do you make everything yourself?" he asked.

"Yes," she said. "Everything's made daily." Her eyes strayed to some three-day-old apple cake nearby, and she moved to shield it from view. It wasn't *her* fault no one wanted to buy it. This gentleman must have gotten lost on his way to one of the smarter districts, where the more upmarket shops could be found.

"What's your name?" he said. "Are you a Burgess, of Burgess & Son's?"

"Yes," Thomasina replied. "Father's the owner. I'm just—just looking after the shop until he comes back."

"Ah," he said. "I see."

He looked at her in a peculiar, searching way, then said, as if to himself, "Good."

"Do you want to buy some apple cake?" Thomasina asked.

"Thank you, but no. I haven't any appetite. But it looks wonderful. Perhaps on some other occasion."

She nodded. The presence of this dapper man in the shop made her all too aware of the shabbiness of Burgess & Son's.

Looking around, she felt her stomach twist with shame. She saw through the stranger's eyes the grimy windows peeking from behind the ragged curtains, the sloping shelves made from pieces of driftwood she and Arthur had scavenged from the riverbank, and the jumble of knickknacks in the corner forming a pile of rubbish that Father refused to throw away.

As if hearing her thoughts, the man studied her face curiously for some time before saying, "I'm afraid I must be off. Good day to you."

The bell clanged behind him, leaving her bewildered.

"What an odd customer," she whispered to Arthur. "He didn't seem to want anything."

It occurred to her then that the man had sounded different from anyone she'd ever come across. His words were strange things, bent out of shape. Some of them slipped over each other, others stretched out in odd places, and some were oddly clipped. She couldn't place his accent, which frustrated her for a reason she didn't understand.

It was nightfall by the time Father came home, his face creased into itself with tiredness. He shrugged off his cloak and kicked off his boots before settling into his chair at the head of the workroom table.

"A few people are putting up stalls on the ice," he said, propping his feet by the fire.

Thomasina ladled parsnip stew into two bowls, then passed the larger one to him with a plate of hard cheese and bread. Father blew on the stew before slurping a spoonful, and tore off a corner of the bread with his teeth, like a dog devouring a bone.

"I'm going to pitch a tent next to them," he said. "We'll sell gingerbread to start with." He speared a hunk of cheese with the tip of his knife.

Thomasina swallowed a spoonful of stew.

"Who else is working on the river?" she said.

Father carried on chewing while he opened his mouth to speak, the deep lines of his face shifting from shadows cast by the fire.

"The baker down the road and his sons; the Cornish twins and their tavern, the Green-Eyed Mermaid; and a couple of stray milk sellers." He bit into the cheese. "No competition."

Thomasina nodded.

"You'd best feed your mother," he grunted, avoiding her gaze as he took another bite of bread. "I've got to look over our accounts."

As Thomasina carried her half-eaten stew and Mother's portion upstairs, she heard the door to the workroom thud shut. She fed Mother and combed her hair for her, then she watched while she fell asleep as darkness consumed the room.

The cold bit into her bones. She didn't want to sleep yet. When she did, Arthur would haunt her dreams, like he did every night, and she'd have to relive the painful memory of his death. She looked out of the crack in the shutters to the gloom of the street, and she stayed there staring even after all the candles had been blown out in the neighbors' windows and she'd heard Father clamber into bed on the floor below.

London had a way of changing character, like a giant face twisting itself into different expressions. In summer, when skies were blue and ribbon-clad people celebrated May Day, the city was friendly, watching over its smiling citizens as they danced around the maypole and decorated their houses with blossom. Now it felt like London had closed its eyes against everyone. She saw her reflection in a window opposite. The darker the street became, the clearer her reflection grew, revealing someone she no longer recognized—someone with long brown hair tucked behind her ears, a round, rosy face marked with purple shadows under her gray eyes, and a mouth drooping at the corners. Every day that passed, she wondered if her face looked less like Arthur's.

As she studied the image of herself, a flicker of movement caught her attention. A small light, stark blue like the undertips of fire, was traveling down her street.

Thomasina pressed an eye against the crack in the shutters, trying to see what was going on. As she watched, the blue light floated past her house, then traveled onward.

It must be witchcraft. There could be no other explanation. The thought made her very afraid, and she drew back, wanting to be close to Mother in a small, ancient way she hadn't felt since she was little. She climbed into bed beside Mother, reaching out a hand to touch the older woman's back. Though her heart hammered, she closed her eyes and tried to match Mother's deep breathing, willing herself to fall asleep, even if it meant Arthur would soon appear in her dreams.

Tap, tap, tap.

She opened her eyes and realized she wasn't dreaming.

Someone was at the door of Burgess & Son's, knocking to be let inside.

4

Inigo

Thomasina sat bolt upright in bed, too frightened to breathe. When she eventually did, white mist gushed from her mouth, as if she were a dragon drawn in Mother's household book. She didn't feel much like a dragon, though, with her shaking hands and racing heart.

Beside her, Mother showed no sign of waking. The blankets wrapped around her were rising and falling in a gentle rhythm, the patchwork quilt slipping toward the floor. Downstairs, Thomasina couldn't hear any movement from Father, either. Burgess & Son's was so quiet it could have been enchanted, bewitched by sleep itself.

Tap, tap, tap.

There were the knocks at the door again, though this time she thought they sounded muffled, as if someone were tapping at the door with a velvet-gloved hand. She looked at Mother again, who was turned away from her, facing the wall. If Thomasina woke her, things would be even worse, as she'd have to comfort her. If she disturbed Father, he'd be furious.

Who was knocking at their door? Were thieves raiding the neighborhood? Had the authorities come to call? Was Father in trouble?

Fingers trembling, she fastened her cloak. The thin wool did little to shield her from the bitter cold that sucked the breath from her as she left the warmth of the bed. Thomasina could see nothing except the pale moon creeping under the shutters, casting a narrow sliver of light between her and Mother. Her heart was beating so fast she thought she might be sick.

Tap, tap, tap.

Fumbling for a candle, she crept downstairs to the small workroom, wincing as she felt the cold from the flagstones seep into her knees. She held the candle to the embers of their dying fire, and the scent of tallow soured the dingy room.

Watching the little flame wobble in her hand, Thomasina was amazed she didn't rock the candle from its holder and spill fire down her front as she stumbled to the front door. The bones in her fingers felt like they were made of ice when she set the candle down.

"W-Who's there?" she said as quietly as she could.

There was no sound from the other side of the door. For a moment, Thomasina wondered if she should ask again. Her fingers clenched her cloak around her, and she shivered violently in the winter chill.

Open the door, Thomasina.

Shock twisted in her stomach. The voice was Arthur's. But it wasn't coming from inside her head this time. It was coming from outside.

"Arthur?" Thomasina gasped, staggering back. "What—?"

Open the door, Thomasina. Please. I need to show you something.

Thomasina took a few deep, shuddering breaths, feeling the icy air bite into her teeth. This was impossible! Her brother couldn't be on the other side of the door, in the street. He was dead! Could someone be playing a trick on her?

Please, Thomasina—please open the door.

Arthur's soft intonation and the precise way he rounded off his sentences, as if he always expected to be interrupted, were unmistakable. Surely no one could sound so much like her brother and not be him. Could they?

She needed to know who was speaking. Thomasina scrabbled to unbolt the front door, alert for any sounds of Father thundering downstairs or of Mother crying herself awake. When she opened it, the cold blasted through her, knocking her knees together.

No one was there. Only the empty street greeted her, the

cobblestones iced and sparkling in the moonlight.

"Arthur?" she said, gasping. A lead weight thudded into the pit of her stomach, and tears pricked her eyes. Despite knowing it was impossible, some part of her had been convinced she'd see her twin on the other side of the door.

Frowning, she looked up and down Raven Lane, listening for footsteps, but she couldn't hear any. Even if she'd somehow imagined Arthur's voice, she'd definitely seen that eerie blue light outside earlier, floating past her window. It could have been a lantern belonging to someone, now she thought about it, swinging in the night mist. But why would anybody be out tonight, in such cold weather?

Despite her fears about venturing out into the deathly chill, she had to know what was going on.

Thomasina shrugged her numb feet into boots, shut the door on the latch, and walked onto the cobblestones outside, slipping a little on the ice. It was only when she ventured farther that she caught sight of the tiny blue orb she'd seen earlier, floating near the corner where the street turned into another. She realized it wasn't a lantern.

It was a will-o'-the-wisp.

Mother had told her about them years ago, in the time when she used to tuck her and Arthur up at night with thrilling tales from Scotland. Will-o'-the-wisps were ghosts who stirred themselves awake after dusk had fallen, luring travelers to their doom.

But I'm not a traveler, Thomasina thought. *I just work in Father's shop.* Despite past warnings from Mother ringing in her ears, telling her to go back at once, she needed to know why she'd heard Arthur's voice.

She didn't seem to feel the cold anymore as she submerged herself into London's dark alleyways and backstreets. Nothing was more important now than following the will-o'-the-wisp's path. The entire city had been charmed into a deep sleep, just like her house had been, and she didn't see anyone as she walked: just the blue orb of light, floating on ahead.

Thomasina didn't know how long she'd been following the will-o'-the-wisp, but after some time she found herself in a clearing. The blue orb had now started to float above her. As it illuminated the empty space around her, she saw, with a thud deep inside her chest, that she'd walked to the center of the frozen River Thames. How she'd managed to do this without slipping on the ice was a mystery. Her surroundings were eerie when lit up by the will-o'-the-wisp's ghost-blue hue. Buildings shrouded in snow beckoned from the safety of the riverbank, but an aching gap stretched between her and them. While she stood there trying to work out how long it would take her to get back to the edge, Thomasina realized she wasn't alone.

A figure was walking toward her, wearing a hat adorned with a single, sweeping feather. A figure she recognized.

"What—?" Thomasina gasped, then realized she couldn't continue speaking. She hunched over, suddenly aware of the cold, wrapping her arms around herself as tightly as she could. Her teeth chattered so loudly they drowned out the whistling wind whirling about her. Whatever charm she'd been under when she'd followed the orb, a charm that had made her forget how cold it was, had clearly vanished. This was unbearable. She needed to go back inside at once.

Then a hand tapped her shoulder before she could shudder away. Heat coursed through her as if she were bundled up in the thickest of furs.

Thomasina looked up to see the man dressed in blue velvet she'd met earlier that day. His skin had a blue tinge to it now, and his small beard was spun with frost. He smiled.

"Good evening, Miss Burgess. Allow me to reveal my true self. My name's Inigo, and I'm at your service."

He bowed, extending one foot in an elegant point.

Thomasina stared at him.

"A thousand apologies for inviting you out into the cold," he continued. "I trust you're warmer now?"

She nodded, although her mind churned so much she couldn't speak.

"I'm glad you made it here without too much trouble."

His eyes twinkled, and Thomasina realized they were the same shade as the will-o'-the-wisp. She felt less scared than when he'd just been a shape walking toward her.

"Arthur's voice," she said, voice trembling. "I heard my brother speaking on the other side of the door just now."

"You did indeed," Inigo said.

"Was it you?"

"I conjured up his voice."

"How?"

Inigo smiled.

"Because I can perform magic."

Thomasina gasped. "You mean, you're a witch?" She staggered away, crossing her hands in front of her to ward off any evil, though she suspected it might be too late in the night to protect herself.

Inigo seemed not to have noticed her terror, and instead looked pained. "I prefer to be known as a conjurer," he replied. "The word 'witch' is rather . . . *pedestrian*, if you don't mind my saying so, Miss Burgess. My powers are of a higher order than mere potions or herb lore, despite"—he sniffed—"what my contemporaries may say."

"How do you know about Arthur?" Thomasina asked, her voice shaking. "And why did you use his voice tonight? Is this a joke to you?"

"It isn't a joke at all!" Inigo said, looking distressed. "Please, Miss Burgess, I assure you. It's just . . . well—"

"Well what?"

"Before I tell you," Inigo said, looking nervous, "you should know—not that I care, of course, what you think of me; I just wish for it to be known, more generally—that I'm not usually one to eavesdrop."

Thomasina raised an eyebrow.

"But, er—as it happens," Inigo continued, a silvery blush decorating his cheeks, "when everyone discovered the frozen river, I decided to explore. I haven't walked around London for decades." His eyes flickered across hers. "I found myself in a neighborhood I'd never visited before. In this neighborhood," he continued, "I couldn't help but overhear someone talking about a shopkeeper's young boy: someone called Arthur Burgess, aged only nine years old, who died several winters ago. His twin sister survived, they said. They also said it was a shame young Arthur hadn't lived to see the sight of the frozen river."

Thomasina took a sharp breath in, feeling the cold snake into her core.

"Who could have been saying that?" she said.

"I didn't catch the speaker's name. She was selling parsnips," the man answered, with an aggrieved expression, "and was most insistent about them, even when I tried to brush her off. I've never seen such indecent enthusiasm about a common garden vegetable."

An image of Miss Maplethorpe swam into Thomasina's mind.

"When I entered the shop where Arthur Burgess had once lived," Inigo continued, "I saw you and felt—well—perhaps I could help."

"How do you mean, help?" Thomasina said, the ache within her widening.

"Miss Burgess," Inigo said, "I can conjure your brother back from the dead."

Silence fell. All Thomasina could do was stare at him, her heart beating in a feverish rhythm. Eventually, she spoke.

"What?"

"If you want me to bring Arthur back to life, I can do it."

"How?"

"I can make the impossible possible," Inigo said, spreading his hands. "What better use for my powers is there than to help someone?"

"This is ridiculous," Thomasina said. "You can't—you're not—" She couldn't continue. Yet within her, something powerful was stretching itself awake. *What if he's telling the truth?*

What if he can *bring Arthur back?*

"If you're not lying," Thomasina said, "then conjure me something now."

"I'm happy to do this if it'll help me prove myself. What do you wish to appear?" Inigo asked.

Thomasina cast her mind around, then thought about the sea monster drawings she'd seen in Mother's household book. Conjuring up one of those would surely prove unmanageable for Inigo. And when he failed, she'd know he didn't have any powers, or at the very least was nowhere near as commanding as he'd made himself out to be.

"I want . . . I want to see a sea monster," she announced, then blushed. It felt ridiculous saying this aloud.

Inigo faltered.

"A . . . a sea monster?" he repeated.

"Yes," Thomasina said, placing her hands on her hips. "If you're not lying and you can bring Arthur back, I want to see a sea monster. A giant kelpie—one of those horses that live in the sea. I've—I've heard of them."

"Are you sure?" Inigo said. "It may be—er—quite terrifying."

"I don't care," she said, though her hammering heart told her otherwise.

"As you wish, Miss Burgess," Inigo said.

He clicked his fingers and the will-o'-the-wisp swooped

down, hovering inches above the river's frozen surface. Thomasina stared at it, then back at Inigo, seeing nothing. It was only when she looked at the ice below their feet that she saw it.

A dark shape was moving under the ice.

Thomasina gasped and took a step backward. The shadow seemed huge in size. She raised her head to find Inigo looking at her anxiously.

"Are you sure you want to see this sea monster?" he asked. "The one below us is rather frightful."

Thomasina swallowed.

"Yes. I need to see it."

Inigo's mouth tightened. He nodded and clicked his fingers.

At once, the ice to the side of them cracked and fell, creating a vast hole. A colossal silver horse emerged, eyes white and wild. Lurching from side to side, it whinnied in the wind. It looked almost exactly like the kelpie she'd seen in Mother's household book, as if one of her inky pictures had materialized—only this creature before her looked as if it were made entirely of ice. The kelpie had a curved back, large fins, and glittering silver scales. As it bellowed, the sight and sound of it were more fantastical and terrifying than anything she could have ever imagined.

Thomasina ran away, sliding over the ice and, once,

falling to her hands and knees, but she scrabbled up again, trying to ignore her bruised shins and the kelpie's monstrous calls.

"Miss Burgess!" Inigo shouted as she reached solid ground, the snow stinging her feet.

She refused to look back and wouldn't let herself see anything but the series of narrow roads and sludge ahead of her. Although it frightened her to be running through London at night, she was even more scared of what was behind her on the river. After what felt like hours, but only really took several minutes, she skidded around the corner onto Raven Lane.

Breathless and thanking the moon for lighting her way, giving her just enough of a gleam to make out the Burgess & Son's shop front, Thomasina pressed her hand on the front door, looking up and down the street for any signs she'd been followed. There were none. She crept inside and shut the door as quietly as she could, then bolted it. She was so absorbed in racing to the attic room she scarcely cared if Father had heard her clatter up the stairs. Still, she was glad to see Mother was fast asleep when she opened the door.

Thomasina crept to the window and peered through the crack in the shutters, prickling her nose on the twine fastening them closed.

The blue light had vanished. Bathed in silvery moonlight,

the street outside looked perfectly ordinary.

"It couldn't have happened," Thomasina muttered to herself. "It's impossible."

Legs shaking and chest wheezing, she removed her cloak and stumbled to the bed, grimacing at the biting cold. Climbing in next to Mother, she buried herself under the blankets, her palms sticky from running, and shut her eyes. Tomorrow was going to be a long day and she needed to sleep—but it was some hours later before she surrendered to it, and Arthur called her name in her dreams once more.

5

The Apothecary's Apprentice

The parson at St. Bartholomew's Church was a short, ferrety-looking man. His severe manner, as well as the monocle indenting an angry pink circle around his right eye, made him seem much older than he was. He enjoyed singling someone out in his congregation to terrify every Sunday, swishing his long black sleeves like an overgrown bat.

"Sinners!" he bellowed, spittle flying from his mouth and landing on the people in the front pew. Thomasina was thankful to be out of range. "Be afraid, for God has summoned this bitter frost because of your wicked ways. Yes, Miss Maplethorpe, *summoned*!"

Miss Maplethorpe gasped from where she was sitting in the front pew, and the sound echoed around the ancient, grime-streaked walls. It was evidently her turn to be spooked today, and she quaked under the parson's gaze, trembling as she held a threadbare handkerchief to her mouth.

"God's wrath," the parson announced, widening his eyes so much that his monocle was in danger of falling off, "will smite the evil."

Miss Maplethorpe swooned, clattering to the floor.

As members of the congregation surrounded Miss Maplethorpe, waving amber vials of smelling salts that stank of rotting eels, Thomasina shifted in her seat.

On any other Sunday, she would have been entertained by the scene before her and spooked by the parson's blood-curdling threats. But today her mind was elsewhere, reliving the odd, eerie events of the night before. Despite the strangeness of it all, she knew that what had transpired hadn't been a dream—a certainty that made her hands tremble so violently she dropped her prayer book. It had been real. She *knew* she'd seen a will-o'-the-wisp, and she recalled the otherworldly man, Inigo, strolling toward her, and her heartbeat quickened as she remembered the creature with iced-over eyes he'd conjured, the kelpie rising from the frozen river to greet her.

And Inigo had promised her he could bring Arthur back to life. In all her years listening to the parson's impassioned sermons at St. Bartholomew's Church, she'd never heard anything so terrifying and mystical as what she'd heard the night before on the frozen river.

Forget it, she told herself as her hands fumbled around on the ground to retrieve her prayer book. *You've got to stop thinking about last night. Arthur can't be brought back from the dead.* . . . Or could he? Her heart twisted at this thought, as if a knife had been wrenched through it.

Why can't we try? she imagined Arthur saying.

"Because," she whispered back, "it's impossible."

Everything that happened last night is impossible. But it still happened, though, didn't it? he replied.

"And so I say to you again: repent! Or you'll be sorry indeed!"

A man at the back of the church gave a rich, rasping snore, followed by a yelp of pain as his wife elbowed him awake. Despite her churning mind, Thomasina felt a chuckle bubble out of her, and she turned away so Father wouldn't notice.

After the service ended and Miss Maplethorpe had been revived, the congregation began filing out. Thomasina stood away from the door, watching Father speak with a well-dressed gentleman she didn't recognize. The stranger reminded her of a moldy apple: his skin was shriveled around the bones of his face, his eyes were glaring and strangely hollow. As they began trudging down the church path through the snow, she strained her ears to overhear their conversation.

"I don't think your help is needed," Father was saying,

"but I haven't got a clue what to do. . . ."

"All the same, tell me how your wife gets on over the next few weeks," the man said. "Madness in women is sadly all too common."

Distracted by his words, Thomasina stepped on a stray twig, which snapped under the heel of her worn boots. The stranger turned with a magnificent sweep of his cloak and narrowed his eyes at her.

"Eavesdropping, were you?" he sneered.

Beside him, Father shuffled his feet. She noticed now, with surprise, that he looked very tired indeed. His shoulders slumped over as he spoke, while his eyes, so red-rimmed they looked mauve, were drooping even more than usual.

"Thomasina, run along and start making six batches of gingerbread for tomorrow," he ordered, avoiding her eyes yet again. "You can get more spices from the apothecary on your way home if we're running out." He handed her a shilling, then turned back to the man. She hurried away, scowling at being dismissed.

Making her way homeward, Thomasina's heart hammered as she noticed peculiar figures in front of her. Two men were staring at the people still gathered near the church behind her, their expressions hungry, as if they hadn't eaten anything in a very long time. They looked unlike any of the people she'd ever seen before in her life. Both cloaked in gray, their skin and eyes were whiter than even the snow around them, and—she squinted—some kind of silvery pattern traced their faces, but she didn't want to get close enough to see what it was. She slipped from their sight and walked as fast as she could in the opposite direction, not knowing why they'd caused such panic to rise within her.

Despite her best efforts, thoughts of the previous night kept swirling in Thomasina's mind. Snow sneaked into the holes in her boots and stung her feet as she made her way to the apothecary's. She frowned when she got there and saw its front door was shut, then she reached out and prized a yellow twist of parchment from the frame. She couldn't decipher the tight scrawl written on it, so she banged on the door. A shutter opened overhead.

"Who is it?" the apothecary called. "Ah." He narrowed his eyes at her as she stepped back to view him better, noting an impressive tuft of white hair sprouting from his nose. "The sweetmaker's daughter." He didn't sound in good health or mood. Thomasina felt a prickle of irritation course through her. *She* was a sweetmaker, *too*.

"Are you closed today?" she called.

"What does it look like?" he snapped.

"Er," she said, "like you're closed."

"Ladies and gentlemen, boys and girls—Miss Burgess is

correct," the apothecary announced to an imaginary audience, his watery eyes wide in mock surprise. "Young lady, I'm suffering from an infection of the head," he continued. "You wouldn't understand my pain. The young never do." He broke into a hacking cough and blew his nose on a dirty handkerchief. Thomasina stepped farther away from the doorstep underneath him.

"You'd better go to Hawke's instead," he said with a sniff, wiping his nose. "In Montgomery Street. We shan't be open for"—he sneezed—"the foreseeable future. And as it's likely I'll die from this infernal illness, farewell forever."

With that, he snapped the shutters closed and she heard him stomp off.

Thomasina's insides clenched. She hadn't set foot on Montgomery Street for four years, because Arthur had died there. Today it seemed she had no choice, so she forced herself to keep walking.

Unbidden, Inigo's words from last night echoed in her mind. *I can conjure your brother back from the dead*, he'd told her. *If you want me to bring Arthur back to life, I can do it. I can make the impossible possible.*

The idea had seemed so ludicrous until she'd seen the kelpie rising from the water. As Thomasina turned right into Montgomery Street, the man's words grew more insistent. *Back from the dead . . . I can make the impossible possible . . .*

If anyone could bring her brother back to life, surely it was he?

Montgomery Street was a busy, bustling hive of activity, where street sellers thronged. Young men carrying wicker baskets full to bursting with jellied gooseberries accosted everyone who crossed their path, while sharp-eyed grandmothers offered up jagged, glittering amethysts, claiming they had magical healing properties. A couple of little girls murmured, "Spare a penny for a pretty ribbon, miss? Only a penny?" as Thomasina walked past.

Scanning the crowd before her, she made out a newly painted sign.

ELIJAH HAWKE, APOTHECARY

She felt dizzy and out of breath. Legs shaking, she paused to collect herself, feeling as if a bell were ringing in her ears. Amid the haze, she sensed a tall man in a gray cloak striding down the street, turning around to stare at her unblinkingly. Her insides froze with shock. It was one of the unearthly men with silvery skin and ice-white eyes she'd seen earlier. Anxious to get out of his path, she steeled herself and, swaying slightly, walked up to the front door of Hawke's.

The familiar smell of an apothecary's shop—a combination of damp moss, brine, and dried herbs—hit her nose. Hawke's interior was dimmed by feeble winter light, but expensive wax candles burned in the corners, their soft light illuminating the strange and wonderful sights within.

Instead of the driftwood-plank shelves in Burgess & Son's, gleaming walnut shelves adorned the walls of Hawke's from ceiling to floor, smelling sharply of strong polish. Treasures from many corners of the world were on display: inventive medicines shipped in from afar, stored in sleek emerald and azure bottles stacked on every shelf. As Thomasina drew nearer, she saw that parchment tags attached to the vials bore long Latin names scrawled in looping, violet ink. Thomasina sniffed a confusing array of scents that tossed and tumbled over each other: aniseed, rhubarb, sulfur, and wormwood.

Walking farther inside, she saw a small, smoking cauldron of chocolate bubbling in the fireplace, spirals of steam beckoning her to take a sip. Normally, Thomasina's mouth would have watered, but she was still feeling spooked after seeing the strange man in the street, on top of her thoughts of Arthur. Diagrams and printed remedies adorned the closed shutters, and spread across one of the walls at the back was a huge, peeling map of the world. On it, sea monsters, ships, and stars were lovingly painted in vibrant colors, charting navigations and constellations stretching to the ends of the earth and the heavens above.

Thomasina swayed where she stood, her head spinning. As she reached out a hand to steady herself against the wall, she looked up and noticed the yellow skull of a huge, fearsome creature suspended from the center of the high ceiling. Its mouth seemed to gape with surprise at its own death, and as she peered at its jagged teeth, the skull rocked slowly back and forth in the dim light.

"It's a shark jaw," a low voice murmured, making Thomasina jump. "My uncle bought it two years ago, from a merchant."

A girl walked out of the shadows, drying her wet hands on her apron. As the wax candles threw her face into focus, she was revealed as having black, curly hair tied back in a bun, brown skin, and wide, dark eyes. She looked to Thomasina to be about the same age as herself. Thomasina recognized her as the girl in the crimson cloak who'd spoken to her by the frozen River Thames the day before. Taller than Thomasina by several inches, she wore a deep-blue dress that shimmered as it caught the light at every turn.

"How can I help?" Thomasina heard her say, but she couldn't respond. Her world was swirling in a churning, relentless rhythm, the barrels and jars on the shelves around her floating in and out of focus. All she could think about was Inigo and Arthur, and the kelpie from the Thames, and how she must fight the madness rising within her—

She opened her eyes. A high-backed chair was pressing into her hips, the hard edges of her stays biting into her skin.

The eyes in front of her sparkled.

"You fainted," the girl said. "Here. Drink up."

A warm cup was pressed against Thomasina's lips. The drink tasted sweet and thick, with a peppery kick.

"Thanks," she said with a gasp, wiping her mouth with the back of her hand. "How much?" Dread throbbed in her stomach at having to pay for something she couldn't afford. The shop's interior looked far more expensive than the apothecary Father usually used. Nowhere else she knew of had a shark's skull hanging from its ceiling.

The girl shook her head. "On the house." She grinned, her teeth flashing pearly white in the candlelight.

Shame was burning in Thomasina's insides at having just fainted. She grasped the sides of the chair and pushed herself up onto her feet.

"I've, er—c-come for some dried ginger," she said in a trembling voice, wishing she could run away. "Two bags of it, please."

The girl frowned slightly, but she walked over to one of the wide barrels at the front of the counter, scooping up several knobbly brown roots. A peppery tang sweetened the air as she twisted the tops of cloth bags together.

With clammy hands, Thomasina fumbled for her purse, then placed a shilling on the counter.

The girl swept the coin into her palm, tilting her head with professional interest.

"Have you always had that wheeze?" she asked.

Thomasina felt herself flush still more. It was so difficult not to see Arthur, lying in the snow, unable to breathe. . . .

"Yes," she said, forcing herself to remain in the present.

"What do you take for it?" the girl asked.

"Nothing," Thomasina said. "Sometimes I boil some water and hold my head over it. That seems to help a bit."

"I'm not a physician," the girl said, "but you sound asthmatic. We see plenty of asthmatics in the shop, especially around winter. You wouldn't believe some of the people who come in here, though. Yesterday, someone told me they'd seen a magical goat." She rolled her eyes. "These herbs"— she indicated a bunch hanging behind her—"they help open up the throat."

She picked off some stems and laid them in front of Thomasina, who shook her head.

"Sorry," she said. "I believe you, but I—I can't afford them."

The girl smiled.

"On the house again," she said. "They're cheap, anyway."

She refused to take them back, even when Thomasina pushed them toward her, instead folding her arms across her chest. Thomasina had no choice but to accept.

"I think I saw you yesterday," the girl said. "When

everyone discovered the River Thames had frozen over."

"Yes," Thomasina said. "I remember you—you were wearing a crimson cloak."

The girl grinned again.

"I'm Anne Hawke," she said. "What's your name?"

"Thomasina. Thomasina Burgess. I—I mean, Father runs a sweet shop a few streets from here. It's called Burgess & Son's."

"I see," Anne said. "My uncle and I moved here"—she broke off, gesturing around the shop—"over the summer. The rest of my family are hatters in Spitalfields. My great-great-aunts established a hat business together, but Uncle wanted to train someone in the family to follow him. There are lots of trades over in Spitalfields—it's very competitive. I'm his apprentice here, for now. But one day I'm going to have my own business, just like my aunts with their hat shop."

"What kind of business?"

"Some kind of apothecary shop. I'm not sure yet."

Thomasina was struck by how Anne Hawke spoke with all the confidence and authority of a grown man.

"Boil the herbs," Anne said, looking back down at the herbs on the counter, "then stick your head over them and breathe in."

"I will," Thomasina said.

"Is there anything else?" Anne said.

It was on the tip of Thomasina's tongue to ask Anne about her strange dream of Inigo and the kelpie, to see if she could recommend a cure, but who wouldn't hear such a story and think her anything but mad? Instead, she thanked Anne again and walked out of Hawke's, dazed.

Are other girls in London as confident and clever as Anne? she wondered as she trudged home through a fresh layer of crunchy snow.

As she turned into her street, Thomasina frowned as she saw a silhouette outlined by an amber light flickering around the shop's shutters. Burgess & Son's was closed on Sundays, so why did it look like someone was waiting inside? Whoever it was seemed spindly and slight compared to Father, but maybe it was just a trick of the light.

As she drew closer, however, and opened the door, she realized someone was indeed in the shop—someone she recognized quite well.

"You!" she gasped, a cold trickle of sweat snaking down her spine. Too late she realized that what had happened last night wasn't over in the slightest.

6

A Silver Snowflake

Inigo beamed, his blue eyes twinkling as he gazed at her, his feathered hat askew.

"Good day, Miss Burgess," he said, voice bell-bright, before bowing so low the tip of his nose grazed the knee of his velvet breeches.

"What are you doing here?" Thomasina cried. Looking wildly around, she wrenched a small stool from Father's clutter in the corner and held it in front of her, sending a couple of faded knucklebones, a battered buckle, and a lump of moldy bootlaces cascading to the floor. A pair of bats, disturbed from their roost within the jumble, made indignant clicking noises as they swooped out the door into the afternoon sky, until they were just a couple of dark shadows dancing against the sun.

"Miss Burgess," Inigo said. "I mean you no harm."

"You've got a funny way of showing it," she said. "Sending a will-o'-the-wisp to my door, leading me off into the night, and conjuring up a kelpie!"

Inigo shrugged. "I fear," he said, "we may have started off on the wrong foot."

Thomasina gaped. "You think?"

"Well—yes," Inigo gabbled. "Not that I meant us to, though!" he exclaimed as she raised the stool higher, preparing to throw it at him if needed. "I came here to apologize."

"Apologize?" Thomasina snapped. "You conjured up a monster—you made me walk out into the cold in the middle of the night!"

"I hate to correct you while you're—er—equipped with such an adequate weapon," Inigo said, sidestepping the stool in an elegant gavotte as she raised it higher. "However, you did decide to come to the river yourself."

"Only after that thing you sent knocked on my door and talked to me in Arthur's voice!" she retorted.

"Well, yes, but still . . . you chose to come."

In soft daylight, Inigo looked different from the night before. Crow's feet were more deeply embedded around his eyes than she'd remembered. He seemed shorter somehow than the day before. No longer spun with frost and icicles, his beard was as straggly and gray as Mother's hair.

"Please don't worry, Miss Burgess," he said. "I've only

come to apologize for scaring you last night and assure you I won't disturb you again."

Thomasina glared at him from behind the stool, trying to look as dignified as possible.

"It was probably a silly idea to send the will-o'-the-wisp in the middle of the night," Inigo continued, "but I didn't know how else to get you alone on the River Thames. And the kelpie? I'm sorry for her, too. I should have known she was too frightening a beast to conjure. Amelia's been banished."

"*Amelia?*"

"The name of the beast."

"She's got a name?"

"Yes. I thought it might be quite nice for her to have one. It's important to have *standards*, you know." His hands fluttered against his velvet doublet, the starlike embroidery gleaming in the gathering dusk. His skin was blue-tinged, with snow-white fingernails. "I'll go now," he added. "You'll never see me again."

He extended a closed fist, screwing up his eyes so his crow's feet were even more pronounced, and chanted something strange and lyrical under his breath. It was in a language Thomasina had never heard before, but it sounded like smoke and salt water, reminding her of the River Thames. Relaxing his grip, he revealed a delicate, glittering chain, so fine it could have been spun from a single cobweb. Dangling on the end of it was a silver-bright snowflake pendant, the size of a fingernail.

"Please accept this peace offering," he said. "I bid you farewell."

He'd turned to exit the shop when Thomasina said suddenly, "Wait."

Inigo paused, then turned back to face her. In the gloom of the shop, his eyes were now wary, flickering between hers. For the first time since she'd met him, he looked unsure of himself.

Thomasina licked her lips, which were very dry. Slowly, she lowered the stool, then sat on it, feeling it wobble on its uneven legs beneath her.

She'd been struggling to marshal her thoughts ever since she'd entered the shop and found him there, but now she felt a golden, shimmering hope spreading like an ink spill within her chest. Inigo wasn't a figment of her imagination. She wasn't going mad. He was in front of her. She'd indeed seen a giant kelpie last night—and now Inigo had conjured up a beautiful, magical necklace out of thin air. She had to ask him. She just had to—

"Last night," she said, "you told me you can bring my brother back to life."

"Correct."

"How's that possible?"

Inigo smiled, his eyes glittering with a strange, silver mist.

"I've been dormant for decades, Miss Burgess. My powers take a long time to cultivate, and now the Great Frost is here—a winter colder than any before—I find that within myself, my powers are strong once more. Stronger perhaps than ever before. You saw I conjured up the kelpie. I believe I could do the same with your brother, but—given time, of course—I'd do the job properly. Arthur, when resurrected, would be as real as you are, and wouldn't be formed of ice, like Amelia last night."

The hairs on the back of Thomasina's neck stood up. What could he mean, that he'd been "dormant for decades"? There wasn't time to ask. She frowned, her heart starting to give quick, faltering thuds, rattling against her rib cage like a bird.

"You could be using your powers to help anyone," she said. "Why me?"

Inigo slid his eyes away from hers.

"Why *not* you?" he said smoothly. "My powers are useless unless I help someone. It was simply by chance I heard the irritating woman selling vegetables speak of Arthur—it was chance I managed to find you—and I thought I could help. That's all."

"And you're not lying to me?" Thomasina asked, her heart pounding more than ever.

"I swear on my honor," Inigo said. "Now, if you'll excuse me . . ."

He made to turn away again.

"I want you to do it." The words slipped out of Thomasina's mouth before she'd registered speaking them. "Bring Arthur back from the dead for me, I mean. Please," she added, knowing manners cost nothing.

Inigo turned back and looked at her.

"Really?"

"Yes." Thomasina felt her hands tremble against the stool, one of its spindly legs in danger of falling off from being rocked so much. "Now—now that I've seen you conjure things. I don't know how else the kelpie could have appeared. Or the necklace."

Inigo blinked, then a smile appeared on his face, making his bright blue eyes twinkle.

"I don't know what to say, Miss Burgess. I'd be happy to help you—delighted, even—but you must understand something."

"What?"

"If I bring your brother back to life, this will come at a price."

Even though she'd been born and raised a tradesman's daughter, Thomasina's mouth fell open in surprise. She should have realized there'd be a catch.

"A price?" she whispered, gripping the stool still more tightly and feeling a splinter slice into her thumb. "What kind of price? I don't have money—we're not a rich family. . . ."

"Oh no. Not money, Miss Burgess. I require something infinitely more valuable than money."

"What then?"

Inigo appraised her, his blue eyes bright.

"You'll have to give me all the memories you have of Arthur," he said, "so I can conjure him up to be as real and as living as you are. Fear not—I'll return them once Arthur is brought back to life again, but for a while you'll lose all knowledge of him."

Thomasina swallowed.

"How do I give my memories to you?" she asked in a small voice.

"You'll have to visit me on the frozen river at night," Inigo whispered. "Four times, for the four years you've been without him. Do you think you can do that?"

Thomasina nodded, not daring to ask how on earth he knew how long Arthur had been dead. There was something unnerving about Inigo, as if by looking into her eyes he could work out the secrets in her soul. Mother had been the same once—she'd always been able to tell what Thomasina was thinking.

She bit her lip, trying to clear her thoughts. "What

happens when we visit the river?" she said.

"It's an entirely painless procedure, I assure you," Inigo replied, a charming smile dancing on his lips. "All you have to do is accompany me, as my guest. I can conjure up all kinds of fantastical, wondrous things to keep you amused, and you won't even notice me siphoning off your memories of Arthur."

Thomasina remembered a flash of moss-green eyes looking into hers. It felt, for a moment, as if Arthur were in the shop with them.

"I'd do anything to bring him back to life," she whispered, her throat dry. "When can we start?"

"Soon," Inigo said. He indicated the necklace with a long, blue-tinged finger. "I've cast a charm on this. If you wear it when you visit the river with me, you won't freeze to death. I cast the same charm around you when you first visited me on the river, but this makes things easier. Be warned, though, that it won't work to warm you up in the daytime, or at night if you're far away from the River Thames—only when you're at the Other Frost Fair."

"Thank you," Thomasina said, excitement clouding her mind. For the second time that day, she felt dizzy, only this time it was for an entirely different reason.

"Now," Inigo said, sweeping into a final bow, "I must take my leave of you. Remember: four nights, for the four years Arthur's been gone."

He strode out through the door, a gust of cold wind flying in after him. She ran outside, the ice and muck seeping into her shoes once more.

"Where are you going?" she called as he walked away up Raven Lane, laughing as a couple of children nearby fought over knucklebones. He tossed them a bright shilling and chuckled still more as they wrestled each other for it.

"Until we next meet," he called back, striding toward the river with a flick of his silver cloak, his hat feather bouncing in the breeze.

Thomasina stepped back into the shop and closed the door, the copper bell tinkling above her head. She forced herself to breathe in and out in deep, gulping mouthfuls.

It felt like a sharp, bright ache was lodged in her heart, now that Inigo had given her this extraordinary hope. Arthur, the blood and bone she loved more than anyone else in the world, could live again. Maybe the guilt she felt about teasing Arthur, not noticing he was suffering until it was too late, would be forgotten. Maybe Mother would be cured of the overwhelming grief she'd succumbed to the night he'd died, maybe Father would come out of his slump . . . and maybe they could be a proper family once more. Her heart fluttered with hope.

"We can be together again," she whispered to Arthur, beaming.

I can't wait, she imagined him saying.

Thomasina picked up the necklace. It caught the light at different angles, gleaming even in the gloom of the shop, then slithered into her palm. It took her a while to find the catch with her trembling fingers and fasten it into place around her neck, as the chain was finer than anything she'd ever handled before. The snowflake pendant fell beneath her collarbones, cooling the flesh it touched, neither metal nor ice but a strange alchemy in between. If she kept very still, it almost felt as though the tiny sliver of magic she wore had a heartbeat.

7

Father Winter

The morning the Frost Fair opened, Thomasina woke with butterflies dancing in her stomach at the thought of Arthur being brought back to life again soon.

She and Father crunched through fresh layers of snow and ice to the frozen Thames, the river buckling under bulky bundles of rope, wooden poles, and swathes of waxed canvas. Azure sky peeked through white, fluffy clouds, and warm winter sunshine speckled the frozen river like an egg.

Around them, frost decorated the other traders' cheeks as they set up stalls near Thomasina and Father, their boots scraping and sliding over the ice. After they'd erected the Burgess & Son's tent together, Father heaved crates onto a makeshift table and Thomasina arranged rows of gingerbread with numb fingers. She darted nervous glances over at the people watching them in bemusement from the safety of the riverbank.

"Do you think any of them will come over to see our stall?" she whispered to Arthur. "Or do you think Father and I, and the others here, will become laughingstocks for thinking we could trade in such a strange place?"

It's worth a try, she imagined him replying. Again, she tried to suppress her guilt at the thought that she was here instead of him, trading with Father on the frozen river.

In total, there were four tents on the ice, and, nearby, two women selling canned milk from trays, their cheeks already blotched red by the wind. All the traders waited, shuffling from one foot to another in the cold, wondering if anyone would be bold enough to visit them.

Over on the riverbank, the bystanders' curiosity was growing into a real interest now. After several heart-stopping moments, a few of them started making their way toward the tents on the river. They weren't used to walking on such a slippery surface, however. Some who, like Thomasina, wore shoes with little grip grabbed at each other for support, but others skated and glided confidently over to the stalls. They gulped down the Green-Eyed Mermaid's piping-hot drinks, bought canned milk from the two rosy-cheeked women, and finally came to the Burgess & Son's tent, where their faces split into grins upon seeing the neat rows of gingerbread.

Before long, she and Father had sold nearly all their stock. Father was beside himself, his eyes shining like a boy's. They'd never had such a swell in business, and they had collected the same amount of money in a single day that they'd usually make in a whole month.

Thomasina worried, however, that their customers would soon grow bored of gingerbread. Now it was clear that people were interested in visiting the stalls on the river, Burgess & Son's would have to come up with some other treats to sell as well, to compete with other businesses that she was sure would set up on the ice before long.

"Father," she said hesitantly, as he handed a penny in change to their final customer of the day. "I was thinking— we have plenty of apples still in the apple barrel. Do you think we could make some coated in syrup and honey, to sell alongside the gingerbread?"

Father blinked.

"Good idea," he said, the glimmer of a smile passing over his face.

Thomasina stared at him. She couldn't remember the last time he'd praised her—certainly not since Arthur's death.

After packing up for the day, she carried a crate back across the ice as quickly as she could, though her boots caught on jagged clumps of it and her feet slid everywhere she stepped. It was all she could do not to drop what she was carrying and grab at the nearest person whenever she stumbled over. Reaching solid ground, she stepped back to allow a boisterous crowd pass by her with a cacophony of voices and shouts. She was just recovering her breath when she heard her name being called.

"Thomasina? Thomasina Burgess?"

She looked up. It was the girl she'd met yesterday at the apothecary's—Anne Hawke—and she was smiling at her. She cut a striking figure in her crimson cloak against the snowy landscape.

"Oh . . . hello!" Thomasina said, feeling her face light up into a beam.

"What a fantastic idea to trade out here!" Anne said, gesturing toward the tents on the river. "I hope it catches on."

"Thanks," Thomasina said shyly, adjusting the crate in her hands, feeling her fingers bruise under the weight. "I think it might."

"I'm going to visit what's left of the fair now," Anne told her with a smile. "I hope I see you again soon!"

Thomasina grinned again. She felt something curious flicker in her chest: a warm feeling that she'd been noticed and spoken to kindly, as if Anne really were glad to see her. She hadn't felt this way for such a long time. Even the races with the butcher's boys had stopped after Arthur's death.

Arriving back at the shop, she ducked inside to avoid Miss

Maplethorpe, who was hastening after her, saying she'd sell her old, moldy cabbages to Thomasina at a discount price. After Thomasina had locked and bolted the door, she started making sweets for the following day, dipping apples that she'd stored away the month before in sticky syrup and then in honey. Her fingertips tingled with excitement. Everything in her world felt like it was looking up: Father had listened to her idea about the new sweets to sell, and Anne Hawke seemed keen to befriend her. Most thrillingly of all, Inigo was going to bring her brother back from the dead very soon—he'd promised her he'd visit again imminently.

Tap, tap, tap.

Thomasina's insides churned when she heard Inigo's knock, just after St. Bartholomew's Church struck midnight. She hadn't thought he'd call so soon. She'd spent a restless few hours tossing and turning in bed, hardly daring to believe what was going to happen.

Checking on Mother, who was fast asleep, a mound of blankets gently rising and falling as usual, Thomasina crossed the attic room. The floorboards creaked as she tiptoed downstairs with a candle, and occasionally she froze, wondering if Mother or Father would wake up, but the house was as asleep as it had felt the other night, almost as if it were enchanted in a dream spell.

She was surprised she didn't feel cold, but then she remembered that the silver snowflake necklace Inigo had given her was protecting her from the night elements. With shaking fingers, she laced up her boots, fastened her cloak, and walked to the front door, setting down her candle on a stool and pressing her lips against the cold oak.

"I'm here," she whispered, her breath a white gust of air around her.

As her fingers fumbled for the bolt, she was reassured to hear Father's snores reverberating through the floorboards from the room above.

She'd been expecting to see the will-o'-the-wisp but was surprised to find Inigo grinning at her when the door swung open with a deafening creak that bounced back at her from the walls on the other side of the street. Immediately, she tensed, wondering if any flickering candlelight would appear at a neighboring window, throwing a suspicious face into relief, or—worse—if Father would be roused from his slumber. Her panic subsided when she heard the snores rumble on and no lights appeared.

"Good evening, Miss Burgess," Inigo murmured.

She hadn't realized it would be possible for him to be even more extravagantly dressed. Tonight, Inigo wore a glittering silver cloak, studded with sapphires, pearls, and opals. Rather than being brightened with silver embroidery, his blue velvet doublet was bedecked with starlike diamonds that twinkled in the moonlight, and he wore an ugly, elaborate headpiece covered in white feathers.

"Lovely, isn't it?" he said, preening as she stared at him, openmouthed. He turned so his knife-sharp cheekbones were illuminated by the moonlight. "Don't worry. Many have been speechless upon first seeing it. You're not alone in your reaction."

"O-Oh," she faltered. "Um—yes. It's . . . wonderful."

"Shall we, my dear?" he said, offering her his arm.

After a shivering moment's hesitation, she took it. It felt as cold and stiff as glass, as if there were no flesh and blood beneath the soft fabric of his sleeve.

"Tonight," Inigo announced, "is the first night of the Other Frost Fair."

"The Other Frost Fair?" she said. "What's that?"

"A magical Frost Fair, unlike anything you'll see in the daylight. The Other Frost Fair is created from magic and sea smoke; it's a living, breathing thing, with traces of ancient magic. It's as curious as the breath before song, and as strange as the glimmer of moonlight on water. Yet it exists, and you'll visit it tonight."

Thomasina didn't know what to say to this. Inigo's words felt magic in themselves, as if he were casting a spell over her. Even though she was visiting the Other Frost Fair to bring

Arthur back, she now wanted to see it, just . . . *because*. And what was sea smoke? Her head felt muddled just attempting to picture what Inigo meant.

While they navigated the tangle of Southwark's streets, Inigo kept Thomasina entertained with stories of how much London's face had changed.

"The last time I was here was well before the Great Fire," he said. "The city looked positively *ancient*. Ghastly architecture. Wooden houses everywhere—all rather *slovenly*. Not to my taste at all," he told her as they walked along. "The streets were so narrow—much pokier than the ones you have now! But St. Paul's, my dear—Oh! You have no idea how spectacular it was. Not that you could imagine such a thing. . . ." He sighed. "There's nothing there now, apart from building works."

Again, Thomasina wondered exactly what he meant . . . and how *old* he was.

"How long did you live in London before the Great Fire?" she asked.

"Ah!" Inigo said, blue eyes flickering between both of hers, a silvery flush decorating his cheeks. "That's an excellent question. Now, close your eyes, Miss Burgess—we're near the Other Frost Fair."

Thomasina bristled at his deflection, but she sighed and

closed her eyes anyway, resolving to ask him again later. Her heart was hammering at the thought of seeing the Other Frost Fair.

Hands as thin and icy as stalagmites guided her gently around a corner.

"Open them!" he exclaimed.

She did and immediately staggered backward, her heart skipping so much she was surprised it didn't burst out of her chest.

Tents of all shapes and sizes stretched along the river, colored silver, white, and midnight blue. Prowling around them were snarling, silver-colored beasts, scraping the ice with their claws, their fur rippling in the winter winds. Their eyes were frosted white, and blue flames flickered out of their mouths. One of them was . . .

"Oh my goodness!" Thomasina gasped. "That's a magical goat!"

A goat came clattering across the ice to greet them both, its coat a sheen of sparkling white ice. Rooted to the spot, Thomasina saw her frightened face cracked and mirrored in its stern gaze. The creature sniffed the air around her, then swiveled its blank eyes to Inigo. It bleated and clip-clopped away.

Inigo patted Thomasina's arm.

"Our Frost Beasts are the gatekeepers of the Other Frost Fair. They keep out unwelcome visitors. You're my guest, so they won't hurt you. But cross their path, or come here when you're not welcome, and they might."

Thomasina shivered at this. She watched an assortment of Frost Beasts prick up their ears and sprint across the ice. A cry was echoing miles away.

"I'm scared," she said.

"Don't worry, my dear. They're as harmless as I am."

Thomasina didn't know whether to believe him. The creatures around her seemed very fierce. She could try to make a break for the safety of Southwark, but how did she know the Frost Beasts wouldn't follow her, snapping at her ankles and tearing her apart with their silvery fangs, angry with her for running off? But she wouldn't do this, she told herself. Not when the prospect of seeing Arthur alive again was so close.

"Come, Miss Burgess," Inigo said. "I've so much to show you. And, if I say so myself, I look wonderful and want as many as possible to see my outfit."

While Thomasina's heart was still fluttering at the sight of the Frost Beasts, she was soon overwhelmed by other strange spectacles at the fair, and momentarily forgot her panic. People dressed in blue and silver were emerging from tents on the river. Dazzling white snowflakes shone on their skin. . . .

Just like the two men in gray cloaks she'd seen outside St. Bartholomew's Church.

Thomasina's mouth fell open, and she stepped back in surprise.

"Inigo!" she said in a horrified whisper, huddling close to him. "Those people are made of *ice!*"

Inigo smiled at her, unruffled by her alarm.

"Yes, my dear. A—er—good observation. These are the Frost Folk: inhabitants of the Other Frost Fair."

"I've seen two people like that before," Thomasina said, her legs feeling like they were made of jelly as she still continued to back away. "They were outside the church, wearing gray cloaks—and one of them looked at me later, in the street. Their eyes were completely iced over!"

Inigo gave her a gentle smile, though his eyes seemed a little wary.

"Don't worry about them," he said in a voice that sounded a little too hearty. "They're friends of mine—and there's so much they, as well as I, want to show you at the Other Frost Fair! Look!" He pointed. "See what they're doing now!"

Thomasina still felt nervous after the shock of seeing the Frost Folk, but she reasoned to herself that nothing was normal in the strange, ethereal world of the Other Frost Fair.

She'd already met animals made of ice here, so why should meeting people with shimmering silver snowflakes patterned all over their skin be any different? Her gaze traveled to where Inigo's finger pointed.

Some of the Frost Folk were river hawkers, selling a kaleidoscope of items she'd never seen before. A few shouted about crystal tiaras and ice-colored pendants, while others waved bottles emitting indigo sparks. Everyone was dressed in a different style: some wore togas, their silvery knees and calves bare to the elements, some were clad in sparkling suits of armor, and others wore enormous breeches like Inigo's. Dancing girls in glittering blue dresses leaped about, spinning in midair. Thomasina gaped at them all, amazed.

Someone was drawing near, like the Frost Beast had done: a little girl clad in a nightdress, her white eyes and skin puckered with snowflakes. She was carrying a hoop and stick, and she laughed at Thomasina's incredulous expression, revealing silver teeth that shimmered in the moonlight.

"Are the Frost Folk conjurers like you, Inigo?" Thomasina asked, her legs still feeling wobbly.

"Not quite. Now, Miss Burgess, you must come with me," Inigo said, looking grave. "There's someone you must meet before you can enjoy the Other Frost Fair."

"Who?"

"Father Winter."

Despite her snowflake necklace, Thomasina felt a chilly breeze sweep through, ruffling the flags on the tents surrounding them. Goose bumps crept up and down her neck.

"Who's Father Winter?" she said.

"He rules over us all and resides in the biggest tent," Inigo said, pointing to one at the river's center. It was decorated more lavishly than any other. Silver ribbons fluttered, and stars were embroidered on thick navy-and-white stripes. Burning braziers blazed in front of it, emitting eerie, stark blue flames.

"Come," Inigo said.

Thomasina noticed it was easier to walk on the ice than in the daytime and wondered if the snowflake necklace didn't just protect her from the cold, but roughened her path as well.

She and Inigo walked toward the huge tent belonging to Father Winter. Standing guard were two figures. One was a huge Frost Lion. Its fur was composed of shards of ice, sticking out of its body like fine, spiked armor, while its mane was formed of sparkling blue icicles. Thomasina stepped behind Inigo as it growled. Beside the Frost Lion was a man dressed in a simple white tunic.

"Reason for visiting?" he demanded in a reedy voice.

"I'm presenting a visitor to Father Winter," Inigo said.

"Her name is Thomasina Burgess. He knows about her."

Something in the man's ice-bright eyes flickered. He and the Frost Lion stepped aside for them to enter, and they walked through the tent flap.

"Oh!" Thomasina gasped.

Father Winter's tent was filled with so many awe-inspiring decorations that at first it was hard to tell where he was. Thousands of glittering snowflakes and icicles were suspended from above. In the middle of the room was another brazier that, despite crackling, didn't emit any heat. The longer Thomasina watched the flames, the greater the number of shades of blue, then purple, then silver she saw them turn. Thomasina looked beyond it and made out some figures at the far end of the tent.

A strange smell filled her nostrils. It reminded her of the ancient crypt at St. Bartholomew's, where generations of a noble family from centuries ago lay entombed under marble. She and Arthur had dared each other to creep inside once. They'd both had nightmares about the cold expressions of the statues for weeks afterward. As her nose wrinkled, she wanted to hurry back to Raven Lane. She'd have preferred to face the Frost Beasts outside than meet the figures at the end of the tent. She was aware of Inigo's hand on her arm, however, and felt a little calmer.

"You'll be fine, my dear," he reassured her.

As they approached him, Thomasina realized how old Father Winter must be. He reminded her of the hollowed-out faces she'd seen in the crypt's gloomy depths, chiseled centuries ago. The wrinkles on his face and hands were deep and silver blue, and the eyes regarding her were bright blue, like Inigo's. He wore a simple white tunic, and a snowy fur cloak adorned his shoulders. On his head rested a coronet of icicles, at the top of which gleamed a sparkling silver snowflake. His beard was a tangle of spun frost, sweeping down to the icy ground.

A couple of Frost Folk stood on either side of him. It was as if they were statues themselves. They were dressed differently. One wore a dress that Thomasina knew, from drawings of her great-grandmother in Mother's household book, had been in fashion decades ago. The other wore a simple shift and seemed impervious to the elements around her.

"Curtsy or bow to him," Inigo whispered.

There was something about Father Winter that made Thomasina not want to do this at all, but nevertheless she swept into a clumsy sort of bob, wobbling as she stood up.

"Father Winter," Inigo said, "I'm here to present to you the girl I told you about. This is Thomasina Burgess."

"You are she?" Father Winter said in a harsh voice, speaking with such an odd accent that Thomasina had a hard time understanding him. The sound reminded her of a cracked coin she'd found while paddling in the Thames with Arthur years ago. His vowels were even stranger than Inigo's, shifting all over the place.

"Y-Yes," she whispered. "I am."

He smiled at her, but his expression wasn't friendly. It was a smile revealing shards of pointed ice instead of teeth, and it seemed to take an age for him to do it, as if every movement cost him a great deal of energy.

"You may enjoy my Frost Fair," he said.

"Thank you," she replied.

Father Winter's eyes then swiveled to Inigo.

"Inigo," he hissed, his smile wider than ever, "do not forget your place here."

"No, Father Winter," Inigo said, and Thomasina was startled to hear bitterness in his voice. "I won't."

"Leave me. I have others to see," Father Winter said, so after another bow and curtsy, Inigo and Thomasina left the tent. She was glad not to be in Father Winter's presence anymore. The longer she'd been there, the more it had felt like her head was swimming with white mist.

"What did Father Winter mean, not to 'forget your place' here?" Thomasina asked Inigo.

He flinched. "Oh, nothing. You know what higher-ups are like," he said, giving her a weak smile. "They want deference at all times. It keeps the feudal system going. Look, Miss

Burgess—you have a new friend."

A Frost Wolf had padded up to her and was sniffing her ankles. It had a gnarled back and glittering blue teeth protruding from its massive mouth. Thomasina tensed, but she was surprised to find it ducked its head under her hand.

"It wants you to stroke it," Inigo said.

Thomasina swallowed but did as Inigo suggested. The Frost Wolf seemed to enjoy her tentative pats, grunting and twisting its face. Thomasina had the peculiar sensation she was stroking a thousand needles, too small to pierce her when she rubbed its pelt in one direction.

The Frost Wolf gave a small growl, then padded away, its claws piercing the ice.

"The Frost Beasts understand that Father Winter has welcomed you," Inigo said. "They can be rather friendly, you know."

Thomasina smiled, watching a large silver Frost Cow and a glittering white Frost Horse chase each other.

"We'll have time to explore," Inigo continued, "over the next three nights you visit. I had to introduce you to Father Winter first. You must remember that you're not to visit the Other Frost Fair without me, or the Frost Beasts will be angry."

Terror clenched Thomasina's heart at his words, and she nodded. She was so scared at the thought of the Frost Beasts hunting her down that she had to remind herself why she was here: for her brother. She'd just have to overcome her fear.

Inigo guided her off the frozen river, and they wound their way down the streets and back alleys once more. When they reached the front door of Burgess & Son's, he bowed low to her.

"I'll call again soon," he said. "You may consider the first visit to be over. There are three more to go, until Arthur is brought back to you. Good night, Miss Burgess."

"Good night," Thomasina whispered. She watched him until he turned a corner, then went inside, locking the door before creeping upstairs. When she reached the attic room, she was glad to find Mother fast asleep on her back.

Thomasina's heart fizzed with excitement at the prospect of seeing Arthur. She knew, however, that if she told anyone about Inigo, they'd think she was mad. To claim she'd seen a kelpie conjured out of thin air was one thing, but to say she'd visited the frozen river at night, in the company of hundreds of Frost Beasts and Frost Folk, was another thing entirely. She had to keep the Other Frost Fair a secret.

With delight still coursing through her, Thomasina sat on the bed and took Mother's hand in hers, noticing how the older woman's skin was butter-soft, her nails clean. The moonlight slipping through the shutters bathed them both in fine silver, so they could almost have been Frost Folk themselves.

"I've had such a strange night, Mother," she murmured.

Mother breathed in deeply, a slow, halting breath, then let it out in a sigh.

"I wish I could tell you all about it," Thomasina continued, rubbing a thumb over Mother's palm. "Maybe I'll be able to, one day, after—after Arthur comes back."

She could hear London waking up as a couple of shouts broke the still of the night, and she knew the traders were stirring. She'd been gazing at Mother's hands while talking to her. Now, she let her eyes travel up Mother's arms to her shoulders . . . then to the ends of her tangled, gray hair . . . and finally her face—and froze.

Mother's eyes were open.

8

A Business Proposition

"Mother?" Thomasina whispered, drinking in as much detail of Mother's eyes as she could. They were moss green, with hazel rings at their centers, like Arthur's had been.

Mother didn't reply. Instead, she reached out and touched Thomasina's hand, closing her own around it, then shut her eyes again. The bones in her fingers felt as delicate as a bird's.

At Mother's touch, Thomasina's heart started to flutter like starlings in flight. Tears crept into the corners of her eyes, burning them and threatening to spill over. She didn't know what else to do except stay like this before her morning chores began.

The light from the waking sun snaked around the shutters, making the twine and ribbons glow. Eventually, when

Thomasina heard the bells of St. Bartholomew's Church announcing the start of a new day, she tiptoed out of the attic bedroom, closing the door and leaning against it.

"Did you see that, Arthur?" she whispered.

I did, she felt him reply.

That was odd. It didn't sound as though he was particularly interested. She'd thought Arthur would have shared her delight at seeing Mother with her eyes open. She'd thought she'd feel his heart, like hers, fizzing with exhilaration.

A frown creased her forehead. Was this what Inigo had meant, about her memories of Arthur fading every time she visited the Other Frost Fair?

She tried to conjure up Arthur in her mind, and his face floated in front of her. She saw his green eyes shining, but there was something different about him. She realized it wasn't just the flatness of his voice: she could feel her recollection of how he sounded slipping away from her like the tide.

She took deep, shuddering breaths to try to steady her racing heart, and she reasoned with herself that this change was temporary. Inigo had promised. Soon, she'd have not just her memories of him back, but him again: alive and well. Before long, she'd hear his voice all the time, and she wouldn't have to resort to imagining it.

She was exhausted after her night visiting the Other Frost Fair with Inigo and seeing the Frost Beasts, Frost Folk, and Father Winter, so it took her a while to register the new tents that had sprouted up that morning at the actual Frost Fair, as if they'd grown out of the ice itself. Taking a few syrup and honey apples with her on a tray, she strayed a little from the Burgess & Son's stall and went for a walk around the others, the wind whipping at her cheeks. In the distance, she could make out a red-and-white-striped tent, standing in the same spot as Father Winter's had been.

"Make way. Dancing bear," a low voice snapped behind her. "Move, girl."

She scrambled out of the way as a huge animal was led onto the ice, its shaggy brown fur matted beyond repair. An open sore on its back gaped near its hindquarters, dripping blood as bright as rubies onto the snow. As Thomasina watched, the bear's two small brown eyes blinked at her, she thought, with sadness, before it was tugged forward by the chain around its neck. It groaned as it plodded on, and Thomasina couldn't help but pity it, even though its bulk was alarming.

"My circus is opening on the river today," roared a man hurrying along in the bear's wake. Sneering at Thomasina's ragged robes, he turned away to address the small crowd forming around him. Pus oozed from a blister on his right hand as he waved it around. "Clowns and performing animals! Terrifying feats of skill and agility! Don't miss it!" he cried.

"Ugh. What a horrible man," she heard someone say behind her, and, whipping around, she saw Anne Hawke narrowing her eyes at the circus ringmaster's departing figure. Thomasina's heart leaped.

Anne switched her gaze to Thomasina. "Hello." She grinned. "I was hoping to find you here again. Where's your father?"

Thomasina grinned back, feeling a flood of pleasure at the girl's words.

"Hello!" she said. "Um—I've been selling sweets from a tray upriver," she told Anne as the pair walked back to the sweet stall. "Father's in the shop today, so I'm on duty here. Why are you on the ice?"

"Uncle asked me to find out what the apothecaries are selling at the Frost Fair—we want to set up a stall here, too. I'm glad to get out in the fresh air and have a break from the shop. There are so many customers in there today it's difficult to move."

"Really?" Thomasina said, passing a couple of syrup and honey apples to a customer.

"Oh yes," Anne said. "So many people with sore throats, coughs, and sneezes come in buying up our stock. *Then* they tell us our medicines taste foul."

"Do they?" Thomasina asked.

"Well . . . yes, most of them do," Anne said with a small chuckle. "I've tried making the remedies taste nicer, but nothing seems to work."

"Lots of people buy our sweets to disguise the taste of medicine," Thomasina said.

Anne sighed. "If only . . ." She stopped, and Thomasina looked at her, frowning.

"If only . . . what?"

"I've got it!" Anne whispered. "You and I could make sweets—medicinal sweets—and sell them at the Frost Fair!"

"What are you talking about?" Thomasina said as they arrived at the Burgess & Son's stall.

"Think about it!" Anne murmured, a feverish glow in her eyes. "I'd bring my knowledge of medicine, and you'd bring your knowledge of sweetmaking, and together we could create medicinal sweets! We could make a fortune."

"Will that work?" Thomasina asked doubtfully. "Don't you already sell sugar as medicine? I swear the last time I was at your apothecary shop, I saw some cures that were sweets themselves. . . ."

"Yes"—Anne beamed—"but they don't taste very nice. Believe me, Uncle and I have tried so many. Besides, no apothecary has your sweetmaker knowledge, Thomasina—and no sweetmaker has mine of how to turn herbs, roots, and minerals into medicine. And no one in London has a business just selling medicinal sweets! We could work together to invent all kinds of treats: not just pills drenched in sugar, like the apothecaries and doctors sell, but really delicious cures."

"Excuse me," a disgruntled voice said. "I'm *trying* to buy one of your apples."

Thomasina jumped and handed a syrup and honey apple to a young lady, who took it, sniffed, and tossed a coin onto the table.

"We don't have to make many medicinal sweets at first," Anne continued. "We just have to think of one invention—something simple to make—that we could try to sell at the Frost Fair. We'd soon see whether anyone liked it or not. This is the place to try out new ideas—look how many people are out here! And if no one wants to buy our invention, so what? We can just think of something else."

Thomasina bit her lip. Though she was pleased at Anne's faith in her sweetmaking abilities, she didn't know if she could help her at all. But she felt determined to try.

"Well . . ." she said slowly, trying to be helpful. "What's the cure you sell for a sore throat?"

"It depends," Anne said. "We give most people honey or ginger to gargle down with water and, for our richer customers, we mix celery or parsley with anise and pepper and wine. . . . Pretty disgusting, really, but it seems to do the trick."

"I suppose," Thomasina said, thinking aloud, "if you want us to come up with a medicinal sweet, honey and ginger could be a good place to start. We could harden the honey somehow—maybe crystallize it—and add bits of cut-up ginger to make a sweet."

"I love that!" Anne said, eyes shining. "Would you mind if I made a batch at home, then showed you in a couple of days? I won't be able to cook anything until tomorrow night, as Uncle and I are so busy—but we're going to start trading at the Frost Fair tomorrow, so I'll be able to see you."

Thomasina grinned. "I don't know if they'll taste any good," she said. "Crystallized honey can be quite clumpy. And . . . do you think we'll even have enough time to try them out? No one knows how long the Frost Fair will be around, or how long the ice will hold. . . . What will we do when it's melted again?"

"*No one* knows, so we might as well try something out

now," Anne said, eyes bright with enthusiasm. "If the ice melts, we can think of another way to sell our sweet cures—maybe on the street, to see if people are interested. But I think we'll have a while yet before that happens. Anyway," she continued, regret crossing her face, "I must go—I need to investigate as many apothecary stalls as I can at the Frost Fair, I'm afraid. But I'll experiment with the ingredients and tell you how I get on!"

"Of course," Thomasina said, smiling at a gaggle of small children eyeing the last of the apples.

"See you soon, I hope!" Anne said. "It's been so nice spending time with you. You've given me so much to think about!"

Thomasina felt herself blush beetroot red and gave a hesitant smile back.

"See you soon," she murmured.

She watched Anne scrape her way across the ice. Though crowds kept milling around her tent as everyone scrambled to see the latest additions to the Frost Fair, she hardly noticed them. She didn't even mind when someone stood on the back of her cloak or when a child screamed right next to her, followed by his mouther shouting, "Bad Timmy! No more gingerbread for you today!"

It's been so nice spending time with you. The words kept

echoing in the back of Thomasina's mind. It wasn't Arthur's voice who was speaking this time, but Anne's.

She had no idea how inventing medicinal sweets together would go—but hope blossomed in her chest at the thought that she might, at last, have made a new friend.

9

A Night at the Theater

The following day at the Frost Fair, despite her misgivings, Thomasina couldn't get the idea of inventing new medicinal sweets out of her head.

She knew sugar and sweet cures were already sold by apothecaries—however, she also knew their remedies didn't taste very nice at all. As Anne said, the two of them had something other apothecaries didn't have: Thomasina's skill at making sweets and treats that would make anyone's mouth water, combined with Anne's astute medical knowledge.

Ideas appeared in her dreams, interrupting her memories of Arthur: concoctions she and her new friend could sell together at the Frost Fair, like sweet cough remedies and cures for stomach pains and toothache, as well as delicious healing drinks.

She couldn't help but watch Anne that day at the Frost

Fair, as she sold wares with her uncle at their newly pitched apothecary stand. Though she couldn't hear what Anne was saying above the hubbub of the crowds, she knew she was very good at her job. She spoke confidently, and Thomasina saw her customers' worries slip away; watched them smile with relief as Anne prescribed them remedies.

She isn't me though, is she? she heard Arthur mutter. Almost like Inigo's strange accent, her twin's voice felt bent out of place today, his words slipping a little. She couldn't put her finger on why that was.

"No one's like you," Thomasina whispered back. "Don't worry. When you're back, you can be friends with her, too."

As it turned out, this was her only happy moment during an otherwise frustrating day. When she returned to the attic bedroom over Burgess & Son's, Mother was in such a state, the like of which Thomasina had never seen her in before.

"What's wrong?" she said as Mother tossed and turned, pinching and wringing her hands together, tears streaming down her face.

Sitting on their bed, Thomasina tried to prize her mother's hands apart, but Mother wouldn't separate them. For the first time in four years, Thomasina put her arms around her. It felt uncomfortable to hold her close as Mother was lying down, and her hands jabbed into Thomasina's front. Thomasina felt her right shoulder grow damp from Mother's tears.

Eventually, the crying subsided. Thomasina sat up, drying Mother's face with her sleeve.

"There now, Mother. Did you have a nightmare?" she murmured.

Mother didn't reply and turned away to face the wall.

"I'm trying to help," Thomasina said to Mother's back, but Mother remained still.

Thomasina sighed. "I hope you feel better soon," she said, so quietly she wasn't sure if the older woman had heard her or not, and left the attic room.

Her stomach churned painfully, as if a storm were brewing.

"Every time I talk to her, it feels like it's one step forward, then two steps back," she whispered to Arthur. "I *hate* that Mother's this way. I *hate* it. And I don't like myself for being angry at her. It isn't her fault she's unwell."

Yeah.

Thomasina frowned at Arthur's lackluster response, and her heart clenched as, again, she realized his voice was different. Inigo's charm was working—he'd told her that her memories of Arthur would start to disappear, and this seemed to be coming true: Arthur's voice sounded different, and she knew it was because she'd visited the Other Frost Fair. *But*, she reasoned to herself again, *it won't be like this forever.* Soon, he'd be back, and she'd listen to his voice all day long and be happy about it, even when he was being annoying.

Still frustrated, she scrubbed out the fireplace until it was spotless, and her face, hands, and apron were covered in grime and soot. Why did everything have to be so hard? Why couldn't she have a life like Anne's, skilled at making medicines, not having to look after an ill parent? *And even if we do manage to bring Arthur back from the dead*, she wondered, *how do I know Mother will be cured?*

After she washed her face and hands, she laid out a pie for dinner. She and Father sat in gloomy silence while eating, and he trudged off to bed without finishing his plate. She went upstairs with a tray for Mother, resting it on the bed.

"Dinner's next to you if you want it," she said shortly.

She changed into her nightdress but then realized she didn't want to be around Mother right now, so she stamped back downstairs, sat down at the table, crossed her arms, and glared at the wall. It was only when St. Bartholomew's Church struck midnight that she realized how much time had passed.

Tap, tap, tap.

She hadn't expected Inigo to come again so soon. She nearly forgot the day's frustrations as she shrugged her feet into her boots and crossed the room to unbolt the door. Somehow, she knew this trip would be different from the last.

"Miss Burgess, you're a vision," he said.

Thomasina snorted. She was wearing her rattiest, oldest nightdress, which was wearing away at the hem. It was ridiculous for Inigo to compliment her when she knew she looked very grubby indeed.

"I've no idea what that sound was meant to represent," Inigo said, "but I maintain that you look delightful. Not as delightful as me, I grant you"—he gestured smugly at his elaborately curled, silvery hair and his glittering doublet—"but then, no one does. Now, come along."

As with the first time they'd visited the Other Frost Fair, he held out his arm, and she slipped hers through it. She again experienced the strange sensation she'd felt the last time she'd touched him, as Inigo's arm was frozen stiff. They started walking down the street.

"What are we going to see tonight?" she asked.

"Tonight, we're going to the theater," Inigo said, grinning. "I promised I'd do my best to entertain you while you visit the Other Frost Fair. Have you ever been to a play before?"

"No," Thomasina said. "I'm always working, and it's too expensive, anyway."

"I thought as much," Inigo said.

Thomasina frowned. "Are there actors in the Other Frost Fair, then?"

He smiled. "You'll see."

They proceeded in silence along the tangle of streets that made up her corner of the world. When they reached the edge of the frozen river, Thomasina's mouth dropped open.

In the middle of the ice lay the most dazzling building she'd ever seen: even more impressive than Father Winter's tent had been. It was made of ice and glowed as she watched it. Braziers of blue flames stood at its entrance, crackling in the night breeze. The whole building was circular. Frosted walls rose before her, with midnight-blue oak timbers and beams supporting the structure. Crowning it was a snowy-white thatched roof.

"What do you think?" Inigo asked her.

"It's beautiful," she whispered.

Outside the theater, a crowd of Frost Folk were hurrying inside the sparkling main doors. As on the previous night, they were dressed in a bizarre array of clothes. Some wore attire similar to hers—long, sweeping nightgowns so gauzy she could see silvery legs underneath them—while others wore huge ruffs sticking out from their necks, making it difficult for the Frost Folk around them to walk past.

"It's not quite the Globe, obviously," Inigo said with regret. "My word, that was wonderful in its day."

"The Globe burned down decades ago," Thomasina said, frowning. She was about to ask Inigo how old he was when a Frost Bear ambled up to them, with huge, frosted-over eyes and a silver nose. It rubbed its head against Thomasina's left arm. She winced as tiny shards of ice pricked her skin a little, but not enough to pierce it.

"Hello," she said, and she gingerly reached up an arm and patted it. "Are you checking I'm allowed here again?"

The Frost Bear put his nose into Thomasina's palm and sniffed. She felt as though her hand had just touched a huge block of ice that had just begun to melt, and when she looked at her hand, she saw a tiny silver snowflake melting to water against her skin.

Satisfied, the Frost Bear grunted and plodded away. As it did so, Thomasina noticed there was a circle of sapphires grouped around the lower-right part of its back. There was something about this that stirred her memory, but she couldn't think what of.

"Come, my dear. The doors will close soon," Inigo said. "We won't be late if we hurry."

The last time Thomasina had visited the Other Frost Fair, she hadn't moved near enough to the Frost Folk to scrutinize them, so she hadn't realized quite how ghostly they were until now. Up close, their skin was translucent, with silver snowflakes frosted on it. Narrow blue lines decorated their wrists and mouths.

"Inigo," she whispered, pulling him aside while they walked past, "how can the Frost Folk exist? They don't look real. Why are there silver snowflakes on their skin?"

"It's the way people look here," Inigo said, shrugging. "Don't trouble yourself, dear girl. You won't have to talk to them. Some members of the public can be rather *exhausting*, after all."

Thomasina bit her lip and didn't question him further, and yet the more she saw the Frost Folk up close, the more she felt concerned. For instance, they didn't blink at all and stared with frosted-over eyes instead, and the way they moved was jerky and rhythmical, as if they were all performing some kind of dance she didn't know the steps to.

Inigo led her to a silver staircase in the heart of the theater, large sapphires and amethysts glittering in the posts and spindles of the banister, and together they climbed. Occasionally, Thomasina bumped into one of the Frost Folk by mistake, and she felt like she'd touched a pail of cold water.

When she started to wheeze, and pain started blossoming in her chest, Inigo stopped and gestured toward two empty seats.

"We're almost at the top of the building," he said. "I prefer not to be with the groundlings—the people who stand on the floor," he explained, when Thomasina looked confused. "Call me old-fashioned, but the last time I visited, I was carrying a cup of ale with me—it was *The Tempest*, you know—and one of the impudent actors drank from it!" Inigo shook his head at the memory. "Anyway—what do you think?"

Thomasina looked at the stage. Light filled her insides at the sight before her.

She and Inigo were almost at the top of a mountain of people crowded around a raised platform on which stood two marbled pillars. Above it was a balcony, decorated in blue and white. On top of this was a silvery facade, with navy-blue leaves growing around it. Dark skies above were encircled by blue lights from yet more burning braziers. As Thomasina looked around, she saw that all her fellow theatergoers were tinged in this light, and so—she inspected her hands—was she. She saw the ethereal color spread through her skin.

"Now," Inigo said beside her, "I'd recommend a straight-forward play to start with. This one was popular in my day."

"Ah yes. When *was* that?" Thomasina asked, trying to match his thoughtful tone to see if she could trick him, but he couldn't be fooled.

"The play," Inigo continued, "is called *Twelfth Night.* It's about twins who are separated and find their way back to each other. I thought it might be appropriate for you."

"Do you mean all this was conjured up for me?" Thomasina whispered, but Inigo only smiled.

A ripple of movement passed through the Frost Folk

circled around the theater, and Thomasina's nostrils filled with a strange scent. As she looked back at Inigo, she saw his expression tighten.

She looked down to where the smell was coming from, and her heartbeat slowed.

Father Winter was gliding across the stalls below her. Thomasina frowned. The last time she'd seen him, Father Winter had barely been able to move due to old age. Now he was walking easily to his seat.

This wasn't the only thing different about him tonight. His appearance was as surreal as it had been when Thomasina had first glimpsed him, yet from where Thomasina was sitting, he now looked a little younger than before. The deep wrinkles she'd noticed grooving his face and hands seemed to have faded a little, and his long beard was shorter and less wispy than she remembered.

Thomasina felt a creeping sensation that she was being watched, even though Father Winter's gaze was elsewhere. She felt the hairs on the backs of her arms rise. The Frost Folk surrounding him seemed incredibly afraid and, while Thomasina didn't know why, she felt the same way. Father Winter had an aura that seemed to suck the energy from everyone around him.

"Don't look at him," someone muttered beside Thomasina. She turned and saw a girl perhaps a couple of years older than herself, skin pearly-white, staring at her. A blue birthmark formed a half-moon above the right side of her mouth.

"Why not?" Thomasina asked.

"Don't look at him," the girl repeated, then folded her hands on her lap and stared out at the scene before her.

Bewildered, Thomasina looked over at Inigo, who raised a gloved finger to his lips.

"The play's about to start, now that Father Winter's here," he said in an undertone.

Thomasina couldn't help staring at Father Winter from where she sat. Before she had time to avert her gaze or jerk away, she watched his head tilt upward, his eyes swiveling until they met her own. She gasped and trembled in her seat. Though Father Winter was smiling that same, chilly smile of welcome he'd given her the night they'd first met, there was something about it that pierced her soul and made her feel incredibly vulnerable.

She found she couldn't do anything but stare back at him, transfixed and horrified, until he jerked his head away to focus on what was happening onstage.

After a few moments, Thomasina looked away, too, and she strove to concentrate on the play, trying to calm her heartbeat down.

Twelfth Night was unlike anything Thomasina had ever

seen before. The audience were whipped up into a frenzy, and she with them. They gasped as Viola told of the storm at sea and the shipwreck, and when she heard how Viola's twin brother, Sebastian, had drowned, tears blurred Thomasina's vision; the storyline felt too close to home.

But Arthur will be back soon, she told herself sternly. *I only have two visits left before Inigo conjures him back to life. It's all going to be fine.*

In no time at all, it was the end of what Inigo told her was the first half. He left her side for a few minutes while she remained in her seat, beaming from ear to ear.

"Isn't this wonderful!" someone said. It was the girl next to her with the blue birthmark.

"Yes," Thomasina said, "it is. Do you come to many of these performances?"

The girl's white eyes shifted, and her smile wavered for a moment or two before it reappeared, frozen, on her face.

"Isn't this wonderful!" she repeated.

"Y-Yes," Thomasina said, feeling fear twist inside her stomach. "Yes . . . it is. Er—do you come to many plays?"

The girl's smile faltered again, then became rigid.

"Isn't this—"

"Excuse me, Miss Burgess," Inigo said, reappearing at Thomasina's other side and nudging her. Thomasina dragged her gaze away from the girl.

"The interval has concluded," Inigo told her.

"Yes—er—yes. Good," she replied.

After that, try as she might, she couldn't concentrate on the second half of the play. Even when the twins were reunited, and eerie claps echoed around her, she couldn't join in. All she could think about was the girl beside her, and how strange it was that she'd repeated the same line, and those silver snowflakes on her skin that sparkled in the moonlight as she gave her peculiar, frozen smile.

"Didn't you enjoy the play, my dear?" Inigo asked as they walked out. Behind them, Thomasina felt, rather than saw, Father Winter move from the doors and melt into the surrounding crowds of Frost Folk.

"Why did that girl say the same thing over and over to me?" Thomasina asked. "I know you heard her."

Thoughts collided in Inigo's eyes. His mouth pursed, and it felt to Thomasina like he was making his mind up about something.

"Because," he said, "she was told to."

"Like an actor on the stage, you mean? Was she an actor, too?"

"Not exactly."

Silence stretched between them as they walked on. Thomasina could tell Inigo was on the brink of refusing to answer her questions, so she tried to think of a good one to ask before he left her for the night.

Eventually, as they turned into Raven Lane, she said, "Why could she only say one thing over and over again, but you can say whatever you want to me? Are you their leader?"

She knew instantly she'd taken things too far. Inigo's smile became fixed, just like the girl with the birthmark's had, as they stopped outside the shop.

"My dear Miss Burgess, it was an utter pleasure to accompany you this evening," he said, bowing low. "I can't remember when I last had this much fun."

His eyes flickered with something she couldn't identify.

"I'll see you again soon," he promised. "Two weeks from today." His tone was bitter, and she watched as he swept off into the night.

She considered following him—thought about shouting that he hadn't answered many of her questions at all—but she knew it was no use. Her mind twisted this way and that, trying to understand what was going on, but she was far too tired. All she wanted to do was sleep, so she let herself in and trudged upstairs, only remembering at the last minute to kick off her boots.

10

The Second Snowflake

The morning after her second visit to the Other Frost Fair, Thomasina made an important discovery when she woke up, shivering from the icy morning wind.

For the first time since Arthur had died four years ago, Mother was standing at the foot of the bed, gazing out the window. Thomasina was still annoyed with her about the day before, but she couldn't help feeling amazed. Her breath caught in her throat as she watched her mother for a while. It felt so extraordinary to see her doing such a mundane activity, and she wondered if she'd do anything else. Mother stayed quite still, however, studying the street below.

Thomasina got up and started her daily chores. As she changed Mother's warming pan and placed a tray of food on the bed, her thoughts were full of what had happened the night before—the ghostly, magical theater, the eerie girl who'd repeated the same thing over and over again, Inigo's refusal to answer her questions . . . and the thought, too, that she was halfway toward having Arthur with her again for good. She was startled, therefore, when her daydreaming was interrupted. Mother turned around from the window, her wide green eyes searching her daughter's. Thomasina felt a flash of gratitude in that moment that Mother's and Arthur's eyes were the same color. That would be one part of Arthur she'd never be able to forget, no matter how powerful Inigo's enchantments were.

"What is it, Mother?" Thomasina said. "Why are you out of bed? Are you feeling better?"

Mother's mouth trembled, then opened.

"Yes?" Thomasina whispered, walking toward her, her previous night's frustration forgotten in the face of curiosity. Was her mother going to speak for the first time in years?

"Thomasina!" Father's voice came thundering up from downstairs. "We need to get a move on, or we'll be late for the Frost Fair!"

Mother's gaze slid to the door where Father's voice had entered. She looked back at Thomasina, shook her head with a small, sad smile, then reached out a fine-boned hand and took Thomasina's in her own. She gave it a soft squeeze, then let it go, turning away to face the window again, the sun outlining her head in a soft halo.

"We need to hurry," Father grunted after she'd hurtled downstairs. He grabbed a tray off the table and pushed it into her hands. It was so heavy she had to struggle not to drop it.

Together, they trudged through the snow to the Frost Fair. Dawn crept over the buildings around them, infusing the sky with a pink glow.

"What do you think, Arthur?" Thomasina whispered when Father was safely out of earshot. "Mother seemed interested in what was going on outside."

S-Strange.

His voice sounded very weak, and when she tried to picture how he looked in her mind, his features were faded and blurred, as if she were seeing his reflection in a dirty puddle. Her memories of her brother were ebbing away. Although she felt a stab of anxiety in her heart about this, she tried to calm herself down.

"It won't always be this way," she murmured to Arthur. "This needs to happen so you can come back for good."

When they arrived, she and Father worked in silence, scraping off the ice covering their stall, adjusting anything swayed by the wind overnight, then setting out baskets of sugared almonds and jars of jellied cranberries in rows. Thomasina was fascinated that, despite the spectacles conjured at the Other Frost Fair, all the real Frost Fair's tents and stalls were back in place by morning.

As the sun rose, Thomasina saw even more customers than before wobbling and skating across the frozen river to browse what was on display and make their purchases. Their stock sold out by midday. Thomasina was watching her neighbor Miss Maplethorpe swaying across the river with a heavy tray of parsnips, singing snatches of a folk song, when she heard a gruff voice behind her.

"You've done—er—very well today," Father said.

She turned to look at him in surprise, and saw a blotchy red flush spread across his cheeks as he stared at a patch of ice near her left foot. Before she had time to think of how to respond, he'd already swept off, muttering something about needing to buy more spices.

"Thomasina!"

Anne was waving at her from a new stall. She hurried toward Thomasina, bearing a small wicker basket.

"I've made the medicinal sweets we talked about." She grinned, rummaging around in it. She leaned over and dropped amber-colored pastilles into Thomasina's palm. "Honey and ginger sweets, to cure a sore throat—simple, but very effective. I added a few drops of lemon juice into the mixture to make their medicinal properties even stronger."

Thomasina's mouth fell open in delight.

"Anne!" she gasped. "These look wonderful!"

"It took a few tries to get the mixture right," Anne said, blushing. "I went through several batches. I crystallized the honey at first, like you suggested, but it came away in clumps when I tasted it. So, instead, I boiled the honey—it burned at the bottom of the pot the first few times I did it, but on my fifth attempt I managed to save it."

"What did you do then? Thomasina asked, examining the sweets in front of her. They were squashy and looked incredibly appetizing; she could imagine customers coming back for seconds . . . and thirds.

"I tipped the honey out into another bowl, mixed it with chopped ginger and lemon juice, then molded it into a strip after it had cooled," Anne said.

Thomasina felt a huge yawn coming on, and though she clamped her jaws down tightly, she couldn't mask what had just happened.

"Sorry," she said. "I had a really late night last night."

Anne's eyes flicked down to the sweets again, and Thomasina felt a hot burst of shame course through her.

"Th-Then what did you do?" she prompted.

"Er—then I cut it up into cubes," Anne continued, a small frown crossing her face. "Try one and tell me what you think."

Thomasina picked up one of the pastilles and tasted it. The hint of lemon Anne had added gave the pastille more flavor, and, as she sucked on the sweet, the ginger came through, too—a burst of warmth, all enveloped in the sweetness of honey.

"Mmm, I love it!" she said through her mouthful.

"I'm glad," Anne said. "You and I can both make some more tonight and sell them soon, either on my stall or yours, to see if anyone wants them. Are you busy now?"

"No," Thomasina replied, indicating the empty crates around her. "I just need to pack up."

"Here, I'll help you," Anne said.

Together, the pair piled crates on top of each other, swept away stray specks of sugar, tidied up boxes and ribbons, then made their way across the frozen river. Thomasina gave Anne a sidelong glance, and Anne smiled back at her, her crimson cloak billowing in the wind as they were both swallowed up in the crowds. As Thomasina hadn't had a friend for years, walking side by side with someone her age, who wanted to spend time with her, felt very odd indeed—odd, but wonderful at the same time.

Stepping off the river and making their way home, the two girls made each other laugh as they recounted what they'd seen at the Frost Fair that day. All around them, watermen stamped and shivered in their thin cloaks and ice-covered boots, while merchants, hunched over from the cold, trailed miserably behind their wives as they flitted from one stall to another. The girls drew close to a couple of men wearing what Thomasina recognized to be the uniform of the huge circus tent in the middle of the river.

"And one of my bears just vanished into thin air," one of them moaned. "Just like the lion a few weeks ago. . . ."

"Probably escaped, didn't it?" his colleague snapped back. "So now we've got to find a lion *and* a bleeding bear running around London. . . ."

"What if they're out there *eating* people?" his companion asked.

Anne raised her eyebrows to Thomasina and smirked, and Thomasina grinned back. Judging by the way Thomasina had seen the circus ringmaster mistreat his animals the other day, she knew Anne would agree that the circus workers deserved this. She imagined the lion and bear must have scampered across the ice and into the woodland far away from London, as no one had reported them roaming around the streets.

As they rounded a corner, a gust of freezing wind blew into them both. Thomasina was reaching up her hand to push tendrils of her hair out of her eyes just as Anne started talking.

"Those poor— Oh! What's that?"

Anne had stopped stock-still and was staring at Thomasina—or, rather, she was staring at Thomasina's left hand.

"What's what?" Thomasina replied, bewildered, looking from Anne to her hand. . . .

She froze, too.

A silver snowflake had appeared on her wrist, forming a cold patch on her skin. Thomasina watched it, mesmerized, as it sparkled in the afternoon sunlight when she twisted her palm up and down.

"What . . . ?" she whispered.

"Can I see it?" Anne asked.

Thomasina nodded and extended her arm to Anne, who squinted at the patch on her wrist, almost touching it with her nose as she bent her face down toward it.

"Can I touch it?" she asked.

Thomasina nodded again, and Anne rubbed where the snowflake had appeared, frowning even more. She straightened up and looked at Thomasina with a half smile on her face.

"Are you playing a trick on me?" she said.

"No!" Thomasina gasped. "I promise. Do you think it's some kind of rash? Or something that's appeared because of the cold?"

"No," Anne said firmly. "I've never seen anything like that before in my life."

"Maybe it's because of my visits," Thomasina murmured, more to herself, taking back her arm and examining the snowflake. By now, the design was etched and embedded into the skin, as if it had always been there. It certainly didn't look like a normal rash, or like anything she'd ever seen before either. Except . . . except at the Other Frost Fair, on the Frost Folk's skin.

"What visits?" Anne said, breaking into Thomasina's thoughts.

"Oh—er—nothing," she replied, feeling a flush spread over her cheeks.

But Anne raised an eyebrow.

"Go on, tell me. I've never seen this on anyone before—it could be dangerous. I really think you should come back to the shop with me to talk with my uncle—"

"It's not bad, I promise," Thomasina gabbled, taking a step back and feeling snow crunch beneath her heel. "I think I know why it's there, and it's completely harmless."

Silence stretched between them as Anne stared at her, her eyes widening.

"Sorry, Thomasina, but you need to tell me," she said eventually. "Normally I wouldn't insist, but this looks serious. How do you know you don't have some horrible disease that hasn't been discovered yet?"

"I don't—have a horrible disease, that is," Thomasina assured her.

"So what aren't you telling me? You can trust me with your secrets, you know."

Anxiety fluttered in Thomasina's stomach and her mind raced. She didn't know what to do. Part of her wanted to ignore Anne and race away; another part wanted to tell her everything. On the one hand she was sure that Inigo hadn't told her to keep the Other Frost Fair a secret; on the other she was scared he'd go back on his promise to bring Arthur back to life if she *did* tell someone about it. But Anne was the first friend she'd made in years. And Thomasina knew only the truth could explain the snow-flake's appearance. . . .

Thomasina took a deep breath, heart hammering. "Well," she said, "before I tell you about the visits, I need to tell you about a man who came into our sweet shop a little while ago. . . ."

She dared not look at Anne while she told her about Inigo and the Other Frost Fair, and how he'd promised to bring Arthur back from the dead. Every so often, she had to break off her tale when her nerve threatened to fail her, before summoning the courage to go on.

When she'd finished, Anne didn't speak for a long time.

"Do you think I'm mad?" Thomasina said eventually. "I thought I was going mad, too, only—" She withdrew the silver necklace from under her collar and showed it to Anne. "Inigo conjured this for me a few days ago. It protects me from the cold at night."

She tried to unclasp the necklace to hand it over, but it felt too fiddly.

"Does this have something to do with why you fainted the other day?" Anne said slowly.

"Yes," Thomasina said. "It was the day after I first met him. At first, I thought it was just a bad dream, but then he came back. I know it sounds like I'm going mad, but you've got to believe me."

Anne pursed her lips, then folded her arms across her chest.

"I don't think you're mad," she said, "only mistaken. I've never heard of this kind of magic before."

"But—"

"Thomasina, I think it's best if you get some medicine to help you sleep," Anne said. "I think you're having vivid dreams."

"I'm not dreaming this up!" Thomasina said, a bite in her voice now. "Why do you think I've been so tired lately—why do you think I yawned earlier, when you were showing me the sweets? I've spent every night either visiting the Other Frost Fair or waiting up to see if Inigo will come to the shop!"

"Are you sure you didn't just yawn because you were *bored* earlier?" Anne asked her in a tight voice. "You know, if you don't want to make medicinal sweets with me, you could just say so, instead of telling me this story—"

"I don't find it boring, and I'm not telling you a story!" Thomasina snapped. "Anne, it's all true—I promise. There's a magical world out there on the river, and animals made of ice—Frost Wolves and Frost Lions—and people, too, called Frost Folk—"

Anne shook her head.

"That's impossible, Thomasina. You know it is."

Tears rose in Thomasina's eyes. She'd been on the brink of making her first proper friendship in years, and she was worried she'd blown it.

"I *promise* it's true, Anne," she said, her voice breaking.

"But I can't make you believe me . . . unless—"

A thought struck her. "Come in two weeks," she whispered. "To Burgess & Son's, I mean. Yesterday, Inigo told me he'll visit again in two weeks. Hide in the shop and you can spy on him."

"You're worrying me," Anne said. "Who's at the shop to look after you?"

"I don't need looking after—but I can't convince you of that until you see Inigo for yourself," Thomasina said.

Anne pursed her lips. "You really believe what you're telling me?" she said slowly.

Thomasina nodded. She was aware of how strange her tale must sound, which made shame boil inside her.

"Yes, I do believe it," she said. "At ten minutes to midnight the Wednesday after next, knock on the door. I'll let you in. Inigo always comes at midnight. Then—then, you'll see."

Anne sighed, looked down at the ground and up again, staring straight into Thomasina's eyes as if there were a riddle in her gaze that she was trying to decipher.

"I'll think about it," she said. "In the meantime, come by our shop if you want something to help you sleep. Some medicine might make you feel better."

She gave Thomasina a faint, sad smile, then set off down

the street to Hawke's. The shouts and cries coming from the direction of the river had begun to grow quieter, and Thomasina guessed the Frost Fair was wrapping up for the day. She hoped with all her heart that Anne would come in two weeks. *Because if Anne doesn't believe me*, she said to herself, *then no one else will.*

A single, glittering tear trickled down her face, flashing quicksilver before disappearing into the cracks of the cobblestones at her feet.

11

Anne's Trick

Over the next fortnight, as each morning dawned, many more tents emerged on the frozen River Thames as if by magic, glittering with frozen dew.

To Thomasina's eye, the river was now a sprawling metropolis, crammed fit to burst with every trade she could think of, as well as many she'd never encountered before. Hawkers selling canned milk and all sorts of wares, with shouts of "Spiced cakes!," "Lovely pickled salmon!," and "Get your steaming mutton pastries here!" were everywhere, making her mouth water with a dizzying array of enticing smells. Some wheeled huge barrows crammed with roasted nuts, while others poured out gallons of mulled wine, spirals of aromatic steam spicing the air.

As well as the traders, musicians bounded about the river, bellowing and banging as loudly as they could—fiddle players, bagpipers, drummers, and singers. Acrobats somersaulted on each other's shoulders, and fire-eaters gulped down mouthfuls of scarlet flames, spitting them out in a flourish and making their audiences gasp and cower. Soothsayers and fortune-tellers trundled from group to group, their predictions ranging widely, from death and destruction to love and marriage, while wise women announced they could cure anything from scabies to old age. Gold dealers smiled with glinting teeth as they weighed huge slabs in heavy brass scales. There was even a man in a moth-eaten hat keen to proffer stuffed stoats and geese to anyone who crossed his path.

Inside the huge circus tent in the middle of the ice, Thomasina heard the snarls and grunts of trapped wild beasts. Though part of her desperately wished to see inside, she couldn't stop thinking of the poor dancing bear who'd dripped blood onto the fresh ice. Besides, she doubted anything could be more exciting than the strange Frost Beasts from the Other Frost Fair, their ice-flecked fur sparkling in the moonlight.

There were even rumors that the king himself, Charles II, had visited the river several times. However, there were now so many people of every rank mingling with each other that she had a hard time distinguishing who was who. Lords and ladies from the countryside had traveled great distances to visit. They went about in their soft furs and pearls, peering at everything. Once, an old man wearing a long brown wig and with two spaniels trotting along beside him had winked at her, but it could have been anyone for all she knew.

Christmas was fast approaching, and Thomasina and Anne both had their hands full making and selling wares for their stalls. They still spoke to each other most days, but ever since Thomasina had told Anne about Inigo and the Other Frost Fair, a distance had opened up between them. Taking her friend's advice, Thomasina had bought a sleeping draught for herself, but she didn't feel any different than she had before.

Thomasina knew her friend was still concerned, and she tried to find things to occupy herself with in the run-up to Inigo's next visit, which she hoped Anne would attend. She found any excuse she could to drop by Hawke's Apothecary stall to give Anne little treats, such as marzipan roses, mince pies, and spiced hotcakes. And in the moments she had to herself, when she wasn't caring for Mother, she managed—after several frustrating attempts—to recreate the ginger and honey pastilles they'd thought up together.

After their main stock had cleared one lunchtime, and Father had given her permission to sell the pastilles, she called Anne over, and they were thrilled to discover these sweet cures sold much more quickly than any other wares she and Father had made—in fact, they were completely sold out by the end of the day. When the very last ginger and honey pastille was gone, Thomasina glanced up at Father. To her amazement, she thought she saw a small, surprised smile of approval appear on his face.

This incident, tiny in itself, gave her the feeling that the father she'd grown up with had come back, even if just for a golden, shimmering moment. It made her heart ache.

Thomasina found that, just as Inigo had warned, the silver snowflake necklace she wore didn't protect her from the cold in the daytime. By dusk every day, her fingers were stiff and numb, the skin on her hands, cheeks, and lips red-raw and peeling, and her feet stung and burned with chilblains.

All she could do was wait patiently as the days rolled on, and when Wednesday evening finally came, she was determined to prove herself to Anne.

Hands shaking, she unbolted the heavy front door of Burgess & Son's with five minutes to go until midnight.

"Anne?" she whispered, sticking her head out to look up and down the empty street. All she could see was a glimmer of moonlight illuminating the snow and ice on the cobblestones.

No one answered. Thomasina looked up and down the way for a final time, then closed the door. She wrenched one of the spindly stools out from behind Father's jumble, accidentally dislodging a battered old goblet Arthur used to drink from. She placed the stool near the door and sat on it.

She felt her throat grow warm. Tears pricked her eyes, a couple burning her cheeks as they snaked down her face. She'd so wanted Anne to see Inigo for herself and realize she was telling the truth—even though the truth itself was so fantastical. She'd been so hopeful, and now her heart sank as she heard the deep, dark bell of St. Bartholomew's Church strike midnight, its clanging reverberating in a shiver around the graveyard and streets surrounding it.

Tap, tap, tap.

"Is that you, Inigo?" she whispered, wiping her face with the backs of her hands.

"Yes."

Thomasina opened the door to find Inigo standing outside, frowning and wearing a pair of enormous silver breeches.

"Good evening, Miss Burgess. Is there someone with you tonight?"

"No."

Inigo's gaze flickered.

"You're lying to me," he said, his voice gentle. "We won't

go on our adventure to the Other Frost Fair tonight because of this. What a shame—you were two visits away from having Arthur conjured back to life. . . ."

"Take me with you," Thomasina begged, her knees weak. "Please! There isn't anyone with me, I promise. I checked up and down the street before you arrived: it's just you and me— and I want so much to see Arthur—"

"No," Inigo snapped. He turned away, seemed to think better of it, and faced her again.

"For us to embark on adventures together, Miss Burgess, it's imperative that it's just you and I who visit the Other Frost Fair. Do you understand?"

Thomasina didn't understand one bit, but nevertheless she nodded.

"And I dressed up specially," he said crossly, flicking a speck of ice off the side of his silver breeches.

"Have I ruined everything?" she managed to say, her voice barely a croak. Tears rushed to her eyes, and she choked on her words. "Are you still going to bring Arthur back to life?" Grasping the doorknob, she stared at Inigo, whose pale aquamarine eyes flickered, surveyed hers, and then softened.

"Yes, I am—I will," he said, ducking his head and nodding. "But please don't play this trick on me again."

Thomasina nodded, her throat full with hot tears.

"I promise," she gulped.

Inigo nodded.

"Well, good night," he said with a bow. He departed with a flick of his cloak and was soon swallowed by the night.

"T-Thomasina?" a voice murmured.

Huddled in a thick cloak, Anne crept out of the shadows of the building next door. Her face was frozen in the moonlight, mouth agape in shock.

"Anne!" Thomasina gasped. "I thought you hadn't come!"

"I—I s-saw him," Anne said, shivering. "J-Just now. I saw a man whose beard was sp-spun with frost, and whose skin was s-stained silver blue. I heard him talk about bringing your brother back to life, and about the Other Frost Fair."

"He wouldn't take me tonight," Thomasina said. "He knew you were there."

"I—I wanted to—to c-catch you out," Anne said, her head drooping. "To make sure I was seeing something with my own eyes, and not some kind of performance. I'm sorry," she said, her voice hitching in her throat. "It s-sounded so strange when you told me that I didn't know how it could be real. But I do now."

Thomasina hugged her, then broke away.

"Sorry," she said. "It's just so nice you believe me."

Anne chuckled. "It's late," she said. "I'm so c-cold, and you've given me a lot to think about. I'm going home now, but will I see you on the Thames tomorrow?"

"Yes," Thomasina whispered, "of course. Here, wear this—" She tried to unclasp the snowflake necklace so it could warm her friend, but found she couldn't again. Perhaps it was just because she was very cold, but the tiny silver catch felt like it had been welded tight: it was completely smooth.

"I d-don't suppose he's m-made it stick to you?" Anne shivered. "With m-magic?"

"It's probably just because it's cold," Thomasina said. "It's too fiddly."

She watched as Anne stumbled her way down the street toward Hawke's, then she walked to the workroom and warmed her hands by the dying fire, gasping at the sudden heat that enveloped her. When her fingers had thawed, she tried once more to unfasten the clasp of the silver snowflake necklace, but once again it proved too difficult. The catch now felt completely smooth under her fingers, with no hint of an opening anywhere. After several more minutes of trying and failing, Thomasina knew it wouldn't open.

Why had Inigo given her something she couldn't take off? Was this his idea of a strange joke? Was it connected to the silver snowflake on her skin? As Thomasina rolled up her sleeve to inspect the patch on her wrist again, what she saw made her insides squeeze tight.

There was no longer one snowflake, but three, glistening on the surface of her skin, dancing in the glow cast by the fire.

12

Dr. Silsworth

Thomasina woke to morning bells as usual, clanging from St. Bartholomew's Church. She automatically checked her left arm and saw the three snowflakes were still there on her wrist, glowing on the surface of her skin. She took several deep, shuddering breaths, in and out, hearing her heartbeat rattle against her rib cage. This was Inigo's doing, she was sure of it. Who else could have made them materialize on her body? Why was he doing this?

Despite having reassured Anne that the flakes were perfectly harmless, a question pulsed in her heart. *Inigo wouldn't do anything bad to me, would he?* No, of course he wouldn't. . . . What would be the point? Inigo wanted to help her, not hurt her. She just had to trust him. All she needed to do was make sure no one else saw her wrist until Arthur was back, and then she'd tell everyone in her family what had happened. She smiled to herself, warmth pooling inside her at the thought of her brother's mouth falling open in amazement.

When she felt beside her for Mother, however, to check if she was awake, she only felt blankets.

"M-Mother?" she said, sitting bolt upright and rubbing her eyes.

When her vision adjusted to the daylight, she saw her mother standing by the window again, her shawl around her shoulders.

"Do you like the sound of the bells?" Thomasina said, getting out of bed and crossing the room to stand next to her.

Mother nodded and smiled faintly, and then she did something that to other people might be normal, but to Thomasina was extraordinary because she hadn't heard it for so long—

Mother hummed along with the peal of the bells.

Thomasina felt a smile break out on her face, and joy fill her heart.

Was it possible that her visits to the Other Frost Fair weren't just restoring Arthur to life, but restoring Mother to good health as well? For the four years since Arthur's death, Mother had stayed in bed, moving only to use a chamber pot or take a brief, shuffling walk around their bedroom, but here she was, looking at the world outside again as if she found things in it to interest her.

Thomasina felt a rush of excitement. Though the image of the three snowflakes on her wrist appeared in her mind, as did Arthur's blurred, indistinct face, she waved them aside. If losing her memories of Arthur for a short while and having a few snowflakes appear on her skin were the price she had to pay, it was worth it to get Arthur back and for Mother to be well again.

That day at the Frost Fair, Father seemed rather preoccupied: he jumped when anyone spoke to him and flinched when Thomasina accidentally spilled a couple of squares of aniseed cake onto the ice. Thomasina wondered if he'd suffered a poor night's sleep.

"Is everything all right, Father?" she said as he picked up the cake pieces, throwing them to a stray dog who'd come sniffing hopefully around their stand.

"What?" he said, frowning slightly. "Oh—yes. Everything's fine."

He still looked forlorn, and Thomasina tried to think of something that would help cheer him up.

"Mother was looking out of the window, humming along to the sound of the bells this morning," she said. "And she opened her eyes the other day, too. I think her health is improving."

"Hmm," her father said.

Was it just Thomasina's imagination, or did Father look uncomfortable when she'd mentioned Mother's health? She bit her lip in worry, but there was not much time to dwell on their short conversation, as their customers were very demanding.

Two hours later, after dropping some empty crates back at the shop, she returned to the Frost Fair and wandered around, drinking in the buzz around her.

"The Frost Fair isn't half as interesting as the Other Frost Fair," she whispered to Arthur. "No magical creatures walking around, for one thing, ready to hunt you down if you're not invited to it. It's still good fun, though."

F-Frost . . . Fair . . . , she heard him repeating back to her, and his appearance was more faded than ever in her mind. Was his hair black or brown? She couldn't quite remember, and she bit her lip in worry. It felt as if she were betraying Arthur by forgetting vital aspects of who he was, even though she knew it was part of the process that would lead to his return.

"Thomasina!"

She was glad to have her thoughts about her brother interrupted. She scanned the Frost Fair until her eyes landed on Anne, who was waving at her. Eyes sparkling, she was drinking something from a goblet that had wisps of smoke seeping from the rim and which smelled delicious.

"I was hoping you'd be free this afternoon," Anne said, unfurling a flyer, her hands shaking from the cold. "A physician called Dr. Silsworth is talking today at the fair about his work—I don't know anything about him, but it could be helpful to listen to him, if we want to think about other medicinal sweets we could make. Do you want to come with me?"

"I won't understand what he says," Thomasina said.

"Nonsense," Anne said briskly, grabbing Thomasina's hand. "Come on."

Grateful for something else to concentrate on, Thomasina followed her.

"Next, I want to invent a medicinal sweet that helps with stomachaches," Anne was saying as they slipped across the ice, meandering through crowds. "It's one of the most common complaints Uncle and I hear about in our shop. I have a couple of questions I'd like to ask Dr. Silsworth that could help us develop a recipe . . . something to do with pears, maybe."

"That's such a good idea." Thomasina grinned. "What do you think?" she muttered to Arthur when Anne let go of her hand and walked a little ahead of her to accommodate a large crowd passing near them.

Arthur didn't reply to her this time. She felt a sharp twist in her stomach. Why couldn't she hear his voice anymore?

They arrived at a gathering next to the large red-and-white-striped circus tent, where Thomasina had once seen the poor bear yanked by a chain.

"Welcome, ladies and gentlemen," she heard a rasping baritone proclaim at the center of the throng. She and Anne pushed forward to see who was talking, and Thomasina recognized the figure on the platform in the middle of the crowd as the man she'd seen talking to her father outside St. Bartholomew's Church—the man who'd reminded her so much of a moldy apple.

"My name is Dr. Silsworth," he announced, "and I specialize in madness. I work all across London, and occasionally I treat patients in the Bethlehem Hospital in Moorfields, more commonly known as Bedlam."

He was such an unfriendly-looking man that even when he smiled he seemed to be sneering. Anne showed Thomasina the flyer she was holding. She couldn't read it, as the letters were too small for her to decipher, but she saw a drawing of Dr. Silsworth on the page.

"Bedlam," Dr. Silsworth said, sweeping his gaze around his audience, "is a place where physicians like myself study and cure madness. For a small fee, you can visit the hospital and view the patients from a gallery, to see how strangely they behave."

Thomasina frowned, mulling over his words. Father had seemed despondent when she'd spoken to him that morning about Mother's health . . . and she remembered that, outside the church the other week, Dr. Silsworth had asked Father to update him about how Mother was getting on. . . . Did Father want Mother to be under Dr. Silsworth's care? Was *that* why he'd been so preoccupied—because he was planning something?

She gnawed her bottom lip, worried.

"Madness affects men and women in different ways," Dr. Silsworth continued. "And women, as we all know, are feebler than men. Their emotions often overwhelm them. We call this . . . *hysteria*."

Thomasina's ears pounded.

"Today," Dr. Silsworth announced, "I've brought one of my patients with me, and I'll demonstrate before you all how I can cure her."

The crowd murmured as a young woman with thick red hair was pushed forward onto the platform. Her eyes darted nervously around the crowd. Beside her, a man who seemed to be Dr. Silsworth's assistant held her firmly by the elbow.

"I don't like this," Anne whispered to Thomasina.

"Me neither," Thomasina said. "Let's go."

Around them, however, more people had joined the crowd, and it was difficult to escape.

"This woman here, ladies and gentlemen," Dr. Silsworth said, "is mad. She rarely speaks; she suffers from night terrors."

Thomasina felt something sink to the pit of her stomach. "Mother doesn't talk much, either," she whispered to Arthur.

Again, she was met with silence.

The redheaded woman on the stage looked at her feet, and Thomasina could have sworn she saw a tear drip from her chin. Looking at her, Thomasina realized something—

There isn't anything wrong with madness at all, she said to herself.

The woman just seemed incredibly sad, like there was something within her no one could reach. And anyway, what was wrong with experiencing the world a little differently from other people?

"Come, step a little closer, madam," Dr. Silsworth was saying to her now, and his assistant pushed the woman farther forward, so the crowd could view her better. "I am about to show you how I can cure patients like this woman here. Madam," he said, turning to face her, "look up at the crowd."

"Stop treating her like an animal in a cage!" Thomasina cried out, her hands balled into fists as she stormed across the ice toward the platform as fast as she could to confront Dr. Silsworth. "Stop touching her!"

Dr. Silsworth looked slightly surprised, but then he sneered at Thomasina.

"This woman," he snapped, gesturing at the woman with red hair, "was left in my care because of her hysteria. See here, ladies and gentlemen," he said, looking out over Thomasina's head and addressing himself to the crowd, "how weak and *feeble-minded* this girl is? Why! She can't even understand what I'm doing."

The crowd murmured their agreement, and some of them scowled at Thomasina and tutted.

"Thomasina!" She heard Anne's voice, clear as a bell, across the fray. "Let's go."

Thomasina made to step onto the platform, toward the woman, but her way was blocked by Dr. Silsworth's assistant, who glared at her. He was heavyset and older than her by a few years. She didn't fancy her chances against him.

"Shoo!" Dr. Silsworth said. "Be off with you, girl."

His assistant stepped forward and shoved Thomasina out of the way. Members of the crowd cheered, and a little boy whooped.

"And be careful you don't become hysterical yourself!" Dr. Silsworth called after her. "Now, ladies and gentlemen, as I was saying . . ."

Thomasina felt a gentle hand clasp hers, pulling her away.

"Come on," Anne whispered. "We can't do anything here."

"But that woman—"

"Is in their care."

"It isn't right!"

"Maybe not to you and me, but—"

"Anne, how are you fine with what's happening to her?"

"I'm not, Thomasina! I'm sorry you had to see it, but sometimes it's best for people with illnesses like that to be somewhere safe."

"Safe? You mean paraded around Bedlam, where people pay to gawp at them like they're part of a circus?"

"No," Anne said, her voice grave. "I don't think that. I didn't realize this is what was on display, else I would never have come, nor asked you to come with me. All it said on the flyer was that he's a doctor."

Thomasina's shoulders slumped. They walked across the ice, past watermen demanding payment from people trying to enter the Frost Fair.

"Have you heard what people say about my mother?" Thomasina asked.

Anne blushed. "Yes," she said. "Just dribs and drabs, really. I—I've also heard about your brother. Miss Maple-thorpe told me."

"Mother hasn't been the same since Arthur died," Thomasina said. It felt strange to say this aloud for the first time ever. "She used to behave . . . very differently."

Anne nodded.

"She taught me everything when I was little," Thomasina went on, feeling a sharp twist inside her stomach. "She was showing me how to read properly . . . before. And then, when Arthur died, something changed. . . ." She hesitated. "Something inside her has been . . . shut off, somehow. It's my fault."

"Thomasina—"

"No, it is," she insisted. "Mother knows I'm to blame. I teased Arthur. Told him he couldn't win a race against me. He wouldn't have pushed himself had it not been for me."

"I disagree," Anne said. "Asthma attacks can be fatal. Sometimes you can't stop them, no matter how hard you try. We don't have a good cure for them yet."

Thomasina pursed her lips. She didn't agree with Anne, but she didn't see what good it would do to argue. They walked in silence for a while, then her friend paused.

"Stop," Anne murmured, holding out an arm and forcing Thomasina to a standstill.

"What is it?"

"I think someone's following us," Anne whispered. "I felt

someone creep behind our backs after we left the river, then I thought they'd gone. But I felt them near us again just now."

Thomasina looked around in the gathering gloom but couldn't make anything out that seemed odd.

"You think someone's watching us?" she said.

"She'd be right about that," a voice rasped from the shadows—and before Thomasina could cry out, a hand was clamped over her mouth so tightly she couldn't breathe. Another grabbed her middle, knocking the wind out of her completely. She heard Anne scream as she felt herself being dragged backward into the darkness.

13

The Merchant of Cadaver Street

Thomasina reacted on pure instinct, her expertise honed from years spent in tussles with Arthur.

She felt around for a foot behind her and stamped on it several times as hard as she could, hearing whoever it belonged to yell before they released her, then she turned and shoved them backward as hard as she could. Though she and her assailant were about the same height, she could tell her quick wits had taken him aback and he fell with a yelp. She staggered away, gasping, her hands on her knees, and lurched forward to choke air into her chest.

"Get out of the way, Thomasina!" she heard, and lifted her head.

Anne had wrenched an old street sign, crystallized with ice, out of the muck and snow, and was holding it aloft.

With a groan, Thomasina's assailant sat up, rubbing his feet where she'd struck him and wincing.

"Please . . ." He panted. "Listen to me."

Thomasina was surprised to see him. He was a fair, blond-haired boy around their age, with a softer voice than Thomasina had initially thought, his vowels shorter than someone from London. His clothing and figure showed unmistakable signs of wealth: his well-built frame, a gold signet ring on his finger that caught the dim light, and a thick, fur-lined cloak around his shoulders. His face was so pale it looked colorless in the gloom.

"You have some cheek," Anne said. "How *dare* you!" Then, turning to Thomasina, she said, "Are you all right?"

Thomasina nodded, shaking. "Are *you*?" Anne gave a grim nod, though Thomasina saw her hands, too, were shaking—and perhaps not just from the exertion of holding the sign. Her chest wheezing, she stumbled over to her friend and rubbed her arm in silent thanks for her support.

"You don't . . . understand . . ." the boy said, still clearly in pain. "We mustn't be . . . seen . . . because . . ." But he was still hurting too much from the blow Thomasina had inflicted on him, because his next words were indistinguishable from a groan.

"Tell us who you are," said Thomasina. She coughed,

then, despite her groaning chest, tried to straighten herself up and braced herself to attack the boy again, curling her hands into fists, ready to strike. Beside her, Anne kept holding the sign aloft, but Thomasina saw that her friend's hands were still trembling.

"Anne?" Thomasina said softly, then coughed again. "You don't *seem* all right."

Her friend shook her head.

"I'm not, really," Anne replied. "You really scared me just now," she said to the stranger, her voice shaking. "What do you want?"

"I promise," the boy said, raising a hand. "I mean neither of you any harm." The pain seemed to be subsiding enough for him to squint at them both. Thomasina suspected he'd have wicked bruises on both his feet and ankles by morning. "Please," he said, "we need to get out of the street. I think you're in danger. You're being followed. That's why I dragged you into the darkness—to get you out of their sight, and make sure they had less chance of spotting you. I was told to do that, you see, by—oh, I'll explain soon enough, but for now we all need to get out of here. My rooms are a few minutes away. Sorry I frightened you," he went on. "I realize creeping up on you wasn't the best way to go about it. But I—I just didn't know what else to do. I couldn't just walk up and say hello, or they'd have caught us all by now. Let's hurry—we don't have much time before they find us again."

"They?" Anne said. "Who's following us?"

"I'm sorry, but there's no time to explain," the boy replied. He looked at Thomasina. "Are you hurt?"

Thomasina shook her head.

"A fine thing for you to ask, having just winded her and scared us both," Anne said.

"For which I again apologize—but we must move away from the street now."

"We're—" Thomasina wheezed, then broke into a series of coughs. "We're . . . not going . . . *anywhere* with you unless . . . unless you tell us who you—"

"My name's Henry," the boy interrupted, his voice cracking as he slipped a little on the ice. "Henry Lawley. I'm a merchant—well, an apprentice one to my parents, anyway—and I live on Cadaver Street. I promise I'll tell you everything, but we must get inside first. The people in gray cloaks with white eyes—you've seen them around London, haven't you?"

"What people in gray cloaks? Who are you talking—" said Anne.

"Yes," whispered Thomasina.

Henry looked at her and gave a grim nod, soft eyes roaming around her face.

"You've—You've seen them, too?" Thomasina said, panic welling in her stomach, then she coughed again—her chest felt too tight.

"Yes," Henry said. "They're swarming all over London, and more of them are appearing in this corner every day. I saw two on your tail about twenty minutes ago. That's why I . . ." He lapsed into silence.

"Why you attacked my friend," Anne finished. "The logic is flawless."

"Anne, I want to hear what he's got to say," Thomasina said.

"We don't even know him," Anne replied.

"But he might know something we don't," Thomasina argued.

Tottering unsteadily onto his feet, Henry dusted the snow off his clothes. "Thanks," he said. "Come on—we must get inside." He looked at the sign Anne was holding, then at Thomasina, who still had her hands up in front of her, curled into fists. "Are you, er—are you going to bring that with you?" he said to Anne. "Or fight me again?" he asked Thomasina.

Anne considered the sign, then Henry, then looked back at the sign again. "No," she said, and she tossed it to the ground, where it landed with a deafening crack. Then she winced and pulled a splinter from the index finger of her right hand. "Ow!" She grimaced, shooting a look at Henry. "Besides, it's too heavy to carry. I'm only going with you because Thomasina wants to. But," she warned, "we'll defend ourselves again if you try anything."

He nodded, then gestured for them to follow him as he hobbled into the gloomy, deserted side street.

Thomasina lowered her fists. She could still hear shouts and echoes of the Frost Fair in the distance. She scoured the ground around her, looking past the bones, broken bottles, and rotting food, then bent down, wincing as her chest squeaked and groaned with every breath, and scooped up two jagged rocks from the side of the street. She gave one to Anne and folded the other into her cloak.

"Just in case," she whispered.

After making their way in silence down several fine streets and past grand buildings, they arrived outside an imposing redbrick townhouse. Henry stumbled up the stone steps and tapped on the door. A pompous-looking servant wearing a neat white wig opened it. He raised his bushy eyebrows at the three of them, and even more at Henry's bedraggled state, but stood back to let them all through. They walked into a wood-paneled room lit by several candles that made it smell like the cozy interior of Hawke's apothecary shop. Thomasina shivered as a final gust of icy wind blew in just before the servant bolted the door. Would the Great Frost ever end?

They followed Henry up the creaking stairs to the second floor, where the servant sprang ahead of them and opened a door.

Thomasina's wheeze was still groaning in her chest. Anne heard it, too, and rubbed her back for her. "Are you all right?" she hissed.

"Yes," Thomasina lied. "I just need to sit down." She also needed to hear whatever it was Henry had to tell them.

"Here," Henry said, gesturing to a chair, "sit down. Please." Thomasina sat, feeling her chest complain still louder. Her fingers sank into velvet as she grasped the sides of the chair and closed her eyes.

Though she could no longer see what was happening, her senses were overwhelmed by this room: the sweet scent of wax, the soft chair she was sitting on, and the sound of a clock somewhere, gently ticking the time. She had the feeling that Anne and Henry would be looking anywhere but at each other. After several, silent minutes, Thomasina opened her eyes again, blinking at the brightness of the fireplace in front of her, then nodded at Anne, who took her hand in hers as if it were the most natural thing in the world to do.

"Better?" Anne said.

"Yes, much better."

"Good," said Anne.

The door opened, and a tall servant came in and crossed the room, bearing a vast tray laden with steaming drinks and large slabs of ginger cake. They watched him set the tray down, then walk back to the door, closing it behind him with a gentle click.

"So. Why are we here?" Anne said.

Henry crossed one stockinged leg over the other, looking at them with sad, weary eyes.

"I suppose," he said, staring around the room, "I should start at the beginning . . . years before I was born."

Aristocratic men and women stared down at them from the portraits on the walls, their oil-waxed skin gleaming in the firelight. This wasn't a comfortable place, Thomasina thought, as she drew her cloak around her as tightly as she could. The paintings cast a strange, centuries-old weight she could feel in the air around her, as if there were living, breathing people sitting just out of sight.

"Tell me," Henry said, nodding toward a light-gray wall on the left, on which a single painting hung. "What do you think of him?"

Thomasina and Anne looked at the portrait. Its gleaming lines depicted a youth of no more than twenty-one, with milk-white skin and tousled hair. His light-brown beard wasn't fully grown yet, and he was a small, slight creature, resting a hand on his hip and staring at them with a vacant smile. His clothes seemed ornate and fashionable for the time he'd been painted in—an open-collared ruff trimmed with delicate lace constricted his neck, and his breeches were enormous, ballooning to just above his knees.

"He looks like a nobleman," Anne said.

"Yes. He was my great-grandfather," Henry replied.

The fire crackled and sputtered scarlet and gold flames, as if it, too, were privy to the secret Henry was spilling from his lips, and desperately wanted to join in.

"Why are you telling us this?" Anne said. "You said you had information—something that could help us."

"I promise it's important," Henry said. "You see, this man has become a legend in my family. There's no evidence my great-grandfather died. He simply vanished into thin air one night. His body was never found."

Thomasina looked again at the portrait. A slight smile was dancing on the boy's lips, and she thought that he would have been an impish, mischievous kind of person.

"He was older than he is in that portrait when he disappeared," Henry said.

"What happened?" Anne asked in a hushed voice. Her concentration on Henry's tale seemed to give him confidence, and he straightened his shoulders slightly.

"He disappeared one winter's night," he said. "A night

just like tonight. It's a famous story in our family. My ancestor had been to a party at Court and was due home. He never arrived."

A shiver coursed up Thomasina's spine. It wasn't for lack of warmth. The fire was roaring in the hearth, reminding her of the massive blaze she'd seen at the Frost Fair earlier that day, where an ox was roasting on a spit. The firelight illuminated tired lines around Henry's eyes.

"You asked me," he said, "why I followed you in the first place. It's because of something that happened a few weeks ago. I've been trailing you almost constantly since, knowing that if I tried to speak to you openly, I'd endanger you."

"What happened a few weeks ago?" asked Thomasina.

"Well . . ." Henry began, "there was a knock on my door, at midnight. I opened it and . . . and two people with silver skin and white clothes were waiting for me. Frightened me out of my mind, I can tell you—I thought I was going mad."

Thomasina and Anne glanced at each other, eyebrows raised. Another chill prickled up and down Thomasina's spine.

"They didn't say anything," Henry continued, "but indicated I should follow them, so I did. They took me to the icy River Thames . . . and . . . I didn't feel cold, even though it was the middle of the night."

Butterflies fluttered in Thomasina's stomach.

"When I arrived on the river," he said, eyes scanning both of theirs as if he were afraid they'd laugh at him, "I saw a huge theater with animals and people flitting around. They all looked like they were made of ice. Apart from you, that is . . ." he said, looking at Thomasina. "You were there, too. . . .

"One of the ice people who'd taken me there said you were in danger, and that I had to tell you about my great-grandfather, and who I was, and that I had to keep you out of sight of the Gray Cloaks—the people with white eyes dressed in gray, who were walking around on the river. They pointed to the river again and I saw . . . I saw a man next to you. Though he looked a bit different from his portrait, I knew he was my ancestor. I tried to ask the ice people around me about him, but they all kept telling me the same thing, over and over again: find you, tell you who I was, and tell you about my ancestor—and to make sure the Gray Cloaks didn't see us."

Thomasina's ears were pounding.

"What was the name of your great-grandfather?" Anne whispered.

But Thomasina knew the answer before Henry gave it. . . .

"Inigo," he said. "Sir Inigo Lawley."

14

Mary

Why did the Frost Folk want Thomasina to find out who Inigo really was?

Thomasina turned this question around in her mind as she mulled over everything Henry had said. He interrupted her thoughts.

"Why were you out there on the ice when I saw you with my ancestor?"

"Because I want to bring my brother back to life," she explained. Henry looked taken aback. "Inigo told me he can conjure him back from the dead. He said all I need to do is visit the Other Frost Fair with him four times—a visit for every year that Arthur's been dead—so I can trade away my memories of him. Do *you* have anyone you want to bring back to life? Is that why the Frost Folk showed you the Other Frost Fair?"

Henry shook his head, looking nonplussed.

"My parents are both alive, and I'm an only child," he said. "There's no one I want to bring back from the dead."

"I think you should tell Henry what's been happening," Anne whispered to Thomasina. "There must be a reason why the Frost Folk approached him."

Thomasina nodded. She hadn't planned on telling anyone else about Inigo, or her visits—not, at least, until Arthur was safely back. Now, however, it seemed her only option. By the time she'd finished recounting everything, showing Henry the necklace, and describing how hazy her memories of Arthur were becoming, his mouth was hanging open.

"Never in my wildest dreams . . ." he said, and then fell silent. Thomasina looked at the portrait of Sir Inigo Lawley again. The Inigo she knew was middle-aged, so she found it hard to tell if he could really be the same person. And yet there was something about the set of the young Inigo's eyes and mouth in the portrait that looked familiar.

"There's also my arm," she said, and she rolled up her sleeve a little to show Henry and Anne the three snowflakes near her wrist.

Anne gasped. "You have *three* snowflakes there now," she said. "You only had one before."

Henry was staring in astonishment at her arm, too. "I've seen someone else with marks on their arm like that," he said.

"Who?" Anne said sharply.

"One of my friends who works here—a maid called Mary. I saw silver snowflakes on her arm when she was scrubbing the fireplace last week." He frowned. "I should have asked her about it, but somehow I felt afraid to. Visiting the Other Frost Fair really spooked me."

"Can't we ask her now?" Anne said as Thomasina rose to her feet, excited. Perhaps there was someone else who'd visited the Other Frost Fair like she had? If so, maybe she'd know why the snowflakes had appeared on her arm.

"I would," Henry said slowly, "only she went missing shortly after I last saw her."

Thomasina sat back down, her hopes dashed.

"Do you have any idea where she could have gone?" Anne said.

He shook his head. "No. None."

"Thomasina," Anne said urgently, "do you think Mary's disappearance could have something to do with the Other Frost Fair?"

"I don't know," Thomasina said, her voice barely a whisper.

They all lapsed into silence. Thomasina felt like her head was all jumbled up with this new information. Two of the Frost Folk had told Henry to seek her out and tell her about Inigo. And now, she'd found out about a girl with silver snowflake marks the same as hers, but the girl had disappeared. She'd not paid too much attention to the snowflakes blossoming on her skin, but knowing that they'd appeared on another girl who'd gone missing made her question things. . . .

Outside, night had fallen, casting everything in deep shadow. Thomasina was worried how Father would react when she returned home so late.

Henry was a changed boy to the ruffian he'd first seemed to them, and he insisted on paying for a hackney coach to take them back.

"I'm sorry again for being such a cad earlier," he said. "I do hope that, in time, I can make it up to you."

After a few minutes, a hackney coach came creaking along the lonely street, and Henry was able to hail it for them. It drew up at the curb, and Henry helped Anne and Thomasina in.

"Can we meet again soon if I discover anything new?" he asked, his pale face anxious as he peered up at them both.

"Yes, I think we should," Thomasina said. "Anne—what do you think?"

Anne nodded. "We're all in this together now," she said.

"Thank you," Henry replied. "I'll stop by at Burgess & Son's then, shall I?"

"You'd best come over to Hawke's," Anne said.

"Thomasina spends a lot of time carrying crates to and from the Frost Fair, so you two might miss each other."

"Then I'll visit you soon, Anne," he said. "Thank you again, both of you, for believing me. Coachman—drive on!" And with that, Thomasina and Anne were on their way home.

Back at the shop, Thomasina bolted the front door behind her and crept upstairs, desperate not to wake Father as she passed his room on the first landing, or Mother up in the attic bedroom they shared.

"Tonight's been very strange," she whispered to Arthur, who once again didn't reply.

Mother was fast asleep, snoring quietly in her side of the bed, so Thomasina undressed as quickly as she could in the moonlight, shivering in the winter cold. Before putting on her nightdress, she glanced once more at her arm—then stared at it in surprise.

There were no longer just three silver snowflakes speckling her skin near her wrist, but many more! *They must have appeared after I showed Henry and Anne*, she thought. Perhaps they came during the ride home. Whenever they'd appeared, the snowflakes now covered her skin—her wrist and forearm, and all the way up to her armpit. Shining silver, they winked and glittered at her in the moonlight that streamed in through the shutters.

Thomasina frowned, feeling the hairs on her body stand on end. Three snowflakes were puzzling, but seeing them decorate the whole of her left arm was much more frightening. Her heart fluttered as she touched the cold patches of skin where the snowflakes were dotted.

A curious thought occurred to her as she peered at them: *More and more they remind me of the Frost Folk's skin.*

As soon as this thought appeared in Thomasina's mind, she shuddered and shook her head, dismissing it. It was impossible for her to be turning into one of the Frost Folk. She wasn't made of ice. . . . For one thing, her skin was still visible behind the silver snowflakes. And besides, Inigo had given her his word that she wouldn't be in any danger. She thought of how close she was now to bringing Arthur back. She wouldn't give up now.

She could trust Inigo . . . couldn't she?

15

Black Cat

Christmas arrived. Thomasina woke to find fat snow-flakes falling when she peeked through the shutters of the bedroom she shared with Mother. Despite everything that had happened recently, she couldn't help but smile when she saw them. She opened the windows and stuck her head outside, feeling ice melt on her tongue. Arthur would have loved to have had a snowball fight if he were here.

"We'll be able to have one next year," she whispered to him.

The thought warmed her heart.

Thomasina and Anne had managed to sell more medicinal sweets the day before, on Christmas Eve. Their stock sold out rather quickly, as many people at the Frost Fair bought last-minute treats for their friends and family. Thomasina and Anne had been experimenting with some pears Thomasina had preserved in October, and they had worked together to create spiced pear loaves. Anne had explained to Thomasina that she and her uncle often prescribed pears for customers complaining of a stomachache or nausea, though Thomasina had a sneaky suspicion that not *everyone* who had been eager to buy the sweet, tasty-looking slices was ill.

Making and selling these medicinal sweets with Anne made Thomasina happy in a different kind of way than she'd ever felt before. But she couldn't see how they'd be able to continue their enterprise together once the Frost Fair ended—not when they each had their own family business to worry about. Thomasina knew she could never consider leaving Burgess & Son's.

The shop looked very festive. Garlands of holly adorned nearly every surface, and Thomasina had arranged pots of willow twigs sprouting soft silver catkins on the driftwood shelves. Flushed with their success at the Frost Fair, Father had ordered in more sacks of sweetmaking ingredients, and trays upon trays of fresh treats glowed in the soft light cast by the many candles placed around the room.

Thomasina cut off more holly from the boughs curling around their back door and laid it on the workroom mantelpiece, below which a merry fire burned bright and warm. Even being ignored by Father didn't have its usual sting for Thomasina. Neither did the church service, where the parson rattled on for an hour longer than usual, and she felt Dr. Silsworth's eyes burning into her back.

Knowing the physician's attention was focused on her made her squirm. *Why is he so interested in me?* she wondered. Could it be because he'd been speaking to Father about Mother's health again? What if—her heart twisted—he were to convince Father one day that looking after Mother in Bedlam was the right thing to do, if her health didn't improve? Thomasina had seen how he treated patients under his care, and he'd told the crowd that they could pay to come and watch his patients, just as if the hospital were a circus. She couldn't think of a worse place for Mother to be—or a worse person to have control of Mother's care.

For supper, Thomasina had prepared mince pies stuffed with raisins, sugar, eggs, orange peel, and spices. Father chewed on his, drumming his fingers on the table. When carol singers came knocking at their door, Miss Maplethorpe bellowing among them and looking thoroughly pleased with herself, and the wassail bowl was passed around, he nodded at Thomasina, giving her permission to sip the spiced ale. Afterward, he bundled up his cloak and strode down the street. Whatever was on his mind seemed pressing.

When Thomasina went upstairs to give Mother her mince pie, she found her at the window. She was humming again, but this time she was joining in with the carol singers' tune as the music floated down Raven Lane.

Thomasina sat on their bed, beaming from ear to ear. Although her mother hadn't spoken yet, Thomasina was sure she was getting better, and it was just a matter of time before she would. She pictured them all next Christmas—Arthur, Mother, Father, and herself—all drinking from the wassail bowl, and she was so overwhelmed with happiness and hope at this image that she nearly forgot to worry about the silver snowflakes on her arm. . . .

The marks had by now traveled up to her shoulder and beyond, and were snaking close to her heart.

After Christmas, the Frost Fair was busier than ever. The Great Frost showed no signs of disappearing and more people were streaming in from other towns and the counties surrounding London to make the most of the season.

Anne and her uncle were in Spitalfields celebrating Christmas with their family. With Anne gone, Arthur's voice silenced, no matter how many times she tried to conjure him up, and Inigo not having visited her in a while, Thomasina felt extremely lonely. She developed a habit of playing with the snowflake necklace, and she searched the crowds for a familiar pair of wide brown eyes smiling at her, even though she knew she wouldn't find them. She couldn't even pass the time thinking up recipes for new medicinal sweets, as she lacked Anne's apothecary's knowledge and didn't know what would be effective.

Nothing happened until all twelve days of Christmas were over, by which point Thomasina was bored stiff. She'd spent another tiring day carrying crates to and from the fair, splinters piercing her hands, and was walking home when she heard the thud of stones being pelted somewhere nearby, as well as high, excitable voices.

Rounding a corner, she stumbled into a gaggle of boys younger than herself. It was a mystery to her why they weren't enjoying themselves at the Frost Fair, until she saw that they were throwing stones at a shadow cowering against the wall.

"Oi! What are you doing?" she said, raising her voice.

"Black cat," one of the boys said, cheeks blotched scarlet behind his nutmeg-colored cloak. "Means bad luck. Witches have them, don't they?"

Thomasina pushed past, ignoring their protests, and crept toward a tiny ball of fluff. She expected it to run away, but it stayed rooted to the spot and seemed to have given up on defending itself. She couldn't see any injury, aside from looking like it was skin and bone. The poor little cat was soaking wet from the snow and slush surrounding it, and was shaking all over. Thomasina must have stumbled across him just in time.

"Get out of it!" one of the boys shouted. As she turned

around, making sure she formed a shield between their aim and the cat, she recognized him as the younger brother of the butcher's boys she and Arthur used to race against.

"Can't you see it's half-dead with fright?" she snapped. She scooped up the cat, which seemed too traumatized to even claw or bite her.

"Out of my way," she said, sounding a lot braver than she felt, and she shoved past the group, the cat now snuggled in the folds of her cloak. She heard one of the boys step after her, but heard another mutter, "Leave it, Ned."

"You're a strange one!" the butcher's boy yelled. "Something's not right with you!" But she didn't look around.

The cat in her arms was shivering—whether because of the cold or fright, she wasn't sure—and she held him close while huddling against the biting wind. As she continued on her way home, she spotted two Gray Cloaks walking down the street together, their hoods completely obscuring their faces. Remembering Henry's warnings about them following her, she ducked into a nearby porch, waiting there until she heard them pass, their footsteps echoing into nothingness.

Her heart pounded. Though she'd trusted Henry to have given an accurate account of everything he'd witnessed when he visited the Other Frost Fair, this was confirmation that the Gray Cloaks were definitely after her. But why, she wondered again, had the Frost Folk wanted her to find out that the Gray Cloaks were following her? And why had they wanted her to know about Sir Inigo Lawley? She'd report back to Anne and Henry and see what they thought.

When she got home, Thomasina was surprised that Father wasn't in the shop, and thought he must still be packing up at the Frost Fair. She placed the cat down gently on the workroom table and wrapped a cloth around him, trying to dry him as much as possible. After that, she combed his fur, removing any fleas she found. The cat looked young, perhaps only a year old, and he let her stroke him and smooth his fur back down. She didn't have much food, apart from scraps of haddock she'd meant to turn into a pie, but the cat guzzled the fish as if it were the best feast ever while she set a fire for the night. When she'd finished lighting the fire, and the cat was clean, dry and fed, she carried him upstairs to her and Mother's room.

"Present for you," she whispered, putting the cat down next to her on the bed.

The cat sniffed around the blankets, and at Mother's hair. Mother twitched but didn't open her eyes, and Thomasina went downstairs to prepare food for the evening. When she went upstairs again, the little black cat was curled against the backs of Mother's bent knees, blinking up at her like a furry crescent moon, and Mother was stroking his head.

"I'm going to call you Shadow," Thomasina whispered. He gave a soft purr as if he liked the name.

That night, the wind hurled itself against windows so much that Thomasina was surprised the shutters weren't wrenched off.

Shadow nuzzled his cheeks against hers and fell asleep on her chest. When her eyes adjusted to the dark, she saw his paws twitching while he dreamed.

"Careful," she whispered. "Don't go being too annoying, or I'll have to throw you out. You wouldn't like that now, would you?" But she didn't mean it, and she suspected Shadow knew this, too.

Thomasina stared at the ceiling, thinking of Arthur. He used to sleep in this bed with her when they were younger, and he would have loved to have a cat slumber with them. She closed her eyes, listening to Shadow's purring beside her.

"Soon," she whispered to Arthur. "Soon things will be so different."

She must have fallen asleep, because the next thing she knew, she was watching a shining mist glittering above the ground. There was nothing else she could make out.

Apart from . . .

A shape prowled at the corners of her dream, wearing

a blue velvet doublet. It drew close to her and seemed to be searching for something.

The wind slammed against the window, and Thomasina woke with a jolt. Shadow leaped up beside her. He gave a sleepy growl and prowled to the bottom of the bed to nip her toes. Mother grunted in her sleep.

Thomasina felt a thud of anxiety in her chest. Had Inigo been visiting her dream? And why did it feel like he was trying to tell her something?

16

Garraway's Coffee House

Thomasina didn't see Anne the day she arrived back from Spitalfields, or the day after that. On the third day, she'd just resolved to go to Hawke's when there was a knock on the front door of Burgess & Son's. Thomasina wiped her crumb-covered hands on her apron, having spent the morning preparing gingerbread for the Frost Fair, then hurried to unbolt the door.

Standing on the step was Anne.

In an instant, the girls were hugging each other tightly.

"I've missed you!" Thomasina said. "How was your Christmas?"

Anne grinned. "It was nice to see my parents and cousins, but I'm glad to be back. How are you?"

"Fine," Thomasina said, but the grin she gave her friend this time was forced.

Every morning for the past few days, after waking, she'd been stunned to find more and more snowflakes appearing on her skin. She knew she'd have to tell Anne and Henry soon, but she didn't know how to broach the subject. . . .

"Come through to the workroom," she said, continuing to try and smile brightly. "It's warmer there."

"I passed a group of Gray Cloaks lurking near your street," Anne said as she followed Thomasina into the workroom. "I think Henry's right, you know, about them following you."

Thomasina nodded. "I think so, too. I hid from a couple of them the other day," she said. "We should tell Henry when we next see him. Maybe he's found out more from the Frost Folk since we last spoke."

"The Gray Cloaks seem to be everywhere these days," Anne agreed. "Oh! Who's this?"

There was a pitter-patter of feet down the stairs, and Shadow entered the workroom with his tail up. He looked quizzically at Anne.

"This is Shadow," said Thomasina. "I found him the other day. One of the butcher's boys and his friends were tormenting him."

Anne bent down to stroke him.

"I've been investigating Henry, too, just to be safe," she said. Shadow purred loudly at her touch and rolled onto his back, looking like a furry puddle. "He is who he says he is—his parents are based in Newcastle, trading sea coal from there to London." She took off her cloak and sat down at the table, while Thomasina ladled out a cup of hot spiced tonic for her. "He's been sent to London to learn the trade from this end."

"How did you find that out?" asked Thomasina.

Anne blew on the drink, then took a sip. "Asked around, didn't I? People know him. I think he's genuine. He came to our shop an hour ago to see if you and I could meet him tomorrow. Somewhere called Garraway's Coffee House." Anne wrinkled her nose. "I've never heard of it. Have you?"

Thomasina shook her head.

"He told me it's where merchants like to gather, in the heart of the City. He wants to share what he's discovered. Can you come to Change Alley tomorrow morning? I think we need to tell him there are more Gray Cloaks following you around."

Thomasina chewed her lip.

"I can pretend to Father I'm making more marzipan roses in the morning. He won't be back till nightfall, anyway—he wants to sell from a tray farther up the river tomorrow."

"Good, that's agreed," Anne said, then took another sip. Something seemed to be playing on her mind. After a few moments, she must have settled her internal debate, because she set down the cup and looked at Thomasina.

"Over Christmas, I also started asking for loans to start up my own business," she said softly. "I know you're busy here, with Burgess & Son's, but would you ever think about going into business with me? Just look at how well our medicinal sweets have been doing at the Frost Fair—we could make such a success of things."

Thomasina felt her stomach give a guilty, unpleasant twist. While she knew deep down that she desperately wanted to join Anne in this venture, she didn't see how she could ever leave Mother and Father—or Burgess & Son's.

"Whatever you decide," Anne said after a pause, "I know I'll get a loan. It just takes one person to believe in me. I've been planning what stock I'll sell when I set up shop. If I just set up shop on my own, I'd start with ointments first."

"That sounds brilliant, Anne," Thomasina said, feeling a twinge of sadness deep within her heart. As happy as she was for her, she couldn't help but feel jealous. She wished she had Anne's opportunity to strike out on her own.

Her friend grinned at her, eyes twinkling in the winter light. "Thanks. I've a long way to go, but I'm excited. And . . . I know it's tough for you," she went on, her voice gentle. "The idea of leaving Burgess & Son's, I mean. But would you at least think about it? We'd be great together as business partners—I know it."

Thomasina nodded, heart too full to speak.

Anne swigged down the rest of the steaming drink in front of her, giving Shadow another stroke. "I have to run back. Uncle will be annoyed I've taken so long."

"Be careful of the Gray Cloaks," Thomasina said as they hugged goodbye.

"I will," Anne said. "Promise."

A gust of icy wind blustered in through the shop door as Thomasina closed it again. The snowflakes now snaked their way down her shoulders and chest, toward her stomach. She felt the chill of the wintery gust everywhere but those places where the flakes dotted her body. She bit her lip. Her heart clenched whenever she saw the strange, silvery shapes patterning her skin, and she fretted terribly about what was happening to her body. She knew she'd have to ask Inigo what it all meant the next time they saw each other, but for now . . .

For now, she'd just have to sit tight. She'd tell Anne and Henry at the coffee shop in the morning, she promised herself. And she'd ask Inigo about them, and the Gray Cloaks, the next time he called for her and took her to the Other Frost Fair.

The next day, with Father absent from the sweet stall, having taken a tray of treats to sell farther down the frozen river, Anne and Thomasina seized their opportunity to sell more of their inventions at the Frost Fair. Anne had spent part of her Christmas in Spitalfields researching headache cures, and the pair had worked together early that very morning to create a sweet-smelling tonic made from dried violet and chamomile flowers, which they'd mixed with sugar and hot water. They sold this drink alongside violet-scented biscuits that Thomasina had made the night before—and they sold out all their stock in two hours. Thomasina again felt a guilty pang in her abdomen. Despite the happiness she felt with Anne, selling their medicinal sweets together, she knew she couldn't desert the family sweetmaking business—but this fact was getting harder and harder to bear.

It was just as well the girls finished selling their wares early. The Frost Fair was full to bursting with people, which made it impossible for Thomasina and Anne to cross the river quickly. Their path was blocked by the crowds surrounding the fire-eaters, and they were accosted by traders handing out freshly printed picture souvenirs. People hurtled in all directions around them, eager to soak up the delights the Frost Fair had to offer, and, yet again, Thomasina wished Arthur could be there to witness the extraordinary sights on the river and taste the excitement in the air.

"You'll be here very soon," she whispered to him. "I promise."

"Carrots, girls?"

Miss Maplethorpe was on the river today, proffering a tray of vegetables. Her white hair was wildly disarrayed, blown in all directions by the howling winds around them, and she had an unnerving glint in her eye.

"Um . . . no, thank you, Miss Maplethorpe," Thomasina said, and the girls dived into the surrounding crowds to shake her off.

"Look," Anne whispered after a couple more minutes of battling their way through.

Thomasina looked to where her friend was pointing discreetly to their left and saw a couple of Gray Cloaks staring back at her.

"Will they hunt us down here?" Anne said, a slight wobble in her voice.

Thomasina found her friend's hand and squeezed it tightly, feeling it tremble. "No," she said, "I'm sure they won't." She tried to sound as reassuring as possible.

But they saw more and more Gray Cloaks as they walked past, and now she noticed they didn't seem to be watching just her. Instead, Thomasina shivered to see them focusing on many other people, too.

"Henry was right," Anne said as eventually they hurried off the river. "There are so many of them now."

"I can't see any of them looking at us here anymore," Thomasina said, and Anne breathed a sigh of relief.

When they arrived at Garraway's Coffee House, they found Henry waiting outside. His freckled face stretched into a wide grin when he saw them.

"I wasn't sure if you'd come," he said. "Did any Gray Cloaks follow you?"

"A pair looked right at us," Anne said, in a slightly shaky voice. "But Thomasina and I shook them off. I don't think any have followed us now."

Henry nodded, looking grave.

"Thank you for coming," he said. "I thought it would be a good idea if we met in a different part of London, to keep the Gray Cloaks off our backs. I don't think we'll be overheard here." Then, his cheeks turning slightly pink, he stepped aside and gestured to the door. "Please . . . after you."

Thomasina and Anne walked into a cramped, slanted building with huge wooden beams. The noise that greeted them was a deafening buzz, the dimly lit room a hive of activity: a group of merchants were poring over maps, plotting routes and calculating navigations and arguing over ports.

There was a constant drip of wax from the candles they held onto the maps they studied. On one side, a couple of women sat deep in discussion, as a man listened so intently he was unaware he held his cup tilted to the side and was spilling his coffee onto the parchment in front of him. On the other, a group of young men and women were arguing loudly about Parliament, red-faced and banging their fists on the table. Different languages were being spoken all around them that Thomasina didn't understand.

"A lot of people here must be angry," Anne muttered. "The Great Frost will be ruining their businesses."

Sure enough, when they crossed the narrow room to a small table in the far corner, Thomasina overheard someone who sounded at the end of their tether say, "Really, Mrs. Ponsonby, the spices will be here by May, I'm sure of it. . . ."

They sat down at the table, which was buried under a mountain of pamphlets. The writing on some of them was large enough for Thomasina to read. Her chest wheezing from hurrying across the river with Anne, she tried to calm her breathing down by looking at them. She saw that while some advertised stalls at the Frost Fair, others called for revolution; some told of new medicinal treatments, while a few looked like simply dreadful poetry.

A slender woman swooped upon them, looking stressed.

"Yes?" she snapped.

"Three cups of coffee, please," Henry said to her as Thomasina jerked her head up at the interruption. "And some cake."

The woman nodded and left, making no attempt to clear away the pamphlets on their table.

"I know you two don't have much time today," Henry said, "but I've found out something, and I need to tell you about it. Something odd."

"What is it?" Thomasina said, her heart racing.

"It's about . . ." Henry said, but he had to break off as the woman returned with three cups, which she filled so impatiently with a thick, brown substance that some slopped over the sides. She slammed down three plates, each with a generous slice of cake on it.

"Enjoy," she said, and stamped off.

"As I was saying," Henry said, "I told you last time that a maid I was friends with, Mary, had gone missing, and that she had snowflakes on her arm, like Thomasina has."

Thomasina flushed, thinking of the many more snowflakes that had appeared since she'd last shown them to Anne and Henry. She blew on her coffee, feeling worry churn in her stomach, then took a sip—and discovered she hated it.

Why anyone wanted to drink this bitter, muddy water was beyond her.

"She's still missing," Henry said, his freckled face frowning, "and when I asked the other servants about her, I discovered something strange."

"Oh?" Anne said, putting her coffee cup down with a clatter. Thomasina tried the cake. It was soft, buttery, and delicious, and it more than made up for the unpleasant liquid she'd just swallowed.

"I asked the other maid who works in my building about her. She shared a room with Mary, you see. Well . . . this girl told me that Mary's mother died last year, and that Mary kept a lock of her hair in a locket, which she slept with under her pillow every night. The thing is—"

He broke off as the woman flew past again, refilled Anne's and Henry's cups, then looked at Thomasina's full one, sniffed, and stalked off.

"The thing is," Henry continued, "Mary's clothes and boots were still in the room after she went missing. The maid swore she didn't have any other secret clothes tucked away—the room is so small Mary couldn't have hidden them anywhere. She thinks that Mary walked out in her nightdress, in the middle of the night, leaving everything else behind—even her cloak and boots. The only thing she took with her was the locket."

Anne raised an eyebrow.

"So you think Mary woke up one night and, without disturbing the other maid, she picked up the locket, didn't pack anything, then wandered off, without even taking a cloak?"

Henry flushed scarlet. "I know it sounds ridiculous. . . ."

"No, it doesn't—not if she went to the Other Frost Fair," Anne said.

Thomasina gave a small, sad sigh as she thought of Mary alone in the cold, in only her night things.

"What does Mary look like?" Anne asked.

"She's short and pale with strawberry blonde hair"—he screwed up his face—"and she has a birthmark above her lip. A sort of half circle."

Something clicked in Thomasina's mind, but she wasn't quite sure what and why.

"I'm keeping an eye out for her," Henry muttered thickly through a mouthful of cake. "Anyway, Thomasina . . . let's talk about the snowflakes on your arm."

Thomasina swallowed her own mouthful of cake.

"Well," she confessed, "they've traveled up my arm now, and over my shoulders and down toward my stomach. . . ."

"What?" Anne yelped.

There was a sudden silence as the rest of Garraway's Coffee House stopped talking and turned their outraged faces to their table in the corner.

"Sorry," said Anne, looking around at the other customers. "I, er . . . I just can't believe how good this cake is—*yum.*"

Everyone turned back to their tables, murmuring their disapproval, but Thomasina saw the woman who served them their cake looking very smug.

"If it means Arthur will be brought back to life, then I'm fine with it," Thomasina said, chewing her lip. "It's just that . . . well, Inigo didn't tell me this would happen. All he said was that my memories of Arthur would fade away so he could use them to bring him back to life. But—but I suppose it doesn't mean any harm's come to Mary. Or that any harm will come to me, either."

"How do you know that?" Anne said.

"I just . . . I just do," Thomasina said, frowning to herself. "There's something about Inigo—I think we're . . . friends."

Anne looked skeptical.

"Inigo's the only one who can tell you why this is happening, that's for sure." Henry sighed. His blue eyes, which reminded Thomasina so much of his great-grandfather, flickered between hers nervously. "And why Mary's disappeared. I know you're worried about bringing your brother back to life, but *we're* worried about what's happening to *you.*"

"So will you ask Inigo about this, Thomasina?" Anne

said, looking at her earnestly. "It's really important."

"Yes, all right. I'll try," Thomasina said. "But . . ."

"But what?"

"I'm worried if I do," Thomasina admitted, "that Inigo will get angry about me asking too many questions, and he won't bring Arthur back to life."

And that, she thought to herself, *couldn't* happen. Not now that she was halfway to getting him back.

"You've got a right to know what's happening to your own body, Thomasina," Anne said, setting her cup down. "If it has something to do with the Other Frost Fair, Inigo can't keep that information from you."

"I agree with Anne," Henry said. "He can't keep Arthur away from you just because you asked about what's happening. That wouldn't be fair."

Thomasina nodded slowly. She'd never thought about it that way before, but she knew her friends were right. Maybe Inigo wasn't doing everything right, after all. Did he even have her best interests at heart?

Henry settled the bill, and they walked outside. He paid for another hackney coach to take them home, and promised he'd tell them if he heard any more news.

On the way back, Thomasina and Anne sat in silence, deep in thought. Thomasina felt as if she were walking blindfolded in the middle of a complicated tapestry. She knew she should ask Inigo what was happening: the snowflakes on her skin were spreading so much that she could no longer ignore them like she'd tried to do when they first appeared. But nor could she risk losing Arthur a second time.

17

The Frost Ball

Tap, tap, tap.

Thomasina had waited for Inigo's knock for days. A thrill jolted through her when she finally heard it. Each day he hadn't called had made her worry that, after Anne had almost caught him, he'd changed his mind about taking her to the Other Frost Fair twice more, and that her chances of reuniting with Arthur would ebb away.

Unbolting the door and swinging it open, she was struck by Inigo's appearance. It wasn't because of the decadent mask he wore that covered one half of his face with spun ice, nor his sparkling heeled boots, the shimmering blue feather in his hat, or even his silver cloak, glittering with tiny icicles. Instead, she was shocked to see he looked as if parts of him had withered away. When he smiled, the lines around his eyes were deeper than they'd ever been before, and he stood at an odd angle, knees bowed.

"Good evening," he said in hoarse tones, indicating a bundle he was carrying. "I have a gift for you, Miss Burgess. I thought you must be rather tired of dressing up in such drab little outfits. Especially as I'm always dressed so impeccably."

Before Thomasina had time to ask if he was unwell, he shook out the bundle and she gasped as it flashed to the ground. It was an ornate silver cloak, gossamer-thin and shimmering in the moonlight: the twin to his own.

"Thank you!" she exclaimed, examining it.

It was made from soft, beautiful material. Squinting at it closely, Thomasina could see that tiny icicles and miniature snowflakes permeated the surface, so it was as though she were enveloped in a blanket of winter.

"It's the finest thing I've ever owned, apart from my necklace," she told him, and Inigo beamed. His smile was lopsided, trembling at its corners.

"I'm glad you like it," he said, "because I want you to wear it tonight, at the Frost Ball."

"What's a ball? Are we going to kick a ball about in the street?" She didn't see how such a magnificent cloak could be at all suitable for this.

It looked as if Inigo were having difficulty restraining himself from rolling his eyes.

"My dear, a *ball* is where people *dance*," he said, and then huffed and, in a lower tone, scoffed under his breath, "Kick a ball about, indeed. . . ."

"Dance?" Thomasina said. "Like—like people do around a maypole?" This was the only dancing she'd ever done.

"Well, yes, a bit like that," Inigo conceded, "but with nicer clothes."

He held out his arm as usual, and she took it. Her heart was beating very quickly. She felt like she was suspended on a delicate tightrope. On the one hand, she had to make sure that she kept Inigo in a good mood: he held her future happiness in his hands. She didn't want to risk him breaking off his side of the deal if she angered him by asking questions about his past.

On the other hand . . . the fact that a quarter of her body was now decorated in snowflakes was frightening her. And the thought of Mary, the missing maid, was pressing heavily on her mind. What if her disappearance *did* have something to do with Inigo?

She suspected that, one step wrong, and she'd fall off the tightrope, without Arthur or answers to her questions. She'd need to be very careful.

"You told me you were alive years before the Great Fire of London," she said. "That was in 1666, so when *were* you around exactly?"

Inigo stiffened. "Oh, around the time of King James,"

he said casually. "I knew him, as a matter of fact."

So *that* was why his accent sounded so strange—because he'd existed decades before. Thomasina screwed up her face, trying to remember what Mother had taught her about the kings and queens of England.

"King James died almost sixty years ago," she said at last.

"Indeed."

They continued walking down the street.

"So if you knew King James—"

"My dear," Inigo said sharply. "I've planned a special evening for us. Please don't spoil it by asking impertinent questions."

Thomasina opened her mouth, then shut it, feeling stung. She hadn't expected this treatment from Inigo. But she curbed her tongue—she didn't want Arthur to be lost forever.

"I'm sorry for being sharp with you," Inigo said after a while, in a gentler tone. "I want you to enjoy this evening. Can your questions wait until after the Frost Ball?"

After some hesitation, Thomasina nodded. Hope flickered within her chest. *Maybe I can ask him something about the strange things I've heard, and still get to be reunited with Arthur. . . .*

"Thank you. Now, close your eyes," he said. "We're very close, and I want you to take it all in at once."

Thomasina shut her eyes, and Inigo guided her forward.

"Open them!" he said.

Thomasina had been prepared for a spectacle, but she still gasped at the incredible sight before her.

"I present to you: the Frost Ball."

In front of her was an assortment of Frost Folk dressed in elaborate clothes. Thomasina's silver cloak paled in comparison to their finery. Some Frost Folk were elegant in silver ribbons and feathers and ice-white dresses, while others wore light-blue doublets and tasteful ruffs. All wore the same style, unlike on the previous nights she'd visited the Other Frost Fair. Their skin, irrespective of color, was patterned all over with snowflakes, nails as snowy-white as Inigo's, and their hair, irrespective of age, was white or gray. The Frost Folk danced in complicated formations, hollow footsteps echoing around the frozen river. Ice sculptures of Frost Beasts were dotted everywhere, and the dancers weaved past them.

A Frost Horse cantered up next to Thomasina. It nuzzled its nose against her arm, and she felt again the strange sensation of thousands of tiny filaments of ice piercing her skin. She giggled as it snorted at her, then cantered away.

A girl with a familiar half-moon birthmark above her upper lip, wearing what looked like a white nightdress, detached herself from the crowd and walked toward them. Her eyelashes were spun with frost, just like Inigo's goatee. It was the girl who'd spoken to Thomasina so strangely at the theater that other night.

"Welcome!" She smiled and floated away again, her bare feet and arms glittering in the moonlight, but not before Thomasina felt her insides twist with shock—

She'd seen a large, frosted locket bouncing on the girl's bony chest.

Henry's words echoed in Thomasina's mind, as if from a dream: *She's short and pale with strawberry blonde hair, and she has a birthmark above her lip. A sort of half circle.*

"Wait!" Thomasina yelled, but the girl was now lost in the crowd. She knew it must be Mary: the birthmark and the locket she was wearing that Henry had described as being missing from her bedroom—they were too coincidental. Enough was enough. She needed to ask Inigo to tell her why a missing girl who Henry had seen with snowflakes on her skin was now one of the Frost Folk.

She turned around, expecting him to be beside her, but couldn't see him anywhere. Scanning the crowd, she saw he wasn't next to the traders selling potions that fizzed and popped with spirals of purple, silver, and blue sparks; nor by any of the magical jugglers; nor near the dancing girls or the women who breathed silver flames for the Frost Folk crowding around them.

"Miss?"

Thomasina turned and saw a little girl smile with glittering teeth. It was the girl she'd seen the first night she had visited the Other Frost Fair, the child who'd shown off her hoop and stick.

"Inigo's near Father Winter's tent," she said.

"How do you know that?" Thomasina said, surprised.

The little girl's voice trembled. "Miss, Inigo's near Father Winter's—"

"Yes, you've told me," Thomasina said. "Can you only say one line, too?"

The little girl's frosted-over eyes flickered.

"Miss, Inigo's near—"

Thomasina turned away with a frown. First Mary, and now this little girl? What was going on? How and why had they been enchanted to say only one line over and over?

She crossed the ice to Father Winter's tent. A couple of Frost Bear cubs bounced over, nuzzling her shins.

"What is it?" she said, but they gamboled away to greet the lion with armorlike, icy fur that guarded Father Winter's tent.

She was about to walk elsewhere to try and find Inigo when she heard voices coming from inside the tent. One belonged to Inigo. The other belonged to Father Winter. She shivered as she smelled his familiar, odd scent.

"I've sent my Gray Cloaks to follow several of them," she heard him say in his sepulchral tones.

"Why, Father Winter?" said Inigo. "I've already instructed

the Frost Folk and Frost Beasts to keep watch. . . ."

"You know very well, Inigo, that the Frost Folk and Frost Beasts are the weakest of my servants—unlike *you*." Father Winter's voice took on a menacing tone that made Thomasina tremble.

"But your Gray Cloaks . . ."

"My Gray Cloaks follow the weaker ones," Father Winter hissed. "You have your powers for a reason . . . to bring me the special one . . . the one who will give me the most strength . . ."

Thomasina felt her left arm being enclosed in an ice-cold grip.

"Move away," one of the Frost Folk barked at her. She was so scared that she obeyed. She loitered near a pack of Frost Wolves, pretending to look at them wrestling each other and nipping at each other's tails, but in reality her mind was churning with what she'd just heard.

"Thomasina!"

She turned. Inigo was striding out of Father Winter's tent, beaming at her. She thought he looked even paler than usual. Behind him, Thomasina saw Father Winter walking away with a whirl of his white fur cloak.

Her mouth fell open. Father Winter now looked like a young man! His strides were quick and even, and as he turned to gaze around at the Frost Fair, she saw there were only fine lines decorating his face instead of the deep, scar-like wrinkles she'd seen before. His hair was full and curly, and his beard far shorter.

What was going on? He'd been so ancient when she'd first met him. Why, during this visit, did he now look younger than Inigo? Why was he no longer the hunched-over, ancient shell she'd met, who'd been barely able to smile?

"Miss Burgess?"

She wrenched her gaze from Father Winter back to Inigo.

"Would you like to see what else we have on display?" he said. "Some potion makers have conjured up giggling solutions—"

"Inigo, why is Mary here?" Thomasina asked quickly, heart pounding. "The girl with the locket? And what on earth has happened to Father Winter? Why does he look so young all of a sudden? And—"

Thomasina's head filled with white mist. Though she knew there was something hugely important that she needed to ask Inigo, for the life of her she couldn't remember what it was.

"And what, my dear?" Inigo said. "Was there something else?"

"Um . . ." she said, her mind feeling curiously sluggish. "There *is* something—but I've forgotten it."

"Perhaps you'll remember once we're off the ice," Inigo

said with a tight smile. "But until then . . ." He gestured for her to take his arm.

Inigo introduced her to the potion sellers he'd spoken of, and Thomasina tried some of their wares. The first, a magenta-colored liquid, made her laugh so hard her stomach cramped, while a bright-turquoise solution made her levitate several inches off the ice, cackling with delight. After that, Inigo showed her even more ice sculptures, around which some of the Frost Folk danced. Thomasina's feet itched.

"Care to join in?" Inigo suggested.

"I haven't ever danced before," she said.

"This one isn't hard—just two steps to the side each way, and one jump forward, and then you clap. Easy. Come—try it with me."

Inigo stood next to her and guided her through the steps.

"Do you think you can do that over and over again?" he said.

"Yes," Thomasina replied.

"Come on then," Inigo said, and Thomasina found herself caught up in the fray, surrounded by Frost Folk who seemed as amiable as Inigo.

After hours of dancing, Inigo said, "You should be getting back now. People in your world will start waking up in an hour or so."

Thomasina gave one last look at the Frost Folk, at the potion sellers and fire-eaters, and the Frost Beasts and ice sculptures, as she and Inigo stepped off the frozen river. She felt euphoric, having twirled and skipped for most of the night, but as they journeyed into the heart of Southwark, the white mist in her head cleared. Dismayed, she realized she'd forgotten to ask him what she needed to. Frantic about time running away with them, she was careless about the words spilling out of her mouth.

"I've seen Mary—the girl with the birthmark above her lip—just now. She's missing from the house she works in, in London. Why is she here?"

Inigo pursed his lips.

"I'm bound by enchantments too powerful for me to overcome to tell you why," he said. There was a note of genuine regret in his voice. "I'm very sorry."

Thomasina stamped her foot in frustration, feeling the ice on the road crack underneath.

"What do you mean, you're bound? Who are you bound to? You told me at the start you'd try to answer my questions."

"I can't tell you much," Inigo said. He looked sorrowful. "I wish I could."

Thomasina frowned at him, then realization hit her.

"It was you! Did *you* make me forget my questions

earlier?" She gasped. "Filling my head with that white mist, so I wouldn't ask you about her?"

Inigo's gaze faltered, and he dropped his eyes to the ground, looking guilty.

"I did. I'm sorry. But I had my reasons."

"What reasons?"

"I can't say."

Once again, Thomasina felt like she was walking on a tightrope, wobbling across it to find the truth, but afraid of what would happen if she pressed Inigo for it too much. Bringing Arthur back from the dead was the most important thing to her, and finding out about the snowflakes on her body was second. But . . .

But finding out what had happened to Mary was important, too. And there were now other things she needed to ask Inigo about. From overhearing him speak with Father Winter inside Father Winter's tent, she now knew for certain that the Gray Cloaks had been ordered by Father Winter to follow people—"the weaker ones," he'd said. She and Anne had definitely seen two Gray Cloaks staring at her, and milling around Southwark staring at others, too. Was that what they were doing—searching for "weaker ones"? Why? Was *she* a weaker one, whatever that meant? And there was someone Father Winter had spoken about—someone he said would give him the most strength. Who was it? There seemed to be so much Inigo wasn't telling her. She needed to get answers, now.

She took a deep breath.

"I met someone who says he's a relative of yours," she said, her voice shaking with nerves. "Someone who says you were once called Sir Inigo Lawley. Is this true?"

Inigo drew out a silver handkerchief and passed it over his forehead. His snowflake-speckled hands shook.

"What have you heard?" he said, gray-faced.

"That someone called Sir Inigo Lawley went missing a long time ago."

"Do you know anything else?" Inigo asked.

"That's it," she said. "The person who told me said he's Sir Inigo Lawley's descendant." She gulped. "You've got something to do with Mary disappearing, haven't you?"

Inigo licked his lips. He fumbled with the silver signet ring on his hand, embossed with something Thomasina couldn't make out.

"I—I—can't—"

"Can't what?"

"I can't tell you anything," he said, screwing up his eyes and covering his face. Thomasina stared at his snowy-white fingernails.

"Why not?"

"I just can't," Inigo said. "If I give anything away,

I—argh—I start to . . . But you—you are in—argh—" He broke off, clutched at his heart, and staggered backward.

"What is it? What's going on?" Thomasina said, walking forward to try and steady him, but Inigo shied away from her.

"Listen to me," he said. "I can't tell you the truth because I'm bound by enchantments too powerful for me to overcome. But . . . but there are some things you should know. Your memories of your brother. They've been fading away, haven't they?"

Thomasina nodded. "Yes. And you told me . . . you told me you needed those memories to be able to bring him back."

Inigo screwed up his face. There seemed to be an invisible gag around him, and he didn't seem to be able to fully say what he wanted to.

"The thing is—you need to save me before you can get Arthur back. I can't tell you what I need saving from, but it's of the utmost urgency. Those memories I've been taking from you—the voice you hear inside you that belongs to him—I have possession of them now. But they'll fade away forever, and Arthur will never be able to be brought back, if you don't save me."

"What?" Thomasina gasped, horrified. "No!"

Fear flooded her heart. Not only was there a possibility that Arthur would not be brought back from the dead—something that had kept her feeling joyful and excited for the future for weeks—but her memories of him would fade away completely?

"How can I stop this?" she cried, grasping Inigo's clenched fists in her hands. They were ice-cold, and she could feel frost piercing her palms.

"You have to go to the place where I—Sir Inigo Lawley— used to live," Inigo muttered through clenched teeth, still doubling up on himself as though beset by some blinding pain. "My old residence."

"Where is it?"

"If my descendant is who he says he is, then he'll know," Inigo said. "Go there at once."

"Why?"

"When I was Sir Inigo Lawley, I hid something there— something that can only be found by those of my bloodline. If it's discovered, it will reveal the truth, and how to rescue me," he said. "You have to find out what happened to me all those years ago."

"What did Sir Inigo Lawley—you—hide?"

"I can't tell you. But you need to find it, and quickly. Before your fourth visit. Or all will be lost."

"Inigo," Thomasina said, dread filling her heart. "I have snowflakes all over my arm and chest. Why . . . why are they there? Does this have something to do with you being in danger? Mary had them before she disappeared. And the Gray Cloaks that Father Winter spoke of . . . they're following me, aren't they? Inigo—" She broke off in a gasp. "Am *I* in danger?"

Inigo looked at her, his blue eyes sparkling with ice: they looked like unshed tears. With an effort, he straightened up, fixing her with a smile so dazzling it was one of the most frightening images Thomasina had ever seen—perhaps even more terrifying than Amelia, the kelpie.

"As always, it's been a pleasure seeing you," he said, bowing.

He turned around and set off.

"Wait!" Thomasina said, slipping on the ice to catch up with him. "Can't you give my memories of Arthur back to me now? So I know they're safe? Can't you make the snowflakes on my body go away? Please—Inigo—"

She accidentally trod on his silver cloak.

Inigo turned. In that moment, he was no longer a polite, eccentric gentleman. Instead, he looked fearsome, with narrowed eyes and icy teeth.

"Go," he snarled.

Thomasina didn't need telling twice. She ran to the front door of Burgess & Son's, and clambered inside, shutting and bolting it behind her. She was still wearing the silver cloak and didn't know what to do with it, so she went upstairs and folded it into the bottom of the trunk at the end of her and Mother's bed. As usual, Mother was asleep, but Shadow padded up to her with a drowsy growl, deciding the best place to sleep was on her chest.

Thomasina stroked him to try and calm herself down, listening to him purr. He nipped her hand while she stared at the ceiling, listening to Mother snore.

Her heart was racing. She'd been so sure she was on the brink of reuniting with Arthur, and tonight it felt as if Inigo had reached inside her chest with his icy hands and torn her heart away.

Her friends had been right about him. Maybe he wasn't acting in her best interests after all. His sudden shift to anger had frightened her: she hadn't thought him capable of being like that. She knew she needed to talk to Anne and Henry about what had just happened as soon as she could.

At least there was a chance of saving Arthur still, but first they'd have to rescue Inigo. And if she didn't find whatever Inigo had hidden away soon, not only would her brother be lost to her forever, but her memories of him would be, too. She gritted her teeth, fighting back tears so she wouldn't wake Mother.

She was determined to bring Arthur back, even if it was the last thing she did.

18

The Frost Guard

"I can't believe it," Anne whispered, accidentally knocking over a jug of preserved plum syrup with her elbow as she clapped her hands to her face.

This time, Thomasina, Anne, and Henry were in the workroom of Burgess & Son's, where Thomasina and Anne had been trying out new recipes for medicinal sweets all morning while Thomasina recounted the events of the night before.

Henry stood up so fast he bumped his head on the low ceiling, then sat down again, his cheeks stained the same color as the congealed mess spreading across the floor.

"You must be so scared about your memories of Arthur disappearing!" Anne gasped, bending down to mop up the syrup. "*Ugh*. Remind me why it is we're working with something so sticky?"

"Inigo must be talking about Lawley Hall in Berkshire," Henry said, blushing even redder when his voice cracked. He grabbed a nearby cloth and bent down to help Anne dab away at the syrup, as Thomasina tried to rescue what was left of their concoction, mopping up the sides of the jug with a clean cloth. "My ancestral home, I mean. I'll set off straight away to find whatever it is he's talking about. My parents are still up in Newcastle, so there won't be anyone around to ask what I'm doing. . . ."

"I want to come with you," Thomasina said, wringing out the contents of the cloth into the jug. "But I need to look after Mother, and I don't know what to tell Father. . . ." She trailed off, chewing her lip.

"Henry," Anne said, "can you tell Thomasina's father you want to teach Burgess & Son's gingerbread recipe to your cook? Say it's the best in London, and that writing it down won't do."

Thomasina nodded. "Good idea, Anne," she said, mulling this over. "And I think I could pay Miss Maplethorpe to look after Mother while we're away."

"No, I'll pay," Henry interrupted. "It's my ancestor who's got us into this mess, after all."

Anne smiled at Thomasina, her eyes sparkling in the pale winter light that came sneaking in through the workroom's window.

"Thomasina," she said in a hesitant voice, "I won't be coming with you because I need to be in London this week. I found out yesterday that a family friend in Spitalfields may be able to loan me some money so I can set up a shop of my own. And there are several more lenders in town I've arranged meetings with over the next few days, too. I thought I'd let you know—just in case you'd thought any more about us going into business together."

"That sounds brilliant, Anne!" Thomasina gasped.

Anne grinned. "Thanks. I'm excited. I promise I'll join you on the next adventure."

After Henry talked to Father at Burgess & Son's, presenting a heavy pouch full of silver, Father turned to Thomasina. A faint smile warmed his eyes, yet the groove at the center of his forehead deepened.

"Well done for getting us this business," he said hoarsely. "You'll be safe, won't you? Out there on the roads?"

It took a moment for Thomasina to respond. Father was properly looking at her for the first time in such a long while, his flint-colored eyes roving over her own. As when he'd given her a faint smile at the Frost Fair, it felt as if a whisper of his former self was back, even if just for a moment.

"I'll be all right, Father," she said softly, noticing for the first time how tired he looked. His shoulders were slumped, the speckle of a days-old beard covering his downturned face, which was whiter than usual. New lines were also permanently marking his forehead, crawling above the deep groove that had developed after Arthur's death. "Henry's house isn't far. I'll be back soon."

He gave a gruff nod, then clapped her on the shoulder and abruptly strode to the workroom. She thought she'd seen his eyes water, but she wondered if this was a trick of the light. The part of her shoulder he'd touched buzzed in recognition: a faint wisp of a memory of what home used to feel like, as delicate as a breath, before everything had changed.

The coach Henry hired for them to travel in the following day was jet-black, with such a glossy sheen that Thomasina could see her reflection glistening back at her as if she were an inky spirit. Four midnight-hued horses pawed at the ice in front. A disgruntled coachman, swaddled in heaps of rough blankets so only his eyes and the tip of his red-tinged ears were visible, jerked his head at them both.

Even though it was early morning, the dusk would start to surround them all in a few hours. If they didn't head off soon, they'd have missed their opportunity for the day.

They'd met at one of the main entrance points to the

frozen River Thames. All around her, Thomasina could see a jumble of carriages, carts, and coach-and-fours trundling up and down the river, excitable voices shouting as their wheels scraped the ice and horses puffed and neighed. The Frost Fair was ablaze with color as usual today, due to the crimson-colored flags on top of stalls waving in the wind, the striped circus tent, the roaring fires roasting meat, and the many-hued cloaks of the visitors flitting from stall to stall. Thomasina even saw a fox darting in and out of tents like a spark, carrying what looked like a hot haddock pie in its jaws.

To avoid any questions from the servants at Lawley Hall, Thomasina was dressed as Henry's servant boy, having borrowed clothes from one of Anne's cousins in Spitalfields. They didn't quite fit her, but not so much that anyone would notice unless they were looking closely, and she wore a dark felt cap she could tuck her hair into, though it kept escaping.

Henry's voice quavered in the chill morning wind despite the heavy fur-trimmed cloak he wore.

"If we want to reach Lawley Hall as quickly as possible," he said with a shiver, "we'll need to travel by river. The Thames passes by Berkshire. We should be able to reach it in a day and a half in this weather."

Thomasina knocked the ice off her boots before she clambered into the coach-and-four after him. Inside, swathes of soft lambswool blankets were heaped on both seats, and a glass lantern swung from the middle of the ceiling, a heavy wax candle smoking within.

The coach wheels squeaked on the ice as it waited in a queue, behind impatient horses, carts of every size and shape imaginable, and several gleaming, gold-embellished carriages. Even inside the coach, she could smell delicious scents wafting from the tents of the Frost Fair, making her mouth water. A sweet scent of gingerbread meandered toward her from the ice, making her heart pang for a reason she couldn't understand.

She shivered and pulled her clothes tighter as the coach set off on its journey, wishing it were a bit warmer. The snowflakes on her skin had traveled to her other arm, and there were now so many of them that the places where they collected had turned her skin silver-white. Her heart had hammered when she'd discovered more of them, and her mouth had gone very dry. Thomasina had found that this wasn't the only change she'd undergone overnight.

Somehow, she also felt a little . . . different. Like she wasn't quite herself. When she'd woken up next to Mother that morning, she'd felt an unnatural coldness seeping through the parts of her body covered in snowflakes, as if she were made of ice.

She shivered again.

Though they had to travel by the frozen river some of the way, she reminded Henry they needed to make sure their coach would be off the frozen river by nightfall, as that was when the Other Frost Fair would awaken and—Thomasina shuddered at the thought—the Frost Beasts would prowl at its edges, lurking to accost any uninvited visitors. Earlier that week, news had spread like wildfire around Southwark that a carriage, four horses, a coachman, and two passengers had vanished while traveling via the river one night. While no one else had any idea how this could have possibly happened, she knew the Frost Beasts must have had something to do with their disappearance.

Thomasina tried to ease her nerves about the Frost Beasts by looking out of the coach window. After several minutes, she saw the stalls of the Frost Fair vanish, replaced by rows of houses, taverns, shops, and inns beyond the riverbank. Silver-flecked trees with icicles hanging from their bare branches and frozen boats half-submerged in ice dominated the landscape, and she also glimpsed people learning to skate, having snowball fights, and building snowmen.

As the coach traveled even farther, Thomasina's mouth fell open and she pressed her nose against the window as she saw the countryside for the first time in her life. Acres of snow-white fields surrounded them, with huge stately houses in the distance; and she saw specks of sheep with warm winter coats huddling together, as well as people in the distance riding on horses. Despite the stresses of their journey, she felt a warm glow ripple through her, and she beamed at Henry, who grinned back.

In the afternoon, there was a commotion as a horse a few coaches in front of them threw a shoe. Thomasina watched as blacksmiths skated across the ice, bearing tools wrapped in lumpy sacks on their backs, ready to help out.

"We should think about getting off the river in an hour or so," she told Henry as he took a generous hunk of cheese out of his bag and offered her half with some bread. "The Frost Beasts won't want us here."

As she said this, her heart thudded in panic for all the other people and horses on the river. No one else knew about the Other Frost Fair, so how would they know they needed to get to safety before sunset? She opened the coach door and shivered as a gust of icy wind blew inside. She was relieved to see that most of the vehicles around their coach were stopping off at different points on the riverbank around them. She guessed they'd been spooked by the story of the vanishing carriage that week. . . .

"Agreed," Henry said, swallowing down a mouthful of

cheese and bread.

He opened the coach door, and Thomasina heard him shout instructions to their driver, whose words back to him were swallowed up by the winter winds.

"He says he'll turn as soon as he can, once the ice is safe enough," he said, his head back inside the coach.

"All right." Thomasina sighed.

She leaned back against her seat, exhaling slowly, and realized her appetite had returned. Stomach rumbling, she devoured her half of the cheese and bread, watching the sky outside fade into soft pink and amber. Occasionally, she'd open the coach door and look about to make sure the coaches around them were getting off the river in time.

Darkness started descending more quickly than expected. While all the carriages, carts, and coach-and-fours they could see had made their way to the safety of the riverbank and were traveling by road, Thomasina and Henry felt even more scared to be still on the frozen river. Their coachman had managed to get them farther than expected, but he hadn't accounted for how slippery the ice was when he tried to turn the coach so they could leave the river. As a result, this could only happen very slowly, otherwise there was a real chance of the coach falling on its side. Though Thomasina and Henry had clambered out to push the coach on, they'd only succeeded in nearly toppling it over, and were forced to wait inside, hoping it would turn as quickly as possible so they could leave.

"Please hurry!" Thomasina called to the coachman as the horses snorted and continued to try and turn the coach on the slippery ice. The sky was fading to a deep indigo, and opposite her she saw that Henry's face was even whiter than before, worry lines taut in the amber candlelight.

As the coach finally juddered to the correct angle for them to get off the river, an unnatural growl echoed in the near darkness: a heart-stopping sound that made her hands shake.

The lantern swung above their heads, creaking a lonely reminder of how lost they were.

"Henry," Thomasina whispered, teeth chattering. She realized they were chattering because she was afraid, not because of the cold, which she didn't feel. It must be the snowflake necklace that was keeping her warm—and that was surely a bad sign now, because the necklace was only to have kept her warm when she was at the Other Frost Fair.

"Wh-What is it?" he replied, cocooned in heaps of lumpy blankets.

"I—I think I heard a Frost Beast growl behind us," she said. "We need to get out, now."

Henry gulped.

"I heard it, too," he said. "I don't want to die here, Thomasina. My parents will be ever so angry with me if I do."

"If you die, you won't be around to see it," she snapped. Her stomach twisted. She couldn't be caught by the Frost Beasts. Not now—not when they'd come so close to finding out Inigo's secret, so she could make sure Arthur came back. Not now that Mother was starting to show signs of getting better, and even Father was beginning to soften. She was so close to fixing everything.

More growling echoed around them, up and down the river. It was getting louder and louder.

"Henry!" she screamed. "We need to get off the river, now!"

Their coachman seemed to have had the same idea, too. They could hear him shouting at the horses to get a move on, but the horses couldn't canter as quickly as they'd have been able to on the roads, due to their hooves sliding over the ice. Their coach lurched from side to side as the growls became even louder, and Thomasina felt chills crawl up and down her spine as she heard the Frost Beasts surround them.

As she looked out the coach window, her heart in her mouth, she saw silvery shapes flickering all around, claws scratching and scraping the ice, and fangs bared in snarls and howls of rage. Horses, their coats spiked in silvery armor, hunched over, their white eyes glaring at her, while blue-gray wolves snarled and snapped at the air.

A thud resounded on the left side of the coach, and Thomasina was sure that one of the Frost Beasts had hurled itself against it.

"Grab the door handles!" she yelled at Henry as one of the knobs started juddering: one of the creatures was trying to open it with its paws. Henry seized the one nearest the riverbank, and she caught hold of the other, and they felt a series of blows against the sides of the coach, followed by yelping, as some Frost Beasts lunged for the doors and, whimpering, made contact and fell away.

"We're moving!" Henry moaned as the horses in front neighed and the coach-and-four suddenly started hurtling forward at a much quicker pace. Thomasina knew they'd wrongfooted the Frost Beasts as they sped off and heard the creatures' howls in the distance, but she knew it wouldn't take much time at all until they caught up with their coach again.

Despite her terror, Thomasina heard something that made her wonder what was happening. Amid all the barking, howls, and yelps behind them, there was a snorting, snuffling sound that seemed like it was coming from a slightly different place from where the other Frost Beasts were. As she watched, a huge, silvery shape flitted past their window, in the opposite direction to where the other Frost Beasts were charging.

"Come on," she muttered, still gripping onto the door handle.

With a huge effort, the coach plunged onward, the sound of its squealing wheels muffled by the yelping, howling, snorting, and barking of the Frost Beasts following in their wake. Breathless, their hearts in their mouths, Thomasina and Henry felt a satisfying thud as the coach wheels hit against the crunch of solid earth, the dark night stretching beyond.

19

Lawley Hall

Eerie echoes of the Frost Beasts' growls, neighs, and barks faded into the distance. As the coach-and-four raced forward, Thomasina expected to hear claws and hooves scraping on the ice as the enchanted creatures bounded toward them once more, but she was surprised to hear the sounds of them ebb.

"D-Do you think we've lost them?" Henry asked her, his teeth chattering uncontrollably as he wrenched more woolen blankets around him. His pale-blue eyes looked almost transparent in the candlelight rocking above them, which cast his face into strange, expressive shadows as it swung from side to side, as if he were a boy with many faces.

"Yes," she whispered. "I don't think we need to worry for the time being. The Frost Beasts guard the Other Frost Fair on the River Thames: as long as we don't go too close to it, I think we'll be safe for now. But they know we're not in London anymore, and they might be waiting for us when we journey back."

Henry nodded and stuck his head out of the coach window. As Thomasina heard him shout instructions to their coachman to find them an inn to stay in for the night, she leaned back against her seat, her heart still racing.

They'd escaped the Frost Beasts. She'd been so certain they were done for: after all, Inigo had told her they'd have no qualms in hunting down uninvited guests if they dared enter the Other Frost Fair at night.

But what had driven them off? Was it leaving London that had done it? Or something else? She recalled that strange noise she'd heard right before the Frost Beasts retreated, and turned it over and over in her mind, like a question. It was a low snuffling sound that must have come from the pack of Frost Beasts tearing after them, and yet there was something about this sound that was different from the others, but she couldn't put her finger on what that was.

Still dazed by their narrow escape, she felt numb. After they found an inn for the night, with rooms for them all in the barn and stable space for the horses, she found herself clambering dreamlike into bed. She and Henry had been so close to perishing at the paws of the Frost Beasts.

Shivering, her teeth rattled against the cold as she balled her hands into fists under a thin, scratchy blanket. The silver snowflake necklace was no longer working as a means of warming herself up now that she was some distance from the River Thames.

In her mind's eye, someone was reaching out for her, their hands like weeds trailing in a pond. Their face was blurry: she couldn't picture them properly. But she'd fix that.

Sharp winter air and dusty hay itched in Thomasina's nose the next morning. She sneezed several times, wiping her nose on the thin blanket she'd slept under, as she didn't have a handkerchief, then she stared up at the cobwebbed beams above her, watching a fat spider dangle from one of them.

Her chest throbbed with pain. Several times during the night, asthma had forced her awake, like a hand slowly squeezing her throat. She'd coughed so loudly in the early hours, despite trying to muzzle the sound in the crook of her elbow, that the coachman had shouted at her through the wall. Though she'd packed the herbs Anne had given her, she wouldn't be able to access any boiling water until she reached Henry's house to use them, so she'd just have to try and keep her breathing under control until then.

Fetching her disguise with trembling hands, she changed

under her blanket, shivering as the wind gusted in through the gaps in the walls. She was too nervous to inspect her body, to check whether more silver snowflakes had appeared overnight. She almost didn't have to, however, as the bottom of her stomach and her upper thighs felt so glacial she was certain more of them were covering her skin, and trembled at this thought. She knew by now something must be dreadfully wrong, that the snowflakes coursing up and down her body weren't harmless. She only hoped that discovering Inigo's secret would also unlock the secret to ridding herself of them.

She'd been dreaming of someone throughout the night, who'd slipped through her thoughts whenever she tried to remember his name. Alfred, was it? She felt it was something like that. Her thoughts swirled in a hazy cloud. It was only after she'd fastened the ice-cold boots she'd left next to her bed onto her feet, having extracted a sleeping dormouse from one of them first, and then clattered down the stairs, pausing at the bottom to collect her breath, that she remembered who she'd been thinking of. Her brother, who was called Arthur. Of course. Arthur. That was it.

Soft dawn was blushing the landscape as she met Henry at the front of the inn, the cold wind making her teeth and chest sting. Stretching himself awake, Henry seemed unaware he'd fastened his cloak so it was lopsided. As their coach-and-four rolled into view, Thomasina saw their coachman was buried under even more layers than he'd been wearing the previous day: all they could see was the tip of his nose, frosted with ice, and his bald head, which was decorated with icicles, making him look like an oddly shaped egg.

Their journey to Lawley Hall passed peaceably enough, until two hours in, when Thomasina felt their coach judder to a stop.

"What is it?" she said to Henry. "Are we there already?"

Henry peered out of the coach window and gasped.

"I think it's a Gray Cloak," he murmured, pointing to a shadowy figure in the distance astride a huge gray horse. Thomasina felt her insides freeze. As quietly as she could, she slipped off her seat to the ground, stretching herself out so she was spread-eagled on the floor.

"Get down," she hissed.

Henry clambered onto his knees, then lay down beside her. Thomasina shut her eyes against the dusty floor, turning her head so she could better listen. The dust was tickling her chest, and she desperately tried not to cough.

"I told the coachman to look out for Gray Cloaks," Henry whispered, his breath tickling her ear. "He knows to try and hide us. I must remember to give him a good tip."

Thomasina knew they were at an advantage. The mid-morning light was still soft, which would help hide them, and she heard leaves rustle nearby. Good. She hoped their coach would be obscured by trees.

As she and Henry crouched down, she became aware of his scent: apple blossom, mixed with sweat. He smelled a little like someone else she'd once known, which made her heart pang. For a few moments, she couldn't for the life of her think who it was, and then she remembered. She had a brother. A brother she was trying to help save. What was his name again? Arthur? Yes, that was it. Arthur.

After several heart-stopping minutes, she heard a horse cantering away and their coach began moving again.

"I think it's gone," Thomasina whispered. "I'll look."

"Be careful," Henry said as she opened her eyes and stretched up to peep out of the window. She saw a tiny speck on the horizon.

"It's gone," she breathed. She couldn't be sure it had been a Gray Cloak, but there was something about the rider's slow, strange movements that had unnerved her.

Henry returned to his seat, brushing his clothes free of dirt.

Neither spoke for a while, and Thomasina looked out the window. At first it was to watch out for more Gray Cloaks, but after a while she contented herself with watching the late-morning sunshine creep across the frosted landscape, burnishing the trees pale gold. Compulsively, she touched one of her arms that snowflakes now completely covered, and shivered. She hoped that whatever Inigo had hidden, it would help her discover the truth.

"We're here," Henry said. "This is my family's land."

The grounds belonging to the Lawley family had an aura of lonely beauty. As the coach traveled up a road, under a canopy of gnarled, bare oak trees, Thomasina saw a building in the distance. It was the largest dwelling she'd ever seen in her life; her jaw dropped as the coach wheels crunched on gravel.

In front of them was a yellow-brick mansion with dozens of large, mullioned windows. Before it was an ornate garden with fountains and trimmed hedges. Sneering boars carved out of stone stood guard, their tusks curving upward and their flint-gray eyes glinting as they surveyed Thomasina. Large chimneys rose from the roof, and ivy snaked across half of the house. Lined up on the sloping steps were the servants, wearing neat caps and aprons, their uniform a deep russet. Until now, she'd not appreciated how wealthy and powerful Henry and his family must be.

"I sent a message ahead," he muttered to her. "Don't say anything. Just follow my lead."

She nodded, still not quite believing what she was seeing, and reached up a hand to her cap as the coach came to a stop, checking that her hair hadn't escaped.

"Morning," Henry called as he jumped out of the coach.

Thomasina followed. He was addressing a servant with sleek, tawny hair.

Thomasina thought she saw the servant's eyes flick to her cap. However, as quickly as he'd done this, the servant flicked his eyes back to Henry as they walked up the front steps, and the man didn't pay her further notice.

Thomasina made to follow them, coughing—her chest was still feeling uncomfortably tight—but her way was blocked by a woman in a stiff, starched apron, who glared at her.

"Servants' entrance is around the back," she snapped, her mouth pinched.

"Don't worry," Henry called back to her. "He's with me."

Reluctantly, the woman stepped aside. Thomasina smirked as she followed Henry up the stairs, trying to calm the wheezing in her chest.

They entered a magnificent hallway that housed a large oak staircase and even more portraits on its walls than in Henry's London rooms. An ancient tapestry adorned the far side, depicting a battle, and a collection of jagged swords were strung from another.

"We'll require total privacy in the Great Hall," Henry said.

"And a pail of boiling water," Thomasina added, feeling her breaths grow shallower by the minute. "Please."

The servant bowed. "Er—of course, sir," he said. "Can I ask what . . . ?"

"I'm afraid not," Henry said.

Thomasina followed them both down a narrow corridor, trying not to be too obvious as she gawped. The wealth in front of her eyes was shown off like fresh, plump fish on market day. As they padded past on soft rugs, yet more tapestries stretched across the walls, depicting brave battles and fantastical creatures, some of them like the ones in Mother's household book. Here were fire-breathing dragons and kelpies, and here, too, were mutinous ogres and beautiful sirens. She and Henry were walking in the middle of a swathe of color, gold threads gleaming amid crimson, emerald, sapphire, and amethyst. Ranks of battered suits of armor formed a ghostly army, almost tilting their heads as they passed.

"The Great Hall, sir," the servant said to Henry, clearing his throat when they reached the end of the dark passageway. He opened a set of heavy doors with bronze knobs the shape of boars' heads.

They knew they had to find the secret something Inigo had told Thomasina was hidden in Lawley Hall, in order to save Inigo and make sure her memories of Arthur weren't lost forever.

But where was it? And *what* was it?

20

The Final Hiding Place

Thomasina gasped as she followed Henry into the Great Hall, the wheeze in her chest echoing back as a small groan.

Smelling of sweet candlewax and musty wood, the Great Hall had an aura of frosty nobility, as if centuries of expectations and tradition were trapped in the airless room, like a butterfly pinned under glass. Perhaps this was because of the long table, covered in a snow-white tablecloth, dominating the room, or the polished silver candlesticks gleaming in a line down its center. Or maybe it was the portraits of blue- and green-eyed men and women with alabaster skin dotted around the room, one for every empty mahogany chair around the table, who peered at her as she craned her neck to gaze above. The ceiling was painted dark emerald and sapphire, with wild cornflowers carved into the woodwork.

At the far end of the room nestled a colossal stone fire-place, engraved with the same boars that had studied Thomasina when she first arrived. It was so cavernous she thought ten people could stand inside it. On its mantelpiece was engraved something she couldn't make out.

"It's my family's coat of arms," Henry explained, notic-ing her gaze. He took off the ring on his little finger and passed it to her. "It's on here, too."

Thomasina considered the ring, warmed from his hand. His coat of arms formed two boars glaring at each other, separated by a shield. Why anyone would want this insignia engraved on a ring, Thomasina had no idea, but she nodded and returned it.

"So . . ." began Henry. "You told me Inigo said that whatever he put inside this house was something only his descendant would be able to find." He sighed. "I've been having a think about what that might be.

"Years after Inigo went missing, my family lost Lawley Hall during the Civil War to the Roundheads. The soldiers stole pretty much everything they could carry when they left, and then they blew up half the house. The only places I can think of that might still be untouched are the Great Hall and the stables. If Inigo hid whatever it is anywhere else, I think it would have been taken away."

Thomasina shook her head, remembering what Inigo had said.

"He told me only someone from his bloodline would be able to find it. Even if the Roundheads looted the place, I reckon they wouldn't have come across it."

They were interrupted by a servant bringing in a steaming pail of boiling water, setting it down with a grunt before exiting. After Thomasina scattered some of the herbs Anne had given her and spent several minutes inhaling steam from the concoction, feeling her wheeze ebb a little with every breath, she raised her head to find Henry watching her with an anxious expression.

"Better?" he asked.

She nodded, relief coursing through her.

They explored the Great Hall: under loose floorboards, the fireplace, the table, as well as the backs of the portraits on the walls. Henry's ancestors glared at them as they were removed from their nails. Even though Thomasina knew the old men and women painted here were long dead and buried, their expressions were so severe she had to stop herself more than once from apologizing to them.

They found nothing. Nor was there anything when they searched the stables, which only housed the horses belonging to their coach-and-four. One of them snorted at Thomasina as she crawled in thick muck around its paddock, trying to work out if anything looked out of the ordinary. She suspected it was inching close to kick her, so she scrambled out of its way, wiping muddy hands on her breeches and gritting her teeth as she plunged them into a fresh pail of chilly water, which was already starting to transform into ice.

Desperately, she and Henry combed through every nook and cranny in the original building that had existed before the Civil War, down to the last stone, sweeping aside tapestries to peer at uncovered walls. They finished their search by inspecting the rubble outside: jagged bricks scattered about the place, as well as stony fragments of blown-apart boars' heads and sawn-off candelabras. It felt strange to do this, as if they were disturbing a tomb.

They still couldn't find anything. Thomasina howled at the sky in frustration, causing a couple of robins to fly out of a nearby hedgerow. Inigo had given them so little to go on. How were they supposed to find whatever it was if he wouldn't even tell them what to look for?

"I'm having doubts we'll ever find it," Henry said, echoing her thoughts as, hours later, she sank her teeth into a hunk of juicy venison. This was the best meat Thomasina had ever tasted, but she couldn't enjoy it. She lowered her knife, frowning at him. Another pail of boiling water filled with some of the herbs Anne had given her sat steaming nearby: she'd needed it, as the cold was making her chest tighten once more.

"Inigo looked terrified when he told us to come here," she said, "and I'm sure his fear was genuine. There isn't anyone who could act that well. He said whatever it is lies somewhere no one would have thought of—it's something only a descendant can find. Isn't there anywhere else you can think of?"

Henry took a deep swig from his goblet. A drop of crimson wine slid off the edge of the ornate glass when he put it down, staining the white tablecloth. Thomasina watched it spread, wondering how long it would take to wash out.

"I can't think of anything." He sighed. "I'm sorry. I've failed you and Anne."

As he pressed his knuckles across his forehead, his signet ring flashed in the light from the winter sunshine pouring in through the grand windows.

"That crest is on everything," Thomasina said, gazing around the room. "On the chairs, the portrait frames, the candlesticks . . ."

She looked toward the fire again. In the decades since Inigo had disappeared, the furniture could have been moved around. Portraits could have been sold off by the Roundheads, tapestries could have been rehung, and the silver candelabras and fine decorations could have been replaced.

The fireplace, however, was something that couldn't have been moved. And Inigo had insisted that whatever he'd hidden still resided at Lawley Hall.

What else was more entrenched in a building? She stood up and moved closer toward it.

There was something etched to the right of the coat of arms that she could see. As she drew closer, she saw a carving of two boars, just like in the Lawley coat of arms—only this time, they were facing outward and there was no shield between them.

There was something odd about it. Almost as if whoever had engraved it had *wanted* it to look out of place.

"Let's look in the fireplace," she said.

"Why? We already have," Henry said.

"Farther inside, I mean. We've only looked around it, or at the stones near the grate. Look at this—" She pointed at the engraving, and Henry moved closer to look at it, frowning. "We need to put the fire out."

Henry nodded, then walked out of the room, coming back a few minutes later with two servants. One of them took a candle from a drawer under the table and lit it from the fire's flames, placing it on the table. Another lugged a huge pail of water in front of them, panting.

"Your *third* pail of water for today, sir," he said to Henry, narrowing his eyes at Thomasina.

"Are you sure you want to do this?" Henry asked as the servants shuffled out of the room, looking at each other with raised eyebrows. "It'll be freezing once it's out. Doesn't the cold make your breathing worse? And anyway—the servants are bound to tell my parents about this."

"It's just a feeling," Thomasina said, scratching at one of her snowflake-covered arms and feeling her heartbeat pound in her ears. "But it's important. My chest will be all right."

"Well—fine," Henry huffed. "If you insist."

He emptied the pail of water over the roaring fire, which vanished, leaving indignant spirals of steam in its wake. Thomasina passed him the flickering candle. Once the clouds had cleared, he took it and stood in the great fireplace, on top of the half-burned wood, touching the tips of his fingers to the sides. They came away jet-black.

"It's hot in here," he said, voice bouncing off the chimney walls, which meant there were suddenly a dozen aggrieved Henrys speaking to her. "What do you think I should be looking for? The walls are caked in soot." He coughed into his elbow and turned around, waving the light higher, so his head and arm were obscured. "I can't see anything. Can you come in here with me?"

"Run your fingers over the bricks," Thomasina said. "But be careful—they're probably hot." Her heart was hammering. She knew this was their last chance. She needed to find out how to rescue her memories of her brother, and increasingly it looked as though hope was lost. She hadn't a clue where next to search, unless the place Inigo had hidden whatever it was, before the Civil War, had been dislodged. Or perhaps a distant relative of Henry's had discovered it already. . . .

With a sigh, she climbed into the fireplace with him. She expected heat to envelop her, but it didn't. The snowflakes decorating her skin in silver droves made her feel as brittle as a block of ice. More soot crumbled around her and Henry, scattering onto their clothes.

"Inigo was really clear," she murmured, running her fingers, too, over the bricks, and wincing at the heat that sparked against her icy fingertips. "Only a relative of his can discover whatever it is. It's got to be you."

Henry sighed.

"I'm trying," he growled, stretching on tiptoes to sweep his hand higher up the chimney and waving the candle near the bricks. "But nothing's—"

He froze.

"Thomasina," he said, waving his candle higher. "It's probably nothing, but . . . look up there."

He pointed toward a brick on the wall. Unlike the others surrounding it, it wasn't covered in soot or grime at all, but instead gleamed with unnatural cleanliness—as if some kind of magic kept it spotless. And on it was . . .

"Look!" Henry said in a hushed voice, as he moved the candle even closer. The flickering, jumping flame illuminated two tiny boars' heads, scratched into the brick. Unlike their stance on the Lawley coat of arms, there was no shield separating them. They faced outward this time, as if guarding something invisible between them—just like the picture etched on the fireplace. During her and Henry's search of the house that day, Thomasina had never seen the Lawley boars depicted in this way apart from in these two places.

Could this be where Inigo had hidden his final secret?

"It could be something," she agreed, straining her ears as Henry rapped his knuckles against the brick, a hollow sound echoing back.

"I think there's something inside," Henry said while running his hands over the brick's edges. "It feels slightly raised." He tried to prize the brick out of the wall and gritted his teeth with the effort of doing so.

The brick moved by a minuscule amount.

"Here," he said, passing Thomasina the candle.

He ducked out of the fireplace, then stepped back in again, grunting under the weight of a poker and a pair of bellows he'd taken from the tools hanging nearby. He held the poker at an angle—an impressive feat, Thomasina thought, as it was made of dull, heavy brass—and chipped away at the mortar around the brick.

With a piercing screech that made them both grimace, the brick was slowly wrenched from the wall.

"Close your eyes and hold your breath," Henry said, then blew the bellows onto the brick, so even more soot flew over them, covering their eyes, mouths, and ears, and making Thomasina cough violently.

"There," he said, clenching his teeth against the dust cascading around them both. Shaking herself to be rid of the filth coating her, Thomasina watched as Henry reached out and winced as his skin scraped against the rough brick, prizing it free.

"I've got it!" he cried, jubilant.

They resembled ragamuffins after they climbed out, caked in soot and grime from head to toe. Henry spat out a mouthful of ash as they hurried to a window to make out whatever it was more clearly.

"Look!"

He turned the brick around, revealing a hollowed-out shell. Inside was a vellum pouch. Golden lines, faded from decades of neglect, depicted a couple of hideous animals with horns protruding from their mouths.

"My family crest," he breathed.

As his fingers fumbled to open the pouch, Thomasina

cast her gaze around the room, a smile tugging at her lips. She and Henry were so close to finding out what Inigo couldn't tell her himself—and once they knew what was going on, she'd be several steps closer to bringing Arthur back from the dead.

Her heart faltered.

She stepped forward and peered through the diamond-glazed windows at the gardens outside. Cast in the amber winter light, Lawley Hall's low hedges, sparse vegetable plots, and hazel trees looked perfectly innocent, the last of their leaves being tossed around the ground in the chilly breeze.

Only . . .

Beyond the walled garden, vegetable plots, and orchards, she could have sworn she'd just seen a huge, silver-blue shadow flicker against the oaks lining the estate—almost as if a Frost Beast were waiting for them outside. She frowned. Could it have just been a trick of the light? The low afternoon sun glinting through the trees, perhaps?

"Diary entries!" Henry said next to her, and she tore her gaze away.

"What?"

"I think these are diary entries," Henry said, unfurling a yellowing bundle of parchment and coughing as dust spiraled from its folds.

"Can you make out the writing?" Thomasina asked.

"Just about," he said. "Shall I read it aloud?"

Thomasina nodded. Henry took a deep breath, held up the candle close to the parchment, squinted, and began to speak.

21

The Secret

This is the account of Sir Inigo Lawley, a gentleman at the court of King James, in the year of our Lord 1608. I've decided to leave some crucial diary entries here, and hope a descendant of mine will chance upon them one day. If you're reading this, you have my pity, for what I'm about to reveal is incredibly dangerous.

"This is it!" Thomasina gasped.

Henry nodded, cleared his throat, and turned the parchment over.

2nd February

I drank too much mead while celebrating Lord McLaren's triumph against Baron Laythorne following their annual Duck Race, and reaped the rewards this morning. My head feels like someone's BASHED IN MY SKULL! Last night, I dreamed I saw people in gray cloaks gazing at me. I must have had more to drink than I thought.

15th February
I'm troubled by dreams most bizarre. In one, I danced in a masque, surrounded by people made of ice. In another, I was the guest of honor at a banquet fit for King James himself. When I woke up, I was distraught that these imaginings of mine were not real. Is it the Devil tormenting me with these visions, or a witch most foul? Am I going mad?

16th February
I consulted the Countess of Shrewsbury's physician about my reveries. He told me to go easy on the drink. I'll heed his advice and put these dreams out of my mind. What a silliness these last few days have been!

21st February
I'm shaking so much I can barely write. Lord, forgive me for what I'm about to reveal. While others may think I'm mad, I need to tell the truth, though no one will believe me.

I've discovered a secret land on the frozen River Thames that awakens at night. It's a strange place where people and beasts made of ice reside. I've traveled to this land several times, but in the past I thought they were dreams. A man called Father Winter accompanied me; he's unlike any other man I've ever met, and doesn't seem mortal. He's conjured up dazzling visions for me, time after time: my reveries weren't imagined.

Father Winter's promised to grant my dearest wish: to see my late mother again. It's my deepest regret that I wasn't present when she died; the vain and foolish man I am, I was at a party the night she left this world. Father Winter promises we can be reunited—all I need to do is accompany him to the frozen river at night.

24th February

I'll be lost forever after I finish writing this. God help me, I never expected to uncover what I have, and now this has happened, I don't know what's to become of the truth.

Father Winter told me tonight that he's existed for centuries, and he appears in times of great cold and frost. He tells me he's a creature who collects people with sadness at the core of their beings, whom he calls "sad souls." Father Winter lures sad souls to the river, promising we'll see our loved ones again, only to trap us. He feasts on the misery of sad souls, draining us of our life force and keeping us around him on the river as ice creatures—he calls these Frost Folk—so he's made young again through them.

I've never stopped feeling immense guilt at leaving my poor mother to die alone while I feasted with my friends. Father Winter told me this misery of mine will strengthen him. The more guilt and sadness a sad soul feels, the more powerful Father Winter becomes. He told me tonight I'm a soul with sorrow he hasn't felt from a living person in a long time.

When he told me everything, I pleaded to keep my soul. I didn't want to become one of the lifeless beings surrounding him, who follow his every command and recite the lines he tells them to speak and exist only to strengthen him. I promised Father Winter I'd do some of his work for him, and entice sad souls to the river to be trapped forever. When Father Winter heard this, he agreed to my suggestion. I was able to keep my soul, but in exchange, I must now convince others to follow where I didn't want to go.

The moment I struck this bargain with Father Winter, I knew I'd made a terrible mistake. He gave me a day to sort out my affairs. It's too late for me to escape our deal. He's transferred powers to me already, so I can conjure visions for the poor sad souls I must now entrap for him.

To whoever's reading this: I'm bound by enchantments too powerful to overcome. You must find out how to destroy Father Winter. I

don't know how this can be done, but I'll try to discover it. You must end the misery of thousands of tormented souls on the river. Father Winter has magically bound me not to tell anyone of his wicked ways, so I must find indirect ways to communicate.

I'll seal this parchment and bind it with a folk charm learned from my poor mother, who was a wise woman from Suffolk. It's the only spell I knew as a mortal man, learned from someone I love deeply. This spell is so far below Father Winter's notice, it may slip his gaze. This charm ensures that only those of my blood will be able to uncover this. I'll send my cousin to ride ahead and hide it in the old fireplace at Lawley Hall.

Each day at sunset, CLOSE YOUR EYES. You'll likely have been marked by me already. I sense who a sad soul is through looking in their eyes. Closing your eyes is your only hope of protection against the evil forces surrounding you, as Father Winter and his servants can't see anything but the sadness in people's eyes as well as their own. I'm not entirely affected in the same way, but I find it far more difficult to find you if you've closed your eyes.

Forgive me for being a coward: a crime I'll regret for the rest of my existence in this miserable half-life.

22

On the Run

N either of them spoke for some time after Henry finished reading. The setting sun stained the walls of the
Great Hall amber, and the gnarled trees outside gold.

"I can't believe it," Thomasina whispered at last.

Henry shook his head. He seemed too stunned to speak.

"All this time, Inigo's been preparing to hand me over to
Father Winter," she murmured. "That's why my memories
have been taken away from me. That's why snowflakes are
starting to cover me all over." She gaped, horrified, at the
silver peeking through her shirtsleeves.

"And he said it was all to bring Arthur back," Henry
muttered in disgust.

Thomasina frowned.

"Who's Arthur?"

Henry's soft blue eyes widened as he stared at her incredulously.

"Your brother, Thomasina."

"Yes . . ." she said, hearing her voice crack and falter. She felt exhausted with the weight of trying to remember the person she loved.

"Thomasina," Henry said slowly, "you know what this means, don't you? Your life is in grave danger."

Dread snaked around Thomasina's heart like ivy. Inigo had told her she needed to find something to release him from Father Winter, so he could bring Arthur back from the dead. But it was now dreadfully, painfully clear she needed to save herself as well.

"I think I've worked something out," Henry said, sounding sickened.

"What?"

"Thomasina . . . do you think you might be strengthening Father Winter already, as a sad soul?"

"What do you mean?"

"Well . . . you told Anne and me that Father Winter gets younger every time you see him. And your memories of Arthur are being siphoned off by Inigo every time you visit. . . . Thomasina, those memories must be very painful to you."

She shuddered.

"So . . . he's turning me into one of the Frost Folk," she whispered. "I think the Frost Folk have to be kept around Father Winter so he can feed on their memories . . . but the Frost Folk have to forget their past in order to stay. That's why Inigo's been taking away my memories."

Henry's eyes were wide and pitying, glimmering with unshed tears as she looked at him. Thomasina had no clue how to release Inigo from Father Winter's evil power, so she could get her memories of her brother back and save herself. All she'd been told to do was close her eyes whenever she came close to Father Winter or his servants. *And what use is that?* she thought.

The bundle of documents trembled in Henry's hands, the parchment so delicate it was in danger of being ripped in half.

"We need to get you and your mother away from London. Anne too: you both work so closely together, so Father Winter might be after her as well," he said in a strangled voice. "It's the only way we can protect you from Father Winter—to get you where his powers can't reach you, away from the River Thames. You can stay with my parents in Newcastle. I grew up there. It's a lovely place to live."

"No," Thomasina said. "If there's still a chance I can bring my brother back with Inigo's help, I'm going back to London."

"But—"

"I'm doing it, Henry," she said, glaring at her friend. It was costing her an enormous amount of energy and effort to focus on the person who kept slipping away from her memory, and she was sure that in a few moments she'd forget him altogether.

Henry's eyes, which reminded her so much of Inigo's, flitted between both of hers.

"Do you still trust Inigo? Even after this?"

Thomasina's lip curled as she looked at the parchment in his hands, covered in purple ink. It wasn't just the contents of Inigo's account and diary entries that revolted her, it was also his self-pity.

"I hate him for what he's been doing," she said in a low voice. "For taking away my memories of my brother and plotting to trap me—for being part of Father Winter's awful plans. But I don't think he would have told me to come here if he didn't want me to know what was going on. And—" She clenched her fists, her heart beating like a drum. "I saw Inigo conjure up the kelpie. I *know* he can bring my brother back from the dead. I'm sure that if we release him from Father Winter's power, he'll be able to do it."

Henry sighed, his shoulders slumping over.

"Fine. I can see there's no point trying to persuade you otherwise. What should we do now?"

"We've got to head back to London," Thomasina said. "Right now." Her stomach lurched.

Henry nodded. "I'll ask for the coach to be readied," he said. Tucking the pages of Inigo's account inside his coat, he swept out of the room. After a time that seemed to stretch to several hours, but was probably only a few minutes, he strode back inside.

"The coach is waiting."

As they hurried outside, Thomasina heard the crunch of frost under wheels. Their coachman had bloodshot eyes as he drove up, wearing a nightshirt under his cloak.

"Get us back to London," Henry said, handing over a gold coin that made the coachman's eyes widen. "There'll be more if we get back before sunset tomorrow." The coachman looked suspicious, but he nodded and tucked the money away.

After Thomasina and Henry climbed inside, she heard the coachman click his tongue—and they were off. The coach hurtled forward at a breakneck speed, and she put out a hand to steady herself. Rattling along at a relentless pace, the coach skidded over the ice for several minutes . . . then one hour, then two, then three. The light was fading fast, the golden sky turning gray.

She and Henry sat in tense silence, each too preoccupied with worries swirling around in their minds to talk to each other.

It was only when a cry echoed across the landscape that they looked up.

Thomasina looked out the coach window. What she saw made her heart stop.

It wasn't just one Gray Cloak this time, but an army of them, cantering astride silvery Frost Horses, Frost Lions, Frost Wolves, Frost Goats, and Frost Deer. Their cloaks whipped behind them in a fury, and as Thomasina opened her mouth to scream, she saw the hood fly back off one of them. Ice-white eyes stared at her from a hollow, silvery face, frost decorating it so it resembled a magical skull.

"Henry," she cried, "the Gray Cloaks and Frost Beasts are after us!"

"No," Henry moaned as their coach hurtled down the long country road, rocking them even more from side to side.

"Hang on!" Thomasina said. She knew the coach wheels would skid soon—they were traveling too fast—and she was right. She heard the coachman shout as the wheels juddered and the coach slowed to a stop.

She could hear the soft, silvery padding of Frost Beasts close by. They seemed to be surrounding only one side of the coach, as the trees on the other side blocked their path. Unearthly creatures around them growled, huffed, and snarled.

A warm hand gripped her arm.

"Close your eyes," Henry hissed. "Remember what the account said."

"Are you mad?" Thomasina said. *"We're surrounded by Gray Cloaks!"*

"It's the advice Sir Inigo left us," he said. "Right now, that's the only thing we've got." He took a deep breath and shut his eyes.

"We're stuck in a pothole." They heard the coachman curse. "I'll see whoever it is off. Don't you fret."

"Close your eyes!" Henry yelled as close to the coach window as he dared, then hissed, "Please, Thomasina. Just do it."

"What are you doing?" they heard the coachman say to the Gray Cloaks, his voice rising with the wind. "You from the authorities? You can take your search warrant and shove it up your—"

They heard the coachman giving an awful, piteous gasp, followed by a hollow, rasping sound.

"You are hereby drained," they heard a voice whisper, "and will join the Gray Cloaks."

"He's been turned into one of them," Thomasina whispered, sharp, icy air crowding her lungs as she took a deep breath.

"Close your eyes, or we'll be next," Henry muttered, sounding as shaken as she felt.

Thomasina shuddered. Even though every sinew in her body was screaming at her not to, she shut her eyes so her world was now engulfed in darkness, clutching at Henry's arm so tightly she could feel his pulse.

She didn't know what to do. Every second that passed, the closer they were to being caught by the Frost Beasts and the Gray Cloaks. Even if they both made a break for it, running across the frosted fields or as far into the shadowy woodland as they could, the Frost Beasts would surely hunt them down.

Huddled against Henry, who was shaking violently, her other senses readjusted. She sniffed the air, smelling the deep, rotting scent of fallen leaves and the evergreen trees on one side of them. While Gray Cloaks and Frost Beasts surrounded the side of the coach where their driver had just been drained, she sensed none on the other side toward the trees. It was too narrow for them to pass.

She found the handle on the door of the coach and opened it as quietly as she could. Tugging on Henry's arm, she felt him follow. Both were too scared to speak.

As they crept to the trees, Thomasina could smell a bite in the air. The cold sliced into her skin, almost reaching her bones. She stretched an arm out. Her hand felt the sharp, rough bark of a trunk, while the other held Henry's hand, sweat cooling between their palms. Footsteps crunched toward them.

The Gray Cloaks didn't speak. Thomasina knew now that they were hollow shells, commanded to carry out Father Winter's bidding. She heard no voices: only leaves crunching and sniffs. She thought she heard a group head into the heart of the forest, footsteps muffled in the undergrowth, but someone was moving closer to where she and Henry stood. Beside her, Henry was breathing in shallow, frantic gasps. She squeezed his hand to try and hush him, worried that if she whispered, the Gray Cloaks or Frost Beasts would hear them.

Thomasina crouched down, and Henry was forced to follow. She could feel his hand shake violently. Her fingers felt the ground. As quietly as she could, she sifted through tangled leaves and twigs, until she seized the biggest stick she could find. She felt Henry's curiosity next to her. She passed the stick to him and reached around for one of her own: it felt important to have some kind of weapon even though they would surely prove useless against Father Winter's magic.

Whoever it was that had detached themselves from the pack moved toward them; she could sense a presence so close to her that she held her breath.

A stale smell filled the space where she and Henry stood. She heard ancient, sepulchral tones, and realized it was coming from the same voice that had transformed the coachman into a Gray Cloak.

"You and I've met before, Thomasina Burgess. Have you ever wondered why you can't take your necklace off? It leads me to you, even when you close your eyes. I know you're here—and I'm going to finally drain you forever."

It was Father Winter. Thomasina didn't say anything, but her heart was hammering inside her chest so loudly she was surprised Father Winter didn't hear it.

"Your efforts to evade me are futile. You've been marked by my servant, so there's no longer any point trying to escape. And the snowflakes on your skin are doing my work for me: they will transform you into one of my Frost Folk in a matter of days."

Still, Thomasina didn't speak, though every fiber of her body was screaming at her, begging to run away.

"You've shut your eyes against me, which means I can't see you. That was clever." Father Winter's voice tripped on every syllable, as if the dialect he'd learned was worlds away from the one he now spoke. "You'll know, then, that I find my sad souls through their eyes. Tell me how you discovered this."

Thomasina was silent, Henry's hand in hers shaking so much that their grip kept slipping.

"There are other ways I can hunt you down," Father Winter whispered. She imagined his jagged, icy teeth were revealing themselves in a ghostly smile, shining in the light of the dying sun. "And when I *do* capture you," he hissed, "those around you, who you claim to love, will be taken by me as well. I'll give you a chance to open your eyes. If you don't, your fate, and theirs, is sealed."

Thomasina felt Henry's hand squeeze hers. She knew it meant *Keep your eyes shut!*

"So be it," Father Winter rasped, his voice as hollow as a skull. "You're the saddest soul I've come across in a very long time. Why else do you think I'm here? I've feasted on some of your misery already—doubtless you'll have noticed that I've grown younger because of you, and that your memories are slipping away—but when you become one of my Frost Folk, I'll feast on all your sadness: every last drop, so you're drained entirely. It'll be . . . enjoyable. Don't think you can avoid me for much longer. I always find the most tormented sad souls eventually."

Leaves and twigs crunched, and they heard Father Winter and the Frost Beasts and Gray Cloaks turn and walk away from them. Thomasina's knees buckled, and she felt a rush of hot tears leak from her closed eyelids.

She and Henry had been less than a heartbeat away from being captured forever. She knew their ordeal was far from over.

How were they supposed to get to London safely now?

23

The Frost Bear

"We need to move. *Now*."

As Thomasina whispered this to Henry, she heard him swallow.

When they dared open their eyes, they saw their coach had tumbled on its side, its two raised wheels spinning helplessly. Their squeaking sound echoed in the lonely woodland surrounding them. As well as this, the horses had fled. Thomasina wondered if they'd been transformed into silvery servants of Father Winter, just like their coachman had, or else had cantered past the frostbitten wildflowers around them, spooked. Thomasina trembled in the late-afternoon wind, which froze her silver tears solid so they fell in shards to the earth below.

Henry was hunched over beside her, shivering in the snow.

"How are we going to get back to London?" he said, his voice quavering.

Something rustled in the undergrowth; a loping, heavy gait. There was a sound of several snapping twigs, and as Thomasina and Henry looked, shaking, to their left, a couple of bare-branched, spindly trees swayed. One cracked in half and hurtled down to the earth, sending a couple of waxwing birds flying into the sunset.

Thomasina screamed as an enormous Frost Bear emerged from the evergreen, a startling, bright-white mass against the forest. Its eyes were frosted white, and sapphires decorated its snowy snout. Its matted hide was a million filaments of sparkling ice instead of fur, glinting pale gold in the light of the already setting wintry sun.

"Close your eyes!" she heard Henry shriek behind her.

Cold air swirled inside Thomasina's chest, stinging her teeth as she gulped mouthfuls of it down, staring at the Frost Bear. Heart hammering, she glanced at it for a final time, then squeezed her eyes shut.

She wondered if it had been ordered by Father Winter to stay behind and stand guard, tasked with alerting the others that she and Henry had finally opened their eyes. She expected it to charge at her, the way she knew the other Frost Beasts would have done if she'd kept her eyes open long enough for them to see her. The echoes of Father Winter whirled around in her head, and she braced herself for an attack.

Nothing happened. She heard the Frost Bear paw at the ground and snuffle toward them, dead leaves and twigs crunching underneath his massive paws.

What if the Frost Bear wasn't on Father Winter's side? He wasn't growling like some of the Frost Beasts that had chased after them earlier, and this felt significant somehow.

Heart beating so violently that she was scared she was going to die from shock, Thomasina opened one eye in a squint, then the other.

The Frost Bear was sitting down, his giant back curved as he placed his two massive front paws in front of his stomach, while his two hind legs stuck out at the sides. He tilted his head as he looked at her, his muzzle twisting from side to side as he sniffed the heady scent of the cedar trees around them, wiggling his long, silver-blue tongue to taste the air. Thomasina's heart was still pounding fit to burst. She planned to close her eyes immediately if he charged at her, but he didn't. Instead, she watched, heart in her mouth, as the Frost Bear gave a long, slow blink—a blink she'd seen before, from small brown eyes instead of piercing white ones.

"Y-You're the b-bear from the Frost Fair," she said,

flinching as he gave a colossal yawn, his small, frost-flecked ears wiggling one way then another. "The—The dancing bear in chains. I—" She gasped. "I saw you at the Other Frost Fair, too, after you'd been changed into a Frost Beast!"

The Frost Bear screwed up his eyes as he snorted, then opened them again in a snow-white flash.

As he stared at her, Thomasina felt the same burst of pity she'd felt the first time they'd gazed at each other, when she'd seen him being lugged across the ice on a chain, bleeding from his back.

"Thomasina—" She heard Henry moan behind her. "*Please.* Close your eyes, or we're done for. Father Winter will have sent the bear. He must still be here."

Though Thomasina faltered upon hearing his words, she kept her eyes open.

"No," she whispered. "Henry . . . I think he's here for us."

"What?"

"I think—" Thomasina swallowed as the Frost Bear stood up, stretched by balancing his weight on his massive hind legs, then padded across to her, his gigantic silver claws hooking into the snow across his path. "I think he's on our side."

The Frost Bear was so close to her that she could see ice as delicate as filigree silver on his snout, as well as the deep cracks in his marble-white eyes. Very gently, as if he knew she was terrified, he reached forward and pressed his nose into the hand that was dangling at her side. As with the times she'd visited the Other Frost Fair, Thomasina prepared to wince as she felt the familiar spread of unnatural coldness seeping through her palm. Only this time she didn't feel cold in the slightest. In fact, the Frost Bear's snout felt slightly warm.

Were the snowflakes swarming her body making her more used to this kind of coldness?

"What's he doing?" she heard Henry hiss behind her.

"Open your eyes," she said. "See him for yourself."

The Frost Bear padded over on his colossal legs to Henry, and Thomasina gulped, the sheer enormity of the animal made apparent to her as he crossed her path. If this Frost Bear wanted to, he could rip them both limb from limb without a moment's thought. She had to trust what she thought she'd seen in his white, cracked gaze.

She saw Henry squint out of one eye and his mouth hang open as he saw the huge Frost Bear snort.

"How can he be on our side?" he asked uncomprehendingly.

"I don't know," she said. "But . . . Henry, I think he's come to help us."

"Thomasina— Oi!" Henry squawked, as the Frost Bear nudged him from behind with his muzzle, making him hurtle face-first onto the snow. "No! Bad bear!"

The Frost Bear tilted his head, looking quizzically from Henry to Thomasina. He gave a slow blink to Thomasina again, this time as if to say, *Who's this odd boy shouting at me?* She felt a grin splitting her face as he gave a great shake of his fur, icy droplets scattering this way and that, some raining down on Henry, who yelped in disgust, his hands covering his head. The Frost Bear stopped shaking his fur after a while, snorted so that blue steam puffed from his muzzle, and approached Henry, giving his face a long, icy lick.

"Ugh!" Henry said, staggering back. He fell over a nearby fallen branch, crashing to the earth again.

"I think the Frost Bear wants to be friends with you." Thomasina giggled.

With a shiver of recognition, something clicked into place in her mind.

"You were the silver shadow I saw at Lawley Hall in the trees," she whispered to the Frost Bear. "And you . . . you were there last night, when the Frost Beasts were chasing us!" She gasped. "You must have made it seem like we were with you. That's why they stopped chasing after us."

The Frost Bear snorted again, then padded softly to Thomasina once more, dipping his head and nuzzling Thomasina's hand again. He stiffened. His muzzle sniffed around her arms, then the middle of her torso, then looked at her, giving a long, slow blink of his great white eyes again.

She knew what he was asking, and she rolled up her sleeve, showing the silver-blue snowflakes. There were now so many of them crowding over her skin that her warm pink flesh had disappeared completely.

"I think you know I'm in real trouble," she whispered. "We need as much help as we can get."

The Frost Bear gave a soft growl in response.

Hesitantly, Thomasina brought her hand up to the Frost Bear's face and stroked him with a shaking hand. The Frost Bear seemed to enjoy her pats, and he butted his head into her palm as she stroked his strange fur.

"How are you able to work against Father Winter?" she said, tilting her head to one side as she considered him. "I thought you were all under his power?"

The Frost Bear gave a different growl this time: a harsh, guttural sound. In her peripheral vision, Thomasina saw Henry take several steps back, but she knew the noise the Frost Bear had just made wasn't aimed at Thomasina; rather, it was aimed at Father Winter.

"Can you take us back to London without letting Father Winter know?" she asked.

The Frost Bear didn't answer but gazed back at her.

"We're very lost," she said, stroking his nose. "Please don't betray us, Bear. You're our only hope."

The Frost Bear gave another slow, sad blink back at her,

as if he understood, then grunted again. Thomasina was nervous as she approached him. Her instincts could be completely wrong, but the Frost Bear was the only hope they had left for returning home safely.

She smoothed the tiny shards of ice on the Frost Bear's back so they were all pointing in the same direction and climbed on. She'd gritted her teeth when doing so, expecting the shards to bite into the fabric around her legs, but they didn't.

"Come on, Henry," she called, the sharp, icy air hurting her lungs as she breathed. Her wheeze started to come back as she turned to look at her friend, who was gazing at her and the Frost Bear openmouthed. "I think he's going to take us back to London. We've got to hurry."

Henry gulped, but he clambered forward in the snow, then scrambled onto the Frost Bear's back very inelegantly.

When they were both settled in a way that felt as comfortable as possible while sitting astride a massive bear made entirely of ice, she said, "All right, Bear. Please take us home."

They fled the forest in a breathtaking, relentless sprint, pursued by the snap and bite of the icy winter wind.

They didn't travel back the way they'd come; instead, they hurtled into the evergreen woods, away from the river. Thomasina guessed the bear was taking a different route for their protection from Father Winter's kingdom. The farther away they got from the River Thames, the looser his grip on her soul seemed to be.

They sped past fields and towns at lightning speed. Behind her, Henry was clinging around her waist so tightly to stop himself slipping off she had to snap at him once or twice to let her breathe. The wind scorched her cheeks pink and made her ears ring and her teeth sting. Hawthorn and cowpats, rotting leaves and the pungent scent of sheep filled her nostrils as they hurtled past farms and bounded over stone bridges. Slowly but surely, she started to feel jubilant at their escape from Father Winter.

Occasionally, the Frost Bear would abruptly stop, shake both Thomasina and Henry off his back, then gleefully roll in the snow, paws in the air, before springing up and, with his tongue lolling out of his mouth, gambol and burrow, crunching leaves at random and sniffing around at the forest floor to check for bugs. After a while, he'd scamper over to a nearby tree and scratch his back against its trunk in ecstasy, shaking the frost from its branches.

"Um . . ." Henry would say after a while. "Bear? Can we get a move on, please?"

The Frost Bear would grunt, have a final scratch, then romp over to them both again, grunting for them to climb on once more.

"This is probably the most freedom he's had in ages," Thomasina said wistfully, as the Frost Bear poked his muzzle into a tree stump, falling over backward when a red squirrel scurried out, chirping. "See, Henry? He wouldn't hurt a fly. . . ."

Once or twice, while riding on the Frost Bear's back, they passed villagers who stared at them like they were oddities, which, Thomasina realized with a soft, incredulous laugh, they were—the pair of them sitting astride a massive bear made entirely out of ice.

Adrenaline pounded through her. She felt jubilantly, ecstatically alive, and a boldness awakened in her that she hadn't felt for years. Despite the dangers of the night ahead, she had the Frost Bear on her side, and that meant something, even if she didn't know quite what. She expected the Frost Bear to stop running when night fell, but he continued on for such a stretch of time that she realized they'd be traveling through the night. His breaths were becoming labored, and silver mist had started to gush out of his mouth as he panted, but he kept bolting onward at breakneck speed.

Scarlet dawn was stretching across the landscape as Thomasina spotted the familiar landscape of London before them, ready for another busy day of trade. Smoke and steam were billowing out of the corners of the river in a smile as traders readied their wares for the day.

The Frost Bear came to a sudden halt, and Henry again clasped his hands tightly around Thomasina's waist so he wouldn't be thrown.

"You almost crushed me to death," she hissed when she'd coughed enough air back into her lungs.

"Sorry."

The Frost Bear gave them a huge, sleepy growl, and even before Thomasina had opened her mouth to say thank you, he had turned around and departed at a run. It might have been just her imagination, but Thomasina could have sworn that, after a while, she could no longer hear the heavy thud of the Frost Bear's footsteps. It was as if he'd melted away into thin air.

Thomasina's stomach grumbled.

"Look," she said, pointing to a group of milkmaids, who were churning out fresh milk ready to be sold at the Frost Fair. "Let's get some."

Henry gave a coin to one of the watermen lining the river, and they walked across.

Gulping down the warm, creamy milk and hearing her stomach gurgle in appreciation, Thomasina reflected on the fantastical events of the night before. The last astonishing day and a half had passed so quickly there had scarcely been time to reflect on everything that had happened, but as they sat there quietly, drinking their milk, the thoughts that crowded her mind began to untangle themselves.

Thomasina felt her shoulders slump. She drew out the silver snowflake necklace that she usually kept hidden. When Inigo had given it to her, she had thought it was the most beautiful thing she had ever owned. But now she hated it, because she knew it was the mark that would always lead Father Winter to her.

"Do you . . . do you think—because I'm marked—I'll mark other people around me? Like you, or Anne . . . or Mother and Father . . . even Shadow?"

"I can't be sure," Henry said, screwing up his freckled face. "But I think only the Gray Cloaks and Inigo can mark others. No one came after me when Mary went missing, even though I saw her often before she left. So, no, I don't think you can pass the mark on. Besides, Father Winter seems to like to assess each sad soul himself."

"I overheard Inigo and Father Winter talking, the last time I visited the Other Frost Fair . . ." Thomasina said.

Henry waited for her to go on.

"Father Winter said that the Frost Folk and Frost Beasts were the weakest of his creatures, and then he said something even stranger . . . 'unlike you.' And then he said that Inigo had his powers for a reason—that he had to find 'the special one.' I didn't understand any of this at the time, but now that we've read Inigo's account it makes more sense. Inigo found me and enticed me to the river, so I must be one of the sad souls whose misery is making Father Winter strong. I don't know how much time I've got, but I'm not one of the Frost Folk yet, so it's up to me to discover a way to destroy Father Winter. What do I do, Henry? How can I do it by myself?"

"I don't know how to do it, Thomasina, but one thing you can be sure of: I'll do everything I can to help you. I promise."

Wearily, they trudged through the snow as the winter sun lit up the London landscape still more. Despite their triumph at escaping Father Winter, Thomasina was exhausted from the journey, and her nerves were jagged and raw. All she wanted to do was scrub away the soot from the fireplace that still covered her, then sleep. But as they turned into Raven Lane, Thomasina frowned.

The street was haunted by shrieking, and, as Thomasina began to run, fear mounting, she realized it was coming from the attic room of Burgess & Son's, the knotted twine and faded ribbons blowing through the window, the shutters swinging to and fro in a dreadful wail.

She knew something was terribly wrong.

24

The Disappearance

"Mother?" Thomasina gasped, shivering in the chill morning wind. "Mother—could it be you?" The noise swept down Raven Lane in a freezing gust, rattling the shells suspended on the ragged string outside Miss Maplethorpe's window.

As the screams continued, Thomasina hurtled through a heap of fresh, sugar-light snow, banging so loudly on the door of the shop that her clenched fist cracked its frosting of ice, which splintered into shards and fell to the ground. There was a tightness in her chest that spread still more when a distressed Anne appeared from around the corner. Tears glimmered in her friend's eyes, and Thomasina instinctively put an arm around her, holding her close.

"What's wrong?" she murmured, fumbling around for her key with her other hand, as no one seemed to be around to open the door from the inside.

"I just passed Miss Maplethorpe in town—she was get-ting some fresh air," Anne gulped as Thomasina opened the door, and Mother's screams became louder. "She told me your mother's been having nightmares." The morning sun-light illuminated worry lines creasing her forehead.

"What about?" said Thomasina, panting for breath.

"Miss Maplethorpe said she won't tell her—she just keeps saying your name. Your brother's, too."

"My brother's . . . ?"

"Arthur—she's asking for Arthur, too," Anne said, frowning slightly as she looked at her.

Thomasina pushed past her, clattering upstairs to the attic room, heart pounding. She found Mother thrashing and twisting around in bed, tears streaming and cheeks sticky as she gasped and shuddered, her eyes screwed shut.

"Mother," Thomasina said, sitting on the bed and grab-bing hold of Mother's hands, stroking them with her thumbs. "It's me. It's Thomasina."

"Thomasina," Mother whispered, and Thomasina's mouth fell open in shock, while her heart pounded even more vigorously inside her chest. This was the first time she'd heard her mother speak in four years. She'd almost completely for-gotten what the older woman sounded like, and shivered to hear her name uttered by someone she loved so much.

"Yes, Mother—I'm here," she said, thumbs still kneading Mother's fluttering hands as she heard Anne hurrying up the stairs. Dimly, she was aware of her friend closing the window, twisting the knotted twine and faded ribbons safely in place.

Mother nodded, tear stains grooving her cheeks, then turned in a rustle of bedclothes to face the wall. With a soft purr, Shadow wound his way into the room, jumping onto the bed and licking the silvery hair escaping from Mother's nightcap.

"How long has she been like this?" Thomasina murmured to Anne, stroking Mother's back.

"Since you went away; Miss Maplethorpe told me. I think she's been missing you."

Thomasina nodded.

There was a gentle knock on the door. "Er . . ." Henry's voice floated in. "Thomasina? Anne? Shall I wait for you both downstairs?"

"No," Thomasina said. "I don't want to leave Mother. Come in, Henry. I reckon she'll fall asleep soon anyway."

Henry crept in. After glancing awkwardly at the figure on the bed, he forced his face into a smile and, in an unnaturally bright voice said, "Er, hello, Anne . . . how are you?"

"I'm feeling a bit better, Henry. Thanks," Anne said, reaching out to pat Shadow and wiping a glistening tear away from her cheek. "It was just a shock, that's all." She breathed out in a sigh. "So tell me—what happened at Lawley Hall? Did you find whatever it was?"

"Henry will tell you," Thomasina said. Shadow stretched himself out on the patchwork quilt beside her, his holly-green eyes blinking up at her.

Henry recounted their strange journey, pausing on occasion as Anne gasped, putting her hands to her mouth, or else leaped from the bed and paced around the little room, making the floorboards groan and wail. He described the coach journey and being chased by the Frost Beasts, their arrival at Lawley Hall, and their search of the house for something they still didn't know the identity of. He described how they discovered Inigo's account of his pact with Father Winter hidden behind the brick in the fireplace. Then he described their mad dash from Lawley Hall, and how the Gray Cloaks and Frost Beasts had caught up with them and forced the coach to stop, and the transformation of the coachman into a Gray Cloak (Anne let out an especially huge gasp when she heard this). And he described how Father Winter had threatened them, and how they'd kept their eyes shut tight, so he wouldn't see their eyes and drain their strength from them.

". . . and then all the horses bolted, or else were changed into Frost Beasts, and we didn't know how we'd get back to

London. But then a Frost Bear appeared—we think he's on our side, but we don't know why or how—and he was kind to us, and let us ride on his back, and he brought us safely back here to London," he finished.

Anne looked stunned.

"I can't believe you both escaped," she breathed. "But, oh, Thomasina . . . the danger you're in! Did you bring Inigo's account with you?"

"We did," Henry said, reaching into his pocket for the bundle of parchment and handing it over. Anne held the pages up to her eyes and spent some time reading Inigo's account, eyes widening.

"Where are we going to keep these?" she said when she'd finished.

"I'll take them and hide them in my rooms," Henry said.

Thomasina nodded, her fingers gripping a handful of the blanket on her and Mother's bed.

"I'm so angry with Inigo," she muttered. "I know he's your ancestor, Henry, but he's been double-crossing me all this time. Even if he wants to help now, it can't undo what's already been done because of him. The snowflakes on my skin mean I'm turning into one of the Frost Folk—Father Winter as good as confirmed it. I'm getting colder every day; I don't think it'll be much longer until I transform into one of them completely."

"I . . . I can't believe I'm saying this, Thomasina," Anne whispered, "but I think you've got to speak to Inigo again. Henry—you and I can look in some books for any mention of Father Winter, but—"

"But books won't put everything right," Thomasina finished. "After all, the people who've been to the Other Frost Fair and met Father Winter—they're already drained, their life force sucked out of them. They've already become Frost Folk. They didn't plead for their souls or strike a bargain like Inigo did, so they won't have written anything down. You're right, Anne. I need to speak to Inigo. He's the only person who might know how to destroy Father Winter, and how I can stop myself from turning into one of the Frost Folk forever."

"Thomasina . . ." Henry said falteringly.

"What?"

"I think you need to tell us how far the snowflakes have gone on your body. I can see some on your neck."

Thomasina flushed.

"They're on both my arms now," she murmured. "And halfway up my neck, and all over my chest and stomach. My feet are still bare. I think the snowflakes have reached some of my back."

Henry and Anne looked solemn.

"I know I haven't got much time," Thomasina said.

"That's not the only thing that's worrying me," said

Henry. "You also keep forgetting Arthur's name; sometimes you seem to forget you've even got a brother at all."

"Arthur?" Thomasina repeated. She knew that name should mean something to her. "Arthur . . ."

Anne looked alarmed.

"Can't we come with you when you talk to Inigo?" she said. "I hate the idea of you being alone with him. . . ."

Thomasina shook her head.

"I've got four visits, he told me," she said. "I've visited the Other Frost Fair three times with him: the first time, I met Father Winter; the second, we went to the theater; and the third was when we went to the Frost Ball. I only have one visit left, and I need to make it count. I think he's trying to help me now, even if he's tricked me before."

"What if the next time you see him you're trapped by him, though?" Anne said. "What if the fourth time you visit him is when you'll turn into one of the Frost Folk for good?"

"Yes, that could happen," Thomasina conceded, feeling sick. "But I don't think Inigo wants that."

"I agree," Henry said. "Remember what he wrote about closing your eyes at sunset to protect yourself? Maybe if you keep your eyes closed all the time you're with Inigo, he and Father Winter won't be able to turn you."

Thomasina nodded. "I'm going to have to try." She sighed.

Anne coughed. "There's something else I need to tell you, Thomasina," she said.

"What is it?"

"Miss Maplethorpe also told me something else in town. . . . It's your father," she replied, not meeting her eye. "He's gone missing."

"Missing?" Thomasina said. "What do you mean, missing?"

"Apparently, he disappeared two days ago," Anne said. "At first, Miss Maplethorpe thought he'd perhaps just visited a tavern, but he hadn't been in any of them when she asked around. She told me she then walked to the Frost Fair to try and find him there. The sweet stall was empty and no one had seen him."

"You don't think he could be a sad soul, do you?" Henry said.

Thomasina shook her head. "No," she said. "He's lost in his own world most of the time." Something nagged at her thoughts as she said this, but she pushed it away.

They sat in silence for a while, no one quite knowing what to say.

"I should go," Anne said. "Uncle's going to open up our shop soon, and I need to be there when he does."

"I need to head off, too. Will you both be all right?" Henry said, looking at Thomasina and Mother.

"Yes," Thomasina said. "Thanks so much . . . both of you . . . for everything."

After Henry and Anne left, Thomasina changed into her nightdress, needing to sleep after her blistering race through the ice and snow on the back of the huge Frost Bear. She didn't want to look at her skin now: it made her too upset to see how far the silver had crawled its way across her body in snowflakes. She couldn't bear to think that she might soon be one of those poor Frost Folk who could only say what they were told to say.

"Move over, Shadow," she said. He crept into his usual place on her chest, tickling her nose with his fur.

She waited to get warm and thought of Inigo, wondering what she should say to him to make everything right. She stroked Mother's back gently with her snowflake-stained hands.

"It'll be all right," she whispered to her, unsure whether she believed it would be anymore.

25

Such Dreadful Rumors

Thomasina dozed fitfully through the remainder of the day. When the sun set, she made sure to close her eyes so she'd be invisible to Father Winter, as well as to Inigo and the Gray Cloaks.

Someone kept flitting in and out of her mind. It was someone she felt she loved very much, but whose name she couldn't remember, whose presence she kept sensing in front of her, as if they were just within arm's reach. She woke up several times, taking shuddering, deep breaths in and out, attempting to calm herself down, although she was always sure to keep her eyes squeezed tightly shut.

"Who are you?" she'd whispered in the darkness to the person who felt just out of reach. But they wouldn't reply.

When she got up the following morning, she found that more snowflakes had appeared on her body overnight and were snaking up her neck, so she kept it covered with a thick collar.

The weight of anxiety was crushing her. She went through Mother's household book again, searching for clues about who the person she loved could be. It was difficult to read—Mother's handwriting was so cramped—but there was a word that kept appearing—a word beginning with the letter *A*. Who was A again? She couldn't remember.

Her mind was a blur. Ever since reading Inigo's account and his warning, and coming face-to-face with Father Winter on the journey back from Berkshire, she'd known her life was in grave danger. She was slowly being turned into one of the Frost Folk, and it was a terrifying burden to have to carry around with her. She didn't know how she could possibly destroy Father Winter—her only hope, she felt, was to get more information from Inigo when she next saw him.

Anne tried to distract her from her worries when they met at the Frost Fair. They were selling a new medicinal sweet they'd recently thought up, which Anne had perfected while Thomasina was away: porridge flavored with preserved plum syrup, a good remedy for indigestion.

"Try not to worry. We'll find an answer to all this," she muttered as Thomasina scraped the bottom of their cooking

pot to dole out the last scrap of porridge for their final customer of the day.

But Thomasina couldn't stop anxiety fluttering in her
stomach, even though they'd sold all their wares in just under
an hour: the most successful the Burgess & Son's stall had
ever been at the Frost Fair. Several of their customers had
even clamored to be on a waiting list for whatever their next
medicinal sweet would be. She wished Father were here to
see the success they were having. His mysterious absence was
another thing that tugged at her.

The following day, Father still hadn't reappeared, so
Thomasina went into town herself to buy food. When she
returned, she was so lost in her worries that she didn't notice
the commotion outside the shop until she was almost at her
door. A small crowd had gathered outside, the weak winter
sunshine glinting on their frosted boots.

"What's going on?" Thomasina panted. "Why're you—"

She was interrupted by the butcher, whose sons she used
to play with. He had red blotches on his cheeks.

"I'm sick of that noise!" he raged, pointing a finger up to
the attic room on the second floor. "Night and day, I hear her
wailing and screaming, startling us awake and frightening
the children. Enough's enough. That woman's mad," he said,
turning to face the crowd, "and I for one say she needs to be

locked away. Who's with me?"

The crowd yelled their approval.

"Locked up for *good*, I tell you," the butcher continued. "Carrying on with that ungodly racket—"

"I haven't heard her screaming much," Thomasina snapped.

"And no wonder—you've been prancing off to the countryside, haven't you? Your father told me. Mind you, he's left as well. Probably got sick of her screaming, too."

"Stop it, stop it," Thomasina whispered. She felt dizzy and hated the fact she was on her own. She stumbled against the shop front and heard her neighbors shout around her.

"Put both of them in the stocks—it's what they deserve!"

"Make them pay for this infernal racket!"

"Stop it!" Thomasina roared, her back against the door.

A wail sounded from the attic room, a wail that sounded more animal than human.

Thomasina's heart sank. She'd only been gone for about an hour. She'd thought it would be all right to leave Mother. After all, the last time the older woman had been in a state like this was when Thomasina had been gone for a couple of days. She hadn't thought Mother was having nightmares anymore. What if this meant Mother's health was getting worse, not better?

"Hear that?" the butcher yelled. "She needs locking up, I tell you!"

The crowd pushed forward, and the butcher made to open the door.

"No. I'll get her some"—Thomasina improvised—"some new medicine. She won't scream and shout anymore then."

"She's ruined our sleep for weeks!"

Just then, a different voice piped up: "Free drinks down at the Dog and Duck!" Thomasina recognized the unmistakable bellow of Miss Maplethorpe. "You'll have to hurry—they'll run dry soon enough!"

The butcher looked at Miss Maplethorpe, then spat at the ground near Thomasina's feet. Slimy spit dribbled from his mouth as he glared at her.

"Come on, Dick, it isn't worth it," one of his cronies said to him, and they sloped off in search of their free drinks.

Footsteps pattered over. Thomasina looked up, her eyes wet. It took a while to register through her blurred vision that it was Miss Maplethorpe standing in front of her.

"I heard shouting," the old woman whispered, "and thought I'd see what was going on. I hope they won't be *too* angry when they realize there aren't any free drinks down at the Dog and Duck—I made that up."

She gave Thomasina a weak smile, which Thomasina returned.

"Thank you," she said hoarsely. Scanning the departing figures, her breath caught as she saw a Gray Cloak loitering at the end of the street. Something about the way they stood felt oddly familiar, but Thomasina's curiosity soon became panic as they stepped forward, face still shrouded in their hood, and started walking toward her.

"It's cold," she said quickly, turning back to Miss Maplethorpe and fumbling to unlock the front door. "We shouldn't be outside for long."

"Shall I come in for a bit, while you look after your mother?" Miss Maplethorpe said, following Thomasina in without waiting for an answer. She reminded Thomasina of a sharp-faced bird, and Thomasina realized with a jolt how thin Miss Maplethorpe looked. The winter had been hard for everyone, and for all her chatter about the vegetables she sold, Miss Maplethorpe didn't look as if she'd eaten many at all.

Thomasina stoked the weak fire in the workroom. Henry had given her a generous supply of logs, and she tossed one into the flames.

"Can you take over for me here?" she asked Miss Maplethorpe, who accepted the poker from her. The crying coming from the attic room had subsided by the time Thomasina hurried upstairs, but she was still nervous about what she might find.

"Mother?" she said, creaking the door open.

Mother was sitting up in bed, clenching the blankets around her.

"Has something happened?" Thomasina said, sitting down and taking her hand.

Mother nodded.

"What?"

"I keep seeing horrible things," Mother whispered, her voice barely more than a croak. "All the time. In my head."

"Like what?"

"Arthur, dead . . . and you . . ."

This was the first time she'd admitted what her nightmares were about.

"Do you want me to stay, Mother?" Thomasina said.

The older woman lapsed into silence again, and she slowly shook her head.

Thomasina squeezed her hand before standing up and going back downstairs. She felt even more tired than when she'd got back from Berkshire. Before she entered the workroom, she peeked through a crack in the door and saw Miss Maplethorpe gazing at the stack of logs piled in the corner. Glancing furtively around, Miss Maplethorpe hesitated, then reached out and picked up a tiny log so flat it could have been a twig, then slipped it up her sleeve.

Thomasina crept up the stairs again, then turned and

came back down, stamping her feet so it was clear she was returning. When she went into the workroom, Miss Maplethorpe looked at her guiltily.

"Is your mother better?" she asked her in a quavering voice.

"Yes. She's much calmer now."

Miss Maplethorpe had been a local joke for years: a troublesome spinster, who everyone went out of their way to avoid. Rumors of madness had followed her around for decades, too. Thomasina—she felt ashamed of herself now—usually tried to dodge her in the street, but when she looked at her now, she saw an old woman whose hands were shaking from the cold. Miss Maplethorpe was poorer than anyone else in the neighborhood and perhaps only a month away from starving or being evicted from her lodgings. Thomasina suspected that the money Henry had given her for looking after Mother had been spent almost entirely on rent, as prices were getting higher and higher.

"Miss Maplethorpe," Thomasina said slowly. "I've got a cheese pie that needs eating up. There's too much for me alone. Would you like to join me?"

Miss Maplethorpe looked at her and gave a tremulous nod, blinking in surprise.

"Well, you sit down here, and I'll get everything ready,"

Thomasina said as gently as she could.

She busied herself, refusing Miss Maplethorpe's offers of help. Despite the fire blazing merrily in the grate, she realized she couldn't feel the heat anywhere on her body apart from her legs, hands, and head, a thought that made her shiver. She desperately hoped that Inigo would come soon.

She'd baked a large cheese pie that very morning, and it would certainly be good for a couple of days. Miss Maplethorpe wasn't to know that, though. She put the pie in the middle of the table and heard her neighbor's stomach rumble as she cut two generous slices and dealt them out. She saw Miss Maplethorpe trying to eat as delicately as possible but still biting into her food as hungrily as Shadow had done when Thomasina first brought him home.

Silence fell as Thomasina and Miss Maplethorpe both enjoyed a second piece of pie. Finally, they pushed back their plates.

"Thank you, my dear," Miss Maplethorpe said softly. "That was a wonderful feast."

Thomasina felt a flush creep up her face.

"Don't worry about it," she muttered.

She had a strange impression that Miss Maplethorpe was debating whether to tell her something or not, her blue-veined fingers trembling as she laced them together on the table. Eventually, the old woman broke the silence between them.

"Thomasina . . . have you heard of a Dr. Silsworth?" she asked in a small voice.

Thomasina frowned and nodded. "Yes, I've met him. He's horrible," she said. "He was behaving badly to a woman on the ice a few weeks ago. And he was rude to me, too."

Miss Maplethorpe didn't seem surprised by Thomasina's opinion. She drew her shawl around her, her hands quivering still more.

"Yes," she said. "He's a . . . a rather frightening man."

Thomasina stared at her.

"He's spoken to Father about Mother," she muttered. She didn't know why she was telling Miss Maplethorpe this, but there was something about her neighbor's kind expression that made Thomasina feel like she wouldn't be judged.

Miss Maplethorpe looked uncomfortable. "Thomasina . . . I think you should know that there are rumors. Rumors about you—you and your mother—both being mad. . . ."

"What are people saying?"

"Some of the neighborhood children say you've taken in a black cat. There was joking here and there, at first, of you being a witch and the cat being your familiar. But then the talk got nastier. Your father hasn't been seen in a

couple of days, and your mother's crying upstairs. . . . Well—
people like to gossip. They've even started talking about your
brother."

"My brother?" Thomasina asked vaguely.

"Yes—Arthur," Miss Maplethorpe prompted.

"Arthur," Thomasina repeated. "Arthur . . . Arthur . . .
Arthur . . ." she murmured to herself. "I have a brother called
Arthur. I mustn't forget that."

"Er . . . Thomasina?" Miss Maplethorpe said, looking
distressed. "Some people say your mother's a witch. That she
isn't a woman grieving her son, but that . . . well—that she's
either a witch or mad. Dr. Silsworth's been asking questions
about her."

"So he's after Mother?"

"I think so, yes."

Thomasina's stomach sank. So it was certain now: Dr.
Silsworth wanted to put her mother in Bedlam.

"*I* don't think she's a witch," Miss Maplethorpe said. "I
don't think witches even exist. But your mother needs help.
I'm sure you can see that for yourself, can't you, Thomasina?"

"Yes," Thomasina said. "But, Miss Maplethorpe, I can't
let Dr. Silsworth take her away. I think she's getting better—
she just needs a bit more time, and maybe a doctor who
understands her. Dr. Silsworth won't."

"But, Thomasina," Miss Maplethorpe said. "You heard her screams just now . . ."

"She's started listening to me," Thomasina said. "She's getting stronger."

Miss Maplethorpe sighed, then nodded. "Well, you know her best," she said.

The light was fading fast. Soon, it would be nightfall, and Thomasina needed to make sure her eyes were closed by then.

"I should check on her again," Thomasina said.

Miss Maplethorpe still looked concerned. To placate her, Thomasina took down a box of gingerbread, into which she also put some jellied fruit and some pear cake, then she wrapped several logs in sackcloth, and handed it all to Miss Maplethorpe. *I'm getting too soft for my own good,* she thought as her neighbor's eyes welled up.

Miss Maplethorpe hesitated and took a deep breath. "Thomasina," she said in a tremulous voice, "earlier, when you were upstairs, I took a—"

"Don't worry about it," Thomasina said.

She smiled at Miss Maplethorpe. Though she was anxious about everything her neighbor had said about Mother, something inside her told her that Miss Maplethorpe needed kindness. The beam the older woman returned at first was uncertain but grew. She transformed into another person entirely: radiant and beautiful, with gentle, kind creases around her eyes.

"Goodbye," Thomasina called, as Miss Maplethorpe walked back home, clutching the box of food and logs. Thomasina scanned the street in the gathering darkness to see if the Gray Cloak from earlier was still loitering around, but she was glad to see they'd disappeared. After locking the door, she closed her eyes at last and listened to Miss Maplethorpe's footsteps fading away.

So it wasn't just Inigo and Father Winter she had to deal with. She had to keep Mother out of harm's way, too.

26

Inigo's Final Clue

Something in the air tasted like magic that night. Hours after Miss Maplethorpe left, Thomasina felt she'd developed an acute awareness of when Inigo was nearby, and she wondered if it was because so many icy silver snowflakes were now biting into her skin.

She didn't wait to hear a tap on the door. Instead, she stood outside, keeping her eyes closed. The snowflake necklace meant that the parts of her body not covered by silver snowflakes weren't too cold, but she kept her cloak wrapped around her all the same. She was surprised not to sense Gray Cloaks flitting around, but she reasoned this was part of Father Winter's plan to unnerve her. After all, the more tormented a sad soul was when he hunted them down, the more life he could drain from them.

Beneath her eyelids, she sensed a sparkling blue light bobbing toward her. Inigo was approaching, and he appeared to be holding a lantern from the Other Frost Fair. When he spoke, his voice sounded hoarse, like it was fading fast.

"Good evening, Miss Burgess," he whispered.

Thomasina bared her teeth, heart pounding. Her icy fingernails bit into the soft, warm flesh of her palm—one of the few parts of her body still unmarked by Father Winter's enchantment. "I've snowflakes covering me nearly all over," she said, sounding calmer than she felt. "And even though I know I love someone who's now gone, I can't remember who they are anymore."

"I'm sorry," Inigo said. "I didn't want to curse you, but I—I had to. Father Winter made me."

"I see," Thomasina said coldly.

Silence stretched between them, and when Inigo sighed, she heard a peculiar rattle that hadn't been in his lungs before.

"Did my descendant find what I'd hidden?" he asked.

"Yes," she said. "He found your account."

"I'm glad," Inigo muttered. "I only have enough energy to give you one clue. That's why I couldn't tell you much about what to look for, or where. You see—"

"The thing is, Inigo," Thomasina said, feeling her heart

pound even more, "we discovered I'm a sad soul, and that you've been working to entrap me all this time—to turn me into one of the Frost Folk. This hasn't been about bringing the person I loved back, even though I know you could do it if you wanted to. I thought you were kind and wanted to help me, but it was all a trick. You've made a bargain with Father Winter, and you don't care about me."

"Stop," Inigo whispered.

"I don't understand why you pretended to help me," she spat. "Telling me to find the account you wrote in the first place. Are you playing a game, stringing this out for me? As cowardly as you are, I didn't think you were truly cruel as well."

Inigo gave a small cry, as though he were an animal in pain. Despite every instinct begging her not to do this, Thomasina couldn't help it. She had to see what was going on.

She opened her eyes.

Inigo's silvery eyelids were closed, his face contorting. Horrified but unable to look away, Thomasina wondered how she could have ever thought him to be anything other than under a spell. His skull shone through his translucent, blue-tinged skin, while his knuckles strained white as he balled his hands into fists. Snowflake marks just like hers swarmed up and down his hands and over the skin of his neck, edging upward from his jawline. They hadn't been there before, she realized. Was Inigo falling under the same powerful snowflake charm that she'd been cursed with, too?

"There's one last thing . . . you need . . . to do," Inigo said, "to . . . destroy Father Winter." His eyes were shut, and the more he tried to speak, the less he seemed able to. His body looked like it was collapsing in on itself. "I couldn't tell you . . . until I knew that you knew . . . who I really was, because when he finds out . . . that I've broken my promise to him . . . to keep his secret . . . I'll be overpowered by his . . . enchantments." He grunted, holding a hand to his side.

"I don't—"

He raised a hand to show her he had more to say. "Most sad souls . . . have a beloved item. It's this beloved item that Father Winter fears—more than everything else . . . Beloved items are things that remind sad souls . . . of—of their loved ones. For me"—he winced, gesturing toward his blue velvet doublet, which Thomasina had admired for so long—"it was my doublet. . . . My mother gave it to me . . . before she died . . . and I treasured it above everything else."

"But I don't have a doublet," Thomasina said. "What's my beloved item? What can I use to destroy Father Winter?"

Despite her anger at Inigo, she had a feeling he was telling the truth. A sparkling blue mist was starting to swirl around him, and it was glowing brighter as every second passed. She wondered if this was the powerful enchantment Father Winter had placed upon Inigo, which would enact revenge once his servant betrayed his biggest secret.

"Only you know what it is," Inigo grunted. "You'll have to find it out yourself. . . . But be quick—" He gasped, staggering on the pavement.

There was a faint sound of a terrible music that grew louder and louder as he spoke. It seemed to be coming from the glittering mist surrounding Inigo, and Thomasina knew it wouldn't be long before Inigo was silenced.

"It's—it's nearly too late . . ." Inigo croaked. "You only have a—a day or so, before he—before he hunts you down for—for good. Make him—make him come into contact . . . with your beloved object—throw it at him . . . or hold it up against his skin—and he'll be vanquished."

"But," Thomasina said, her mind racing, "why do you have the object you most love attached to you? If coming into contact with your beloved object could destroy Father Winter, why doesn't he destroy it?"

"He *does* destroy it"—Inigo winced—"if he—if he gets to the sad soul first. It's his way of making sure there are fewer—fewer objects in the world that can destroy him. . . . So he binds them to the sad soul, to make sure they're no

longer a—a threat. That's why I *always* wear this doublet. . . .
That's why Mary—Mary always wears her—her locket."

The sparkling mist was contorting, glimmering particles
forming themselves into a giant, long-nailed hand.

"If Father Winter can't touch a sad soul's beloved object
without being destroyed," Thomasina said quickly, heart
pounding feverishly, "how does he get them to bring it to him
in the first place? Why hasn't he been destroyed already?"

"Because," Inigo grunted, his voice barely more than a
whisper now, "he casts a powerful charm to—to lure the sad
souls to him. . . . No one else has been able to destroy him—
because no one else knows what I know—what I've managed
to discover . . ."

The moment he said this, his face blistered white, and he
cowered. A ripping, tearing sound came from the fresh, silvery snowflakes marking his entire face. Thomasina saw him
hunch over in anguish, keening, as blinding pain seemed to
overcome him completely.

"Inigo!" Thomasina yelled. She ran forward to stop
whatever was happening, but she found herself knocked back
by an invisible force that sent her hurtling to the ground,
bruising her shins. The pressure around her was so intense
that Thomasina couldn't help but close her eyes as she felt a
huge gust of wind blow over her.

When she opened them, all she saw were the street's cobblestones, crystallized in ice.

"Inigo," Thomasina whispered from her knees. She'd just had a flashback of her doing the same thing, years ago, with someone else.

Arthur.

27

The Night Market

"Thomasina! Thomasina!"

A face swam before her, with wide brown eyes full of concern. Warm hands grasped her arms. It was Anne.

"What's happened?" Anne said in a low voice.

"Inigo's gone. I said something horrible to him—just like . . . just like I did with . . ."

Thomasina had no idea why she could remember who Arthur was now. Had the spell she'd been placed under by Inigo—making her forget her brother—lifted the moment Inigo had been cursed by Father Winter's enchantment? Though she knew who Arthur was again, her thoughts were hazy and disorientating, but nevertheless she tried to give Anne an account of everything that had happened. All the while, Arthur's face swam before her, but she couldn't make him out clearly enough: it was as if she were looking at him through a translucent veil. His voice appeared in fits and bursts, as if he were calling to her from a long way away, and she couldn't understand what he was saying. Her throat choked up with remorse and fury as she spoke, her heart pounding so much she could feel it in her temples.

"I—I told Inigo he was a coward, and he—he told me how to destroy Father Winter, and something, something happened . . . and he vanished . . . I think Father Winter's enchantment overpowered him. There was a giant hand and—he—he's gone, Anne, just like Arthur—"

"Shh," Anne said, pulling her close. "It's all right."

"No," Thomasina whispered. "No, it isn't."

By now, muttering surrounded them. Neighbors were gathering.

"She's barking mad," Thomasina heard one of the butcher's boys sneer.

"Her *and* her mother," his brother agreed.

"Dr. Silsworth needs to sort them out," another voice piped up. "And where's her father, eh? They've done away with him, I'd wager. I haven't seen him for a week."

"We need to get you out of the street," Anne said. "Come, I'll help you."

"We don't need to be cured of *anything*, thank you very much," Thomasina spat, feeling herself being steered into the shop. "And anyway, madness isn't *bad*."

Dimly, she was aware of the door being bolted, which didn't entirely drown out the noise from her neighbors outside. Anne guided her to the workroom. A chair was scraped away from the polished table, squeaking on the flagstones, while her friend's hands pressed on Thomasina's shoulders. She sat down and heard her friend poke the dying fire so it sputtered to life, then sit down beside her. Shadow appeared, meowing at the girls. He jumped onto the table, where he wasn't usually allowed, and started nibbling at a hunk of cheese pie. Thomasina was in no mood to tell him off.

"What happened?" Anne whispered.

Thomasina let out a sob. Arthur's face was floating in front of her, and remembering him all of a sudden was a shock. It *must* be because the charm Inigo had put on her to make her forget Arthur had lessened. Did this mean—her heart twisted—that Father Winter had been weakened somehow, too?

Taking a deep, shuddering breath, in and out, she told Anne everything that had just happened: Inigo's final clue for how to defeat Father Winter, the swirling mist around him, and his warning that she didn't have much time left before she'd be lost forever.

Anne's eyes widened in the firelight.

"Thomasina," she whispered. "This means . . ."

"That I have a chance of destroying Father Winter,"

Thomasina said, finishing her sentence for her. "Yes."

"What's your beloved object?" Anne said, standing up. "You can go to the river and destroy Father Winter now!"

"I don't know. That's what I need to find out," Thomasina replied, looking down at her hands. She realized icy snowflakes were now completely covering her palms. Her time was running out fast. To be so close to destroying Father Winter but without the final piece of information she needed felt excruciating. Even though she was still angry at Inigo, Thomasina couldn't stop wondering what had happened to him. Was he being punished by Father Winter this very minute? She knew he'd tried to help her, and he was probably suffering greatly because of it.

Anne paid an errand boy to fetch Henry, and when he'd arrived she told him everything, while Thomasina stared into the fire, stroking Shadow and trying to conjure up Arthur more clearly in her mind. Henry and Anne both insisted on helping her search for what her beloved object could be, so they worked deep into the night.

First, they investigated Father's pile of jumble in the corner of the shop, which Thomasina came to realize was almost entirely composed of Arthur's old belongings and things he used to play with. They dislodged a wooden horse, a patched, threadbare cloak he'd grown out of, and a battered bundle of parchment he'd used when he was learning to write. Searching through the jumble made Thomasina realize Father must have a great deal of sadness locked away in his soul. Why else would he refuse to throw the pile away? His absence, just like Inigo's, made her miserable.

"I'm just going to check on Mother," she muttered to her friends.

Creeping upstairs, she found Mother fast asleep, facing the wall as usual. Now more than ever, Thomasina just wanted to talk to her.

"If I told you there was another fair, Mother—an enchanted Frost Fair that only awakened at night, and a conjurer who promised me I could bring Arthur back to life, would you believe me?" she said to the sleeping figure. "What if I told you that, unless I find my beloved object, you may never see me again?"

There was no reply. Thomasina wished Mother could swoop in and sort everything out for her, the way she'd done when Thomasina was much younger and had accidentally broken a toy or had a squabble with Arthur. But Mother couldn't help her right now.

Heart heavy, she tiptoed downstairs to find that Anne and Henry had laid out all the items of Arthur's they could find on the table.

"My beloved object could be any of these." Thomasina sighed. "How am I supposed to know which one?"

"Maybe any of them would work?" Anne suggested.

Thomasina shook her head.

"He told me it was one object," she said. "Inigo had his doublet, and Mary had her locket . . ."

She broke off, biting her lip.

"I'm going for a walk," she announced.

"We'll come with you," Henry said.

"No. I want to be alone."

"But it's nighttime," he objected. "Is that wise, with the Gray Cloaks hovering around?"

"I won't be long," Thomasina said, rubbing a hand over her forehead. Snowflakes had traveled all across her feet, and she knew she only had a trickle of time left. She felt unnatural, as if there were no heart beating in her chest now. "I just need to *think*."

Closing the door, she walked outside, choosing a direction at random and not noticing the winter darkness starting to stain the gray sky above. A thought was nagging away at the corners of her mind: something she couldn't quite give shape to yet.

"Arthur," she whispered. "Talk to me. *Please*. I need you."

In her mind's eye, her brother opened his mouth, but she couldn't work out what he was saying.

Dreamlike, she walked on, trying not to slip in the frozen muck coating the cobblestones around her. After several minutes, the scent of roasted chestnuts and spices filled the air. Turning the corner, she found herself on the edge of a night market and she walked on in.

Tambourines jangled earthy tunes that made her feet itch to dance. Stalls draped in a rich array of jewel tones glistened in the dark. Braziers were starting to be lit; she heard the hiss and sputter of them sparking to life fizzing all around her. Jostled in the crowd, her fingers accidentally touched a swathe of different fabrics: soft silk, luxurious velvet, and scratchy damask.

A voice muttered in her ear. "Pretty cloths, miss? We have fine, bright silks for spring . . ."

"N-No," Thomasina murmured, stepping back. She was pushed unceremoniously into the fray again, swept up in a tangle of bodies.

There was something she knew was important to her, but she didn't know how useful it would be against Father Winter. . . .

"Like a block of ice!" A woman shivered after Thomasina accidentally bumped into her. "What was that?"

Struggling to think, Thomasina felt something hard knock against her shins as she was pushed into another stall. Her fingers found soft feathers, and she felt a stab of pain as a beak clamped around her little finger.

"Ow!" she cried, stumbling back.

"Kestrels and owls, I have them all," came a voice glinting jewel-bright in the gathering darkness. "Barn and tawny, or my prize kestrel will hunt for you, all manner of things . . ."

"N-No thank you," Thomasina murmured as she stumbled away. Animals . . . animals . . . why were animals sparking a glimmer of recognition within her? Strange animals . . . animals with long beaks or strange limbs . . . animals that appeared to be from another world . . .

People shoved at each other as Thomasina pushed her way out of the crowd. Lanterns full of flickering orange flames jumped at her. Different accents and languages echoed everywhere in an exciting confusion . . . and suddenly she emerged onto a quieter street again and was leaving the night market behind.

As she made her way back home, her mind kept racing—animals and strange, cramped handwriting . . . She walked on, immersed in her thoughts.

"What could it be, Arthur?" she muttered. "Do *you* know?"

Th-Think, she thought she heard a very faint voice reply, but she couldn't be sure.

As she rounded the corner at the far end of Raven Lane, she was surprised to hear a loud babble of voices nearby, but she reasoned they must be people stumbling home from taverns. A small figure emerged out of the gloom into the weak light cast by a burning brazier. She was humming a tune under her breath. Her hands were shaking so much that they dislodged a couple of carrots from the basket she was carrying, and they fell to the ground.

"Oh, Thomasina!" Miss Maplethorpe said, looking distressed. "I've been looking everywhere for you. You need to— What's that silvery stuff on your chin?"

Thomasina placed her hands to her face. Coldness seeped through her fingers, and she guessed that the enchantment working to turn her into one of Father Winter's Frost Folk was almost complete. Surrounded by candlelit windows, she squinted at her reflection, and saw the silver snowflakes covering her entire jawline. Father Winter's enchantment was growing, and rapidly. Soon, she imagined, the snowflakes would cover her entire face.

"Oh, it's just frost, Miss Maplethorpe," she muttered. "Did Anne and Henry tell you to find me?"

"No," the old woman said, still looking a little disturbed at Thomasina's appearance. "It's our neighbors. I tried to stop them, but—"

A coldness quite unlike the enchantment covering her lodged itself in Thomasina's stomach. She heard Miss Maplethorpe hurrying after her as she ran down the street, her chest wheezing. Her heart shuddered as she saw the scene before her.

Burgess & Son's was encircled by lights, so blinding in the gloom that for several moments, it was hard for Thomasina to work out what was happening, but when her eyes adjusted to the scene, her mouth fell open in horror.

A crowd was surrounding a tall, pallid figure dressed in white, a tangle of gray hair escaping from her nightcap.

Mother.

28

The Woman in White

Horrified, Thomasina stumbled toward the sweet shop, her mind a blur.

What was going on?

Another figure was visible in the candlelight, and she recognized Henry staggering out of the shop, clutching a bloodied cloth to his cheek.

"Stop!" he roared. Anne appeared beside him, fists balled in rage against the crowd.

"Mother!" Thomasina called. "Wait there, I'll—"

But before she could finish, she gasped. Someone she recognized was standing next to Mother and wearing a triumphant, crooked smile.

"Ladies and gentlemen!" Dr. Silsworth exclaimed. "Thank you for trusting me to look after this woman, who's disturbed your neighborhood for far too long. I'll take good care of her, now that she's under my supervision."

"Please," Thomasina pleaded, a lump in her throat as she fought her way to the front of the crowd. "Please, Dr. Silsworth, she's fine where she is. I know she needs some help, but it wouldn't help her to be treated by you, with people being able to watch her all the time: Can't you see that? Don't take her away from me."

Her mother's arm was imprisoned in the grip of Dr. Silsworth's assistant. She looked at Thomasina, who was surprised to see a strange gleam in the older woman's eyes, illuminated by the candles around them.

"Thomasina," she said in a surprisingly firm voice. "Everything's going to be all right."

Thomasina shook her head. "No," she said. "That's not true. *None* of this is all right. It's *never* going to be all right."

Dr. Silsworth's lip curled as he appraised her. Thomasina saw him recoil slightly as his eyes roamed her face—he must have seen the frost encrusting her chin—but his sense of triumph seemed to outweigh any unease he might have felt at her appearance.

"Foolish girl," he spat. "I remember you meddling when I spoke at the Frost Fair. Don't busy yourself with things you don't understand. I'm here to help your mother—"

"You don't understand her, though!" Thomasina cried.

"You don't know what she's gone through, or how she's getting better. You don't care about her—if you take her somewhere like Bedlam, she'll be gawped at all the time! Like some poor animal at the circus!"

"Child," Dr. Silsworth said, his head tilted to one side. He gave a crooked, awful smile that chilled her to the bone. "You're distressing yourself unnecessarily. You sound quite mad, just like your mother. Don't end up like her, or I might have to take you to Bedlam, too."

Thomasina's knees buckled. Behind her, she heard the butcher's sons laugh, and someone splashed a pail of icy water over her head, making her scream in shock. Shivering more from fear than cold, as the snowflakes on her skin insulated her almost entirely, she turned around and saw the silhouette of the parson from St. Bartholomew's Church, as well as that of the apothecary she used to frequent.

"Leave my daughter alone," she heard Mother say in a sharp, strong voice.

Dr. Silsworth paused. Thomasina could tell that, even while he had the upper hand, there was something in the proud-backed way Mother stood before him that unsettled him. And Mother had spoken more clearly and firmly than she'd done in any of the four years since Arthur's death: confident and authoritative, demanding respect. But it was all far too late. . . .

Dr. Silsworth turned to his associate. "Lead the way," he said.

"Mother! Don't go with him!" Thomasina cried.

Her mother turned around to face her for a final time.

"Trust me, Thomasina," she whispered. A single tear fell down her cheek.

Thomasina was so shocked, so bewildered—so angry—that she could only watch, openmouthed in horror, as Mother climbed into Dr. Silsworth's coach without a backward look.

"No!" Thomasina yelled.

"Thank you, good people, for helping me tonight," Dr. Silsworth announced to the crowd, then his coach departed, the horses' hooves echoing down the street.

Now the entertainment was over, the throng surrounding Burgess & Son's dispersed. Thomasina walked toward Henry.

"What happened?" she asked through clenched teeth.

"Thomasina, I'm so sorry," he began, still with the bloodied handkerchief held to his head. "Your mother had a nightmare. She was screaming, and we tried to look after her, but she wouldn't listen. She kept crying out, and we heard your neighbors shouting at her to be quiet. Still, she wouldn't stop, even though we tried so hard—we really did—and a few people went to get Dr. Silsworth. I heard a knock and thought it was you, but it was your neighbors, and Anne tried to stop them coming in, but she was pushed to the side and I was hit on the head, and . . ."

He trailed off, looking anguished.

"We'll get her back, Thomasina," Anne said. "We'll think of a plan."

"Get out," Thomasina snarled. "I should never have left you two alone with Mother. I should've known you'd mess everything up." Even as she said it, she knew she was being sickeningly unfair, but fire was brewing in her chest. She wanted to destroy everything in sight.

"But—"

"Get out!" Thomasina screamed, feeling her hands clench into fists, nails biting down into her skin so hard she felt blood.

Anne and Henry stumbled outside. Before Thomasina slammed the door behind them, she caught a glimpse of Anne's face, which was now creased in worry, her mouth hanging open in shock.

Thomasina breathed in short, sharp gasps. Rage throbbed through her. Her friends had let her down. Mother was gone, and Father was nowhere to be found. Who was left? No one, apart from Shadow. As she paced back and forth, she realized she still had her eyes open, even though it was evening, and they had been for some time.

There's no point in closing them now, she thought miserably.

Losing Mother had made her realize, with burning clarity, what her beloved object was. She had all she needed to journey to the Other Frost Fair immediately and try to defeat Father Winter once and for all.

29

Footsteps in the Snow

G uilt.

It bared its teeth at her, gnawing away at her insides.

With a gasp, Thomasina clutched at her heart. Even more golden, shining memories of her brother started coming back to her, so much so it felt like they were overspilling. Though she'd remembered who he was the moment Inigo had vanished the day before, and had tried to talk to him and make him out more clearly ever since, her thoughts and memories had still felt clouded.

Now, they were clearer than ever. She didn't know why they'd suddenly rushed back to her all at once, and the onslaught was overpowering.

If she hadn't taunted Arthur four years ago, telling him to catch up with her, he'd still be alive. It was her fault he'd died in the snow, hands stretched out to hold hers for a final time—her fault the person she'd loved most in the world was gone.

Father Winter had told her she was the saddest soul he'd seen in years. Though she'd spent all this time planning to vanquish him, she knew he was coming for her: that she was doomed to become one of his Frost Folk.

Inigo's words echoed in her head.

Make him come into contact . . . with your beloved object—throw it at him . . . or hold it up against his skin—and he'll be vanquished. If Father Winter even had a heart, it was as cold and brittle as ice. He'd existed for centuries without coming into contact with any kind of love, and Thomasina imagined he'd crumble like a rock if he touched anything close to it. No wonder he was scared of the objects the sad souls had: their misery was their undoing, but the love they had that had caused their misery was Father Winter's undoing, too.

The agony of losing Mother to the power of Dr. Silsworth had made Thomasina realize what her beloved object was. And she didn't need a charm cast on her by Father Winter to bring it to the river with her. He knew that.

Her fingers trembled as she walked across the workroom and bent down to open the cupboard farthest away from the door. She felt inside, behind plates, knives, trays, and goblets. Her fingers closed around Mother's household book. She drew it out, hugging it against her chest, and wanted to cry against its pages until the ink inside bled tears as well.

What was the use of trying to keep Mother's past with her? The person contained in these pages was forever changed. The woman Thomasina had spent her childhood adoring was different now. While she still loved the person who was left, she could no longer pretend things would ever return to how they'd been before.

Now Mother was gone, there was no one left to say goodbye to apart from Shadow. He pushed his head against her hand, purring as she stroked him for a final time, tail curled in a question mark. She left the rest of the cheese pie out for him and opened the back door, keeping it ajar so he could go out when he wanted. He squeaked at her, but she refused to turn around. She unbolted the front door of the shop, stepping out and locking it behind her.

Raven Lane was bathed in silver as she walked. The moon was wide awake, staring at her. Thomasina wondered if a Gray Cloak or Father Winter was poised to accost her, but all was silent.

Arthur. Arthur. Arthur. As she walked, clutching the book to her chest, her brother's name echoed in her head, matching in time with her heartbeat.

Thomasina's hair was still wet from the water thrown over her. She walked toward the frozen River Thames, feeling the liquid in her hair freezing into ice, cracking against her skull as she moved. *Will it feel like this if Father Winter curses me and entraps me forever?* she thought. A gust of wind snatched a sheet of parchment out of the book. It fluttered into the night sky, lost forever.

So many memories crackled to life in Thomasina's mind, like tiny fires, before being extinguished as quickly as they'd formed. She shivered to remember herself and Arthur as children, screaming or laughing together, bitter enemies one day and thick as thieves the next; herself as a child, running to Mother; Mother wiping her tears away with the end of her apron; Father smiling at Arthur as he showed him the shop accounts; Mother's hands fluttering over the household book that was filled with centuries of knowledge from the women in their family, drawing sea monsters and scribbling things down; Mother tucking her and Arthur in at night, kissing them on their foreheads; herself and Arthur nose-to-nose, dreams shared between them as they slept.

Something rustled nearby, and Thomasina held the household book up in front of her, steeled for an attack by the Gray Cloaks, but lowered it when she saw a huge silver shadow snuffle toward her. A familiar figure emerged out of the gloom: the Frost Bear who'd protected her and Henry from the wrath of the Frost Beasts and given them a safe passage home. He edged close to her, his fur shimmering blue under the moonlight and stars, and he nuzzled his frosted nose into her palm.

He'd come to comfort her. She was sure of it.

"Thank you," she whispered. He tried to nudge her with his snout, pushing her back the way she'd come.

"Hush," she said, stroking his nose. "It's too late for that."

The Frost Bear snorted. It might have been Thomasina's imagination, but she thought he looked deeply sad.

Now, with the Frost Bear padding alongside her, she no longer felt so afraid. After all, what did being enchanted matter, now that she couldn't look after Mother, and didn't have Anne or Henry as her friends, or even Father around anymore? She was the only one left, clutching the tattered remnants of what had been her family before Arthur had died, memories gathered in the book she was carrying.

Her determination to try and defeat Father Winter before she succumbed to his evil magic remained fixed in her as she walked, though step by step she felt her hopes of success ebbing away. But she'd try—at least she'd try.

She could see two figures waiting ahead as buildings gave way to the wide-open space of the Thames. Thomasina knew who they were. They were there to ensure she never left the river again.

As she drew closer, she saw Father Winter and Inigo staring at her, and, behind her, she heard the huge paws of the Frost Bear pad away into nothingness once more. Inigo looked frightened, his hollowed face creased in a frown. Father Winter was smiling, showing his sharp-edged icicle teeth. He looked even younger now, with a strikingly handsome face and no beard at all. His strange, stale smell filled her nostrils.

"Inigo's brought me a gift," Father Winter said. Though he resembled a youth, his voice still sounded impossibly ancient and hoarse. "I have before me the saddest soul I've seen in years."

"Come on, then," Thomasina whispered. "I'm tired of being chased."

It has to be soon, she thought, seeing Father Winter draw near. *I just need to make him touch Mother's household book, then this will all be over.*

"Do you know, child, that I drained your father several days ago?" Father Winter whispered. His voice was ragged in his excitement. "He had such sorrow in his heart, having buried his only son years ago."

A third figure walked out of the mist. It was Thomasina's father—only now, he was a Gray Cloak.

"My son," Father croaked. "I lost him far too young . . . my son . . ."

Thomasina's hands trembled and she stared, unable to breathe for several moments from shock. Father was here . . .

Father. And he was now one of Father Winter's servants, commanded to do his bidding. Sadness at his predicament mingled with even more fury toward Father Winter.

"I have your father's soul"—Father Winter smiled, gesturing for Father to leave; Father turned around and disappeared into the mist—"and now I'll take yours." He raised his hand, staring at her with his unflinching, ice-bright glare.

Instantly, she sprang into action. Feeling the ice below squeaking under her feet as she ran, Thomasina gritted her teeth and, keeping her eyes fixed on the beautiful monster before her, she raised her hand, ready to throw the book directly at Father Winter the moment she was in range. . . .

But with a shock, she heard him mutter something under his breath, and she felt the ice below her crack and splinter. It took all her strength and energy not to fall into the gaping hole that had suddenly appeared before her. She just managed to rescue her precious household book from falling into the watery depths below, throwing it at the last minute across the ice to her right. Chest wheezing, she staggered to her feet again, hearing Father Winter give a low, mocking laugh.

"I thought you'd try a little harder than *that*," he sneered. "Were your attempts to save your brother's life this feeble, too?"

Pain exploded in Thomasina's heart at these words, and she flinched as Father Winter started firing new spells into the ice so that even more gaping chasms opened before her as she scrambled to pick up Mother's book, gripping it to her chest once more and feeling the familiar ridges of its ancient spine brush against her fingers. Again, she charged at Father Winter, trying to get close enough to him so that, when she threw the book at him, it would be sure to make contact. Again, Father Winter blasted deep holes into the ice that forced Thomasina to pivot and dodge, before falling on her side this time, so as not to fall into the watery depths below.

But she wouldn't give up, even though Father Winter was playing his cruel game of cat and mouse with her. She just had to keep going. She had to stop him, somehow, even though her chest wheezed and her hip hurt from where she'd fallen on it.

But as she tried to get up a third time, she found herself being pinned to the ground by a huge, invisible force from which she couldn't extricate herself.

"Playtime's over, Thomasina Burgess," Father Winter said with a cold, deadly smile. She stared up at him, horrified, Mother's book trembling in her hands. "You'll cast aside the book," he commanded, "and submit your soul to me *now*."

Thomasina snarled at Father Winter as she tried to get up, but it was no use. She couldn't move, and she saw the glint of his icy eyes as he watched her struggle before him.

"Do you know, child, that you are about to be drained

forever?" he hissed, his pale eyes gleaming in the moonlight. "You have the most sorrow of anyone I've seen in years. When I look into your eyes, I see your brother, gasping for air. Most of the sad souls I come across have some misery within them, yes—but you have something far more valuable to me. Every inch of you is in torment about your brother. Your sorrow runs so deep that when I drain you of your energy and keep your soul hostage around me on this river forever, it will be many years before I need to consume another sad soul. Your sorrow will nourish me for a very long time to come."

Misery overwhelmed Thomasina. For a moment, it didn't feel like Father Winter was standing in front of her. Instead, Arthur smiled and held out his hand to her, to help her stand. As abruptly as she'd glimpsed her brother, the vision vanished, and she saw Father Winter before her once more.

He was smiling at her like he'd done the first night she'd visited the Other Frost Fair. She knew she was about to be lost forever. She was still just about holding on to Mother's household book, but because of Father Winter's enchantments, she could no longer throw it at him—so there was no longer any hope of him being destroyed. As she looked into his cold, blank eyes, she knew there was no one else to help her . . . she felt herself ebbing away . . .

But someone was there. Someone had clambered out of a rickety carriage, stumbling down its narrow steps; had hurtled into the night air, then ridden on an enormous, silver-streaked beast down cobbled streets, unused to the bitter elements; someone had crouched against walls and gasped in horror at the scene unfolding on the river. Someone had seen Thomasina in the clutches of Father Winter and let another emotion take over entirely: pure, cold rage, so it no longer mattered that they were small and slight. They no longer felt fear or the cold. This was no stranger to Thomasina at all, but she could have been in that moment, so unrecognizable was she. . . .

Mother, gray-haired and as majestic as a queen, stepped onto the frozen river and faced down Father Winter, teeth bared in a lioness's snarl, the Frost Bear rooted behind her like a sentry.

Thomasina's mouth fell open, and her heart skipped a beat.

"Mother?" she murmured. Why was Mother here?

She glanced back at Father Winter and saw his ice-white eyes widen in shock as he stared at the white-faced woman in front of him. His magic was affected, too. Though she was still pinned to the surface of the frozen river by the force of the enchantment, Thomasina found she could turn her head a little more now, to look at Mother; could move her arms slightly, too.

"Stay away from my daughter," Mother growled, and

Thomasina saw that her hands, though shaking—not from cold or fear, but with anger—were balled into fists, ready to attack.

Father Winter stepped toward Mother, raising his hands to cast a powerful enchantment.

"Here!" Thomasina cried. Grabbing the corner of the household book, it took all her remaining strength to hurl it in Mother's direction. "You need to throw it at him to destroy him!"

Mother lunged forward, dodging a blast of blue sparks that Father Winter aimed at her, and caught the household book by the tips of her fingers, losing her balance and crashing forward on the ice, just as Thomasina had done. Though Mother grunted in pain, Thomasina saw her cling onto the book for dear life, and her heart leaped. Behind her, the Frost Bear turned and vanished into the mist once more.

Father Winter gave his deadly smile and started walking with deliberate footsteps toward Mother, as if he were savoring every moment.

"Ah, two sad souls are mine for the taking, it seems," he rasped, and started to raise his arms again. The enchantment binding Thomasina to the ground tightened as his power grew stronger. She could no longer call to Mother, but instead watched hopelessly as Mother, still clutching the household book, gave Father Winter a defiant stare.

"Get up," Thomasina moaned softly, straining against the magical bonds that held her in place. "Or it'll be too late. . . . Throw it—throw it at him . . ."

But Mother didn't let go of her book. Instead, she opened it and began turning its pages.

"What are you doing?" Thomasina gasped. "You have to make him come into contact with it, while you still can!"

"'The eighteenth of October, in the year of our Lord 1670,'" Mother read in a clear, trembling voice, ignoring Thomasina's advice. Thomasina couldn't understand what was happening. With an ache, she heard Mother's lovely Scottish vowels stretching themselves awake. Despite her panic, she couldn't help but be mesmerized as Mother scanned the familiar pages that Thomasina knew were crammed with the handwriting she had never been able to decipher.

"'I have a boy and a girl,'" Mother whispered. "'They're twins. My husband named the boy Arthur, and I named the girl Thomasina after my mother.'"

The black scrawls that Mother was reading aloud . . . were they Mother's old diary entries? And why was she reading them to Father Winter?

"Please, Mother," Thomasina groaned. "Throw it at him, and then it'll all be over."

But Mother kept going, her voice growing stronger by the second.

"'The fourteenth of April, in the year of our Lord 1676,'" she read. "'My daughter has a talent for business, and my son a love of music. How happy my husband would have been if it had turned out the other way around, but this is who they are. I love them all the more for it.'"

Mother turned a page of the household book at random. Tears were streaming down her cheeks, which were frozen to ice by the time they reached her chin.

"'The twenty-seventh of June, in the year of our Lord 1678,'" Mother read out. "'I love my children so very, very much.'"

What was happening to Father Winter? For he was groaning and, as Thomasina watched, she saw his crown of icicles melt, while his body started to collapse, slipping into the ice. His face began to distort beyond anything recognizable.

"No!" he howled, ice-bright eyes spinning out of control. His white hands melted as he clutched at his crown. Transfixed, Thomasina watched as Father Winter hunched into himself, falling onto the frozen river until there was nothing there, aside from a scattering of fresh snow on the ice.

All was silent.

And Thomasina stared at her mother, unable to believe what she'd done.

30

The Frost Folk's Farewell

Mother was bent double in the middle of the ice, wheezing in short, sharp gasps. Beside her, the household book lay facedown on the river. Loose leaves fluttered in the wind, some pages flickering into the black abyss.

Thomasina didn't understand what had just happened, so she did the only thing that made sense to her. Sensing that Father Winter's bonds over her had lifted, she stood up, walked over and started picking the papers up, squashing them back into the book at random and feeling the stitching of the spine fray and unravel.

Eventually, Mother's shallow breathing subsided. She got to her feet, looking weary. Her long gray hair was tousled over her face, sticking to her forehead and neck. Tears were streaming down her wind-flushed cheeks, crystallizing into frost, making her resemble one of the—

"The Frost Folk!" Thomasina gasped. Had the Frost Folk suffered the same fate as Father Winter? Would all that would be left of them be fresh snow on the ice, too? She could hardly bear to think of it.

She turned around—and her heart thudded with relief as she saw the sparkling figures dotted around the River Thames were still there. There was something different about them now, though. They were smiling at her, but sadly. But at least they were still there, still the same figures she'd danced with, who'd watched over her the nights she'd visited the Other Frost Fair.

She was too entranced to notice at first that some of them were transforming, because a mesmerizing scene was occurring before her eyes. It was as if the tents of the Other Frost Fair were being consumed by an unseen fire, catching light from an invisible flame that licked around them. The flaps of canvas sagged and folded in on themselves, split with a brilliant blue glow. Before they fell away, shreds of them were cast up into the sky in a silver mist, until all the tents from the Other Frost Fair up and down the river were razed to the ground.

The Frost Folk watched Thomasina in the still of the night, their white eyes fixed on her as she gaped.

She caught a flicker of movement out of the corner of her eye.

The little girl with a hoop and stick who she'd seen on her first visit to the Other Frost Fair was walking toward her and stopped a few feet away. Her teeth glittered in the moonlight as her frosted-over eyes sparkled.

Another figure joined her, taking her hand. It was an older girl, who had a silver locket hanging around her neck. Mary.

Was it possible for Frost Folk to cry? Because it seemed that was what the older girl was doing. Thomasina saw silver icicles drip down the side of her face, but as the Frost girl who used to be Mary looked at her, a half smile danced on her lips. Amazed, Thomasina watched as her hair transformed from ice-white to strawberry blonde strands, the half-moon birthmark above her lip blossomed into a beautiful purple hue, and a girl made of flesh and bone, instead of ice, appeared before her, beaming.

"Thank you, Thomasina," Mary whispered. "You and your mother saved my life—saved all of us—from Father Winter."

Mary turned and hugged the little girl next to her, who—Thomasina realized—was also becoming flesh and blood once more, her icy strands of hair turning black and a flush creeping into her cheeks. Then the girls both stepped over an invisible boundary to stand on the side of the living, facing what remained of the Other Frost Fair.

Hunched over in the mist, a Gray Cloak stepped forward next and lowered his hood. Though his skin was shimmering silver and his eyes were cracked and white, Thomasina knew it was Father. There were still markings on his body that Father Winter hadn't been able to erase; silvery calluses still adorned his hands, the charm placed upon him not quite enough to take them away. His shoulders sloped in the same way that Arthur's had. And the familiar deep groove that marked his forehead was highlighted in sharp blue icicles on his face.

He looked at Thomasina and then at Mother, his eyes roving over their faces as if seeing them for the first time, and sapphire-colored crystals filled his ice-white eyes. Thomasina realized that, like Mary's, even Father's tears were enchanted.

"I saw you, didn't I?" she whispered. "Outside the shop, when I was with Miss Maplethorpe. You were the Gray Cloak watching me."

Father nodded slowly.

"I was trying to warn you," he said. "About Father Winter's plan to turn you into one of his Frost Folk. But his enchantments were too powerful for me to overcome. I couldn't walk farther than where I was standing."

"If you were a Gray Cloak," Thomasina said softly, "then you must have been a sad soul first."

Father pursed his frosted-over lips.

"I hadn't realized how much everything hurt inside," he said, pain flashing across his snowflake-covered face. "When Arthur died. I didn't talk to anyone about it—didn't feel like I *could* talk to anyone about it. You'd just lost your brother, and your mother . . . grew ill. I didn't want to burden either of you. Not when we were all suffering and grieving Arthur in our separate ways. I thought . . . I thought it was my duty *not* to talk about it."

He looked over to Mother, whose eyes were fixed on him.

"I just kept it inside," he said, his voice cracking. "And I didn't mean to hurt you both, but I know now that I did."

"You never spoke about Arthur," Thomasina said. "Ever. I didn't think you still thought about him, until I came across the jumble of his things in the shop. And you so rarely spoke to me. Or to Mother."

Father nodded. "I didn't know what to say," he said. "I didn't know how to *be*. It's been"—he swallowed, and despite the fact he was made of ice, his voice sounded reassuringly like himself—"so hard. All these years . . . without him. I kept thinking about him and one day a couple of Gray Cloaks started drawing me toward the river. I visited again and again . . . until Father Winter drained me and trapped me on the ice.

"I'm so sorry, Thomasina. And I'm sorry, too, Rosanna,"

he said, looking at his wife.

Thomasina's throat was too full with emotion to speak.

"I never dreamed that charlatan Dr. Silsworth would behave the way he did," Father said, hanging his head. "Believe me. I wanted only for you to be cured, Rosanna. By the time I realized what Dr. Silsworth intended to do, and the kind of man he was, it was too late. Father Winter turned me into a Gray Cloak before I had the chance to protect you both."

Beside Thomasina, Mother gave a deep, weary sigh.

"Losing Arthur . . . it changed me," Father admitted to them both. "I know it will take time for you both to forgive me for everything I've done, but I truly mean it when I say, I'm sorry."

Thomasina and her mother nodded.

It was Father's turn to transform into flesh and bone now. Thomasina watched as his gray eyes, like a misty London morning, returned; she saw the blue icicles turn into a pink groove on his forehead, and the rest of the snowflakes melt into his skin, which flushed pale pink once more. Father strode over the invisible boundary, to join Mary and the little girl and Thomasina and Mother.

Somewhere on Thomasina's left, she heard a soft snuffling sound. The Frost Bear who'd comforted her on her walk there, and who'd brought Mother to her rescue—the Frost

Bear who'd been treated so badly by the circus ringmaster at the Frost Fair—had come back to her. He pressed his nose into her palm, gazing up at her with ice-white eyes as he gave her a slow blink. She was so close she could see the moonlight illuminating every strand of crystal fur.

"Thank you, Bear," Thomasina whispered. She knew he understood her in his own way; knew he loved her as she loved him, in a raw, animal way she couldn't describe.

She expected the Frost Bear's fur to change into a brown, shaggy mass once more, but she was surprised to find it didn't. Instead, the Frost Bear pressed his icy nose into her hand, gave her a final, slow blink, and gamboled away, his soft footsteps thudding into the scattering of fresh snow that was all that now remained of Father Winter. The bear disappeared into the night, until she couldn't hear his paws running on the ice anymore. She wondered why he hadn't changed back into the creature he'd been before. . . .

More sights on the river distracted her. More Frost Folk were transforming. She saw their dazzling gray cloaks, white shifts, and silver togas were turning brown and red, and snowflakes were melting into skin so that flesh appeared once more. Entire families, fully transformed back to who they'd been before Father Winter's enchantment had taken hold, were crying and hugging each other, waving their thanks to Thomasina and Mother before hurrying off the frozen river and onto solid ground once more, to resume their lives. And many of the Frost Beasts, too, were changing, including four horses that Thomasina realized were the team from the coachman's carriage; they cantered away together into the night with the coachman riding on one of their backs.

"Why aren't all the Frost Folk changing back?" Thomasina whispered to herself, gazing at the hundreds of others on the ice.

But the answer came to her as quickly as she'd asked it. The Frost Folk who hadn't changed back must have been people who lived decades, if not centuries, before. If they hadn't been enchanted by Father Winter, they'd already be long dead. These were the people who were still made entirely of ice, who were now waving at her, or curtsying, or doffing their hats, everyone from old men to young children giving great, gusty whoops, the absence of mist coming from their mouths betraying their magical selves. Though they'd been released from their bond of servitude to Father Winter, they were still frozen in time; memories of who they'd been on earth when they'd been alive; their skin still iced over with snowflakes. Thomasina's heart felt like it would burst, but she realized that they were starting to turn away and walk up the river, away from her and Mother, their silvery shadows flickering in the moonlight. Wherever they were going, Thomasina realized she'd never see them again.

Thomasina swept her gaze over the scene. All that was left of the Other Frost Fair's tents and stalls were the snow-white poles that had once propped them up. As she and Mother watched, these silvery props toppled and crashed to the ice below, like Father Winter had done, creating little hillocks of snow on the frozen river.

They were all that was left of the Other Frost Fair.

31

Mother's Nightmares

"This is amazing!" said a voice behind her that Thomasina recognized—Anne's.

Thomasina whirled around. Her mouth fell open as she saw the dumbfounded looks on Anne's and Henry's faces that she was sure mirrored her own. They were standing behind her, gazing at the mounds of glittering snow that had once formed the tents of the Other Frost Fair.

"That was . . . that was incredible!" Henry shivered.

Thomasina stared at them, her mind a mixture of wonder at the events of this strangest of nights and growing shame at her earlier outburst at them for letting Dr. Silsworth take Mother away to Bedlam. Anne and Henry grinned shyly at her in the pale moonlight, slivers of silver from the stars above freckling their cheeks. Thomasina didn't know how long they'd been there, and she couldn't really explain much of what she'd just witnessed, but she realized she was hungry to know more.

She looked back at her mother. How had she gotten there? "Mother . . ." she began, cautiously, "how did you escape from Dr. Silsworth? Did the Frost Bear rescue you?"

Mother tried to speak, but her teeth chattered so much Thomasina couldn't hear her. She reached around her neck and felt for the clasp of her snowflake necklace. It opened with a gentle click.

"Wear this, Mother," she said. "It'll stop the cold. Here, let me fasten it for you."

Thomasina clipped the necklace around her mother's neck. She was surprised to find that, although she herself no longer wore the charm around her own neck, she didn't feel cold, as she'd expected she might.

"Better?" she said, and Mother nodded.

Thomasina was aware of some movement and murmuring behind her, but she didn't turn around. She'd waited years to see and hear Mother like this again, and she wasn't prepared to let the chance slip away now.

"Tell me what happened," Thomasina urged.

Mother swallowed. "The coach stopped during the journey, a few minutes after we'd set off. The door swung open, and a silver girl with white eyes got in. She frightened Dr. Silsworth so much he let me go."

"A silver girl with white eyes?" Thomasina said.

"Yes. Your friends"—she indicated Anne and Henry—"were with her. And they were riding"—she swallowed—"on the huge white bear you saw just now."

Anne stepped forward and smiled.

"The silver girl with white eyes was Mary," she explained, "Henry's friend—the maid who used to work in his building. When Henry and I were walking away from Burgess & Son's, Mary and the Frost Bear found us. I was scared, but . . ."

"I recognized the Frost Bear as the bear who'd helped us before, Thomasina," said Henry, taking up the story. "And the Frost Bear and Mary were jolly helpful. Mary said we'd have to go on a rescue mission to save your mother, in the hope that she'd save you. So Anne and I hopped on the Frost Bear's back and, well, off we went. We scared Dr. Silsworth half to death and freed your mother from the coach. There wasn't enough room on Bear's back for all of us, and your mother insisted she had to go to the river at once, so the Frost Bear brought her here first, then came back for us. We arrived just in time to see Father Winter collapsing."

"Thank you," Thomasina said to them awkwardly. "And I'm—I'm sorry for shouting at you both earlier."

"Thanks," Henry said cheerfully. "We all lose our temper from time to time."

"It wasn't very nice to slam the door in our faces," Anne said.

Thomasina nodded. "I'm really sorry," she said, and after a few moments, Anne nodded.

"It's understandable you were upset," she said gently. "I might have behaved the same. No harm done."

"One thing doesn't make sense to me," Thomasina said. "Mother, how did you know what to do when the Frost Bear brought you here to the frozen river?"

Mother bit her lip.

"I've had nightmares," she said, "for weeks now, about the same thing." Her voice sounded creaky, like unoiled wheels or an old chair being sat upon. Thomasina wasn't surprised by this. After all, Mother hadn't used her voice properly for years.

"Nightmares about what?" she asked.

"About you being in danger," Mother replied. "In my dreams, I saw people dressed in white and blue, with snow-flakes on their cheeks, telling me your soul was in peril. I didn't know what they meant, but I was given a final vision tonight. I was told you'd be lured to the river, and that you were in the clutches of an evil creature . . . I was told to follow you and read my household book to this creature to save your life. They said you'd have the book with you, here on the ice."

Something rustled behind Thomasina, and she looked around at last. Inigo gave her a tired smile. He looked dread-ful. Gaunt and drooping, he reminded her of an old, stuffed doll coming apart at the seams.

"I must apologize, Mrs. Burgess," he said to Mother. His voice had changed. It slid around more than ever, as if he were losing the ability to speak. "What you saw weren't nightmares. I sent Frost Folk to visit you, night after night, to warn you what was going on."

"And I'd heard you talking about the Other Frost Fair in our bedroom," Mother said. "So I knew there was some truth to what I saw in my dreams."

"Why did you make the Frost Folk visit Mother?" Thomasina asked Inigo.

"It was the only way I could think of to save you," he said. "I was under an enchantment from Father Winter, which meant I couldn't tell you directly anything about how to destroy him, or who I used to be. If I did, I'd be summoned back to the river and punished. So I decided to drop hints and give you clues about what you should do, and I've been fading away ever since I started trying to help you. But at our last meeting, when I told you to make Father Winter come into contact with your beloved item, I was finally recalled to the river for punishment."

"You influenced everyone around me at the Other Frost Fair, too," Thomasina breathed. "You made sure the Frost Folk showed me how strange everything was, only speaking the lines you told them to say."

"Correct. I also sent them to Henry, in the hope he'd tell you about me, his great-grandfather Sir Inigo Lawley, and I had just enough power to influence one of the Frost Beasts to help you when you needed it. I chose the Frost Bear, as you'd already seen him on the river being dragged along in front of the ringmaster. The bear was eager to help you. I hoped seeing him would jog your memory."

"But . . . all that was so dangerous. You took a huge risk," Thomasina said, shaking her head. "You could have been caught by Father Winter!"

"Yes," Inigo said, stumbling on the ice and steadying himself. "But I thought it was my only chance of freeing you—and thereby freeing the Frost Folk in turn."

Thomasina's head was spinning.

"I thought you told me that the sad soul's beloved object had to touch Father Winter," she said, "but Mother just read passages from her diary aloud to him. The book didn't touch him. I was going to throw it at him," she explained to Mother.

"Ah, but it cost your mother great pain to comb through her old memories," Inigo said gently. "Her household book, with all the memories it contained within, wasn't just your beloved object, Miss Burgess. It was your mother's as well. And the love within those pages, once read aloud, was enough to destroy Father Winter. As you will have heard, she has so much love for you and Arthur."

Tears pricked at Thomasina's eyes. She looked at Mother, who was standing a little taller, then turned back to Inigo.

"What made you want to help me in the first place?" she said softly.

Inigo hung his head.

"I'd never been commanded to use my powers in this way before," he confessed. "This winter, for the first time, Father Winter asked me to find him a sad soul with more misery than any other. And I found . . . you. I tried to harden my heart against you, but when I saw how much you loved your brother, and how much you were willing to risk to bring him back to life, I knew that I didn't want you to change into one of the Frost Folk. I resolved to try and help you as much as I could."

Thomasina pursed her lips and nodded.

"What happens now, Inigo?" she said after a pause. "Where are the Frost Folk? I mean—the ones who lived a long time ago, the ones who didn't change?"

"I believe, my dear, that they've been allowed to rest at last," Inigo said. "They've passed on. They're no longer puppets at the mercy of either my or Father Winter's bidding, now that he's been destroyed."

"So . . . there aren't going to be any more Other Frost Fairs ever again?"

"I don't think so, no," he replied.

She nodded.

"And why are you still here?" she asked. "Why haven't you vanished as well? Not that I'm not happy to see you," she added, and saw the ghost of a grin flicker on his face.

Inigo nodded. He seemed to be finding it hard to balance.

"Father Winter, in binding my soul to his, ended up transferring a little of his powers to me," he whispered. "So I could enchant the Gray Cloaks and Frost Folk to do my bidding. I still have that power left now, and am keeping myself here because of it."

"And Father Winter's gone? Forever?" she whispered.

"Yes," Inigo said. "I can feel it in my bones . . . except, as my bones are made of ice and don't really feel," he added as an afterthought, "my theory may not be entirely accurate. But I feel it in my heart—wherever my heart used to be— that Father Winter's truly gone."

A light breeze ruffled her hair. Thomasina looked into Mother's moss-green eyes and saw Arthur staring back at her.

"Thomasina," Mother said, and Thomasina shivered to hear herself addressed by name by someone she loved so much after such a long time. "Can you forgive me for not being there for you when you needed me most?"

Thomasina frowned. "There isn't anything to forgive you for," she said.

"But I haven't been . . . myself," Mother said. "For so

many years—since Arthur died. I'm still not fully who I was before his death. I don't think I'll ever be."

"It's all right," Thomasina said, grasping one of Mother's thin hands. "You don't have to be the same as you always were. People change when things happen to them. It isn't a bad thing."

"I lost my son," Mother said, her voice cracked with grief. "If I'd been there when he couldn't breathe, maybe he wouldn't have died. . . ."

"No," Thomasina whispered. "You couldn't have helped him. None of us could have. Anne works at an apothecary's and told me herself." She realized she believed her own words. "We wouldn't have been able to save him."

Mother nodded and closed her eyes.

"At least I was able to help one of my children," she said. "My precious daughter."

Pain burned in Thomasina's throat and chest, but it wasn't an entirely terrible feeling. There was a good feeling in there, mixed up with all the fire.

"Why did I get my memories of Arthur back tonight, Inigo?" she asked.

"Because Father Winter's powers—which included my own enchantments in making you forget about Arthur—were weakened, once I told you how to defeat him," Inigo said softly. "Fortunately, Father Winter didn't realize this himself."

"Thomasina—look!" Anne cried. "The silver snowflakes on your hands have all disappeared!"

Thomasina gasped and checked. It was true—everything was gone. Her hands were reassuringly pink-tinged and warmer than they'd been in weeks.

"You're no longer under any power of Father Winter's," Inigo said, beaming.

Thomasina smiled, and Mother stepped up and gave her a hug. Thomasina had missed this so much, and she hadn't even realized it. Tears pricked her eyes as she lost herself in the embrace, holding on to Mother tightly.

"Thank you," she whispered. "For helping save me."

Mother chuckled through happy tears.

"Thank you," she said. "For helping save *me*."

After Thomasina broke apart from Mother's hug, she watched as Mother and Father gave each other a small, awkward hug, too.

"So . . . you're my ancestor?" she heard Henry say, and she looked around and noticed that he and Inigo were examining each other.

"I see you've inherited my hair," Inigo said affectionately, reaching out and rumpling Henry's hair, wincing suddenly as he did so. Thomasina had no doubt that it was costing Inigo a great deal of energy to perform even this simple gesture.

"Don't worry, it'll get flatter as you grow up," he said. "I take it that it was you who discovered the bundle of parchment I'd left hidden in the fireplace at Lawley Hall," he said.

Henry blushed. His face was stained dark silver by the moonlight, so just at that moment he might very well have been one of the Frost Folk.

"Yes," Henry replied, "but I couldn't have done it without Thomasina's help. And Anne was so brilliant in searching for Thomasina's beloved object, too," he said as Anne stepped forward.

Inigo looked at Thomasina, Anne, and Henry with a sad smile, his bright-blue eyes glittering with an emotion Thomasina couldn't quite identify.

"You've all worked so hard," he said softly. "And done so well. I'm so very proud of every one of you."

Something painful flickered inside Thomasina's chest. She tore her gaze away from Inigo, not knowing what to say, and saw that her friends were shivering.

"We should all get off the ice," Thomasina said. "Come with us, Inigo."

Inigo nodded. They walked over the ice, which didn't feel as steady as it had over the past few weeks, and up the narrow, rickety lanes that led home. Thomasina couldn't help noticing that Inigo was lagging behind.

She unlocked the door of Burgess & Son's and ush-
ered Mother, Father, Henry, and Anne inside. They found
Shadow snoozing on the workroom table with a very round
belly. A great deal of the cheese pie had been eaten, and he
gave a sleepy, contented purr when Thomasina stroked him.
She locked the back door.

"I need to do something first," she said to the four of
them. "I won't be long."

She went to the front door, opened it again, and went out
into the street, locking it behind her.

Inigo was waiting for her, the moonlight and stars illuminating his strange, sharp cheekbones, the jewels in his
doublet twinkling against the dark. They both knew what
was going to happen. They knew that someone was waiting
for them, as quiet as a secret.

32

Arthur

Thomasina and Inigo walked together along a series of narrow, cobbled streets lined with increasingly gnarled buildings. The moon, partially obscured by dusky clouds, illuminated the city, casting shadows at odd angles to their left and right. Glimmers of London flashed past them like crooked smiles: two beams belonging to a high-storied house were dusted in moonshine, while a hat shop's sign was lit up against the dark hulk of the building it swung from, ice lacing over its surface like filigree silver. This ghostly landscape seemed an almost sacred scene for Thomasina, as if a secret world were awakening just for her. She knew she was glimpsing a side of the city she'd never see again.

Enough had passed between her and Inigo that they didn't have to fill the silence with talk. Thomasina was glad. Despite Mother's triumph over Father Winter, there was only one person she could think about.

She didn't slip over the ice and snow-slush, nor did she stumble over the cobblestones as she and Inigo walked, despite the darkness. She suspected Inigo was making the journey as smooth as possible for her. When she glanced at him, she saw his brow furrow as he chanted unknown spells under his breath.

With only the faint hoot of a barn owl for company, they approached St. Bartholomew's Church, its nave hunched in sleep. Thomasina's breath hitched in her throat. Piercing cold seeped through her skin as she twisted the handle of the iron gate that led to the graveyard.

Inigo broke the silence between them.

"Do you know where he . . . ?"

Thomasina nodded. She knew where Arthur was buried. She'd watched Father visit him sometimes, after Sunday services ended.

The half-shrouded moon pearled several headstones around the graveyard as she walked on ahead of Inigo. It felt like a peaceful place here. Frosted winter roses curled around several names, petals peeking up at them both as they passed.

Under a slender silver birch tree in the corner of the churchyard nestled a small headstone bearing Arthur's name. Father must have spent a huge sum of money to have his grief carved into a monument like this that would stand the test of time. Here was a solid testament to how much Father and Mother loved their son.

Beside her, Inigo spoke.

"I'm trying to conjure Arthur up," he said. "I really am. But I can't. I'm so sorry, Thomasina. I've failed you."

Thomasina looked at him and saw silver tears dripping down his cheeks as he hung his head. In the moonlight, Thomasina realized his beautiful velvet doublet now looked worn and faded, his fine, silver beard straggly and limp, and his knees bent inward so his stoop was an old man's. The whole effect made him look even more like a worn-out doll that no one wanted anymore. Thomasina saw his shoulders heave and realized he was sobbing.

"I'm so sorry," Inigo choked. "I thought . . . I thought at first that I could make you an empty promise before helping Father Winter take you. But when I saw you try to defeat Father Winter, I thought, if we could vanquish him, then I'd be able to cast whatever magic I wanted and bring your brother back to life. But now . . . now I realize I still can't do it."

Thomasina took a deep breath, then reached out and patted Inigo's arm. The bones beneath his cloak felt delicate, as if he'd break into pieces at any moment. His presence comforted her, even though he was wasting away.

"It's all right, Inigo," she said softly. "I'd always wondered whether you could do it—but I think, for a while now, I've accepted it's impossible, even though you're free from Father Winter's power. I don't think . . ." She trailed off and swallowed. "I don't think the dead can *ever* be brought back to life."

She pitied Inigo—he looked so miserable and tortured, and casting her eye around the graveyard, an idea occurred to her.

"There's something you can do to help me, though," she said. Inigo raised his head from his hands, his tear-filled, unearthly eyes staring into hers.

"Anything," he said hoarsely.

"Conjure up a memory for me," she whispered, watching as his face tautened. "I know you've learned enough about Arthur through taking away my memories of him. It's the one memory I try not to think of, because it's too painful. But I know you've seen it. Please—just try."

Inigo gave a slow nod and licked his lips nervously.

Around her, the graveyard was very still; not even the rustle of a mouse or the creak of a tree in the wind disturbed their peace in the still of the night air.

"Close your eyes," Inigo muttered. "I'll try my hardest to make this happen."

"Thank you," she breathed, staring at Arthur's headstone. "And . . . Inigo?"

"Yes?" His voice sounded so weary, she thought.

"You're a different man from the one you were seventy years ago. Sir Inigo Lawley would have done nothing to save Mother and me. But you did. You were there for us even when we had no hope left. The Inigo I know tries his best for the people he cares about."

Inigo didn't speak, but something stirred, and she felt a gust of wind sweep over her face. She took a deep breath, closing her eyes.

She heard Inigo mutter a strange, silvery incantation under his breath, and felt herself slipping back through time. . . . She allowed herself to give in to the dream that had tormented her for years as she traveled

down

down

down.

"*Thomasina!*"

Her brother's voice, eager and bright, sliced through her like a knife, making her knees buckle.

Thomasina had expected Inigo to show her the memory exactly as it had been the night Arthur had died. She found, however, she was watching from a distance as Arthur ran toward a girl she realized, with a jolt in her stomach, was her younger, nine-year-old self.

"*Stop running!*" his memory echoed, bouncing off the walls.

She saw her younger self spit a sharp retort and felt a familiar twist in her insides; heard the echoes of her taunt from the buildings around them that she'd tried to erase for so long.

Soon, she saw her brother crumple to the ground. Her younger self ran to the apothecary's that was now Hawke's, then out of sight, then she reappeared with a couple of staggering men who stood around her brother, their mouths agape.

"I'm sorry," Thomasina whispered to Arthur as he died, and her younger self screamed with love and rage. "I'm so sorry I couldn't help you, but I tried my best."

She expected the memory to end there, but it continued, past Arthur's death. Thomasina's memory had blotted out what happened next, until now. She saw the men from the inn carry Arthur's body away, while a girl sobbed in the snow, all alone.

Thomasina couldn't hold back. She walked forward to stand beside the girl and crouched down. Though she knew she could never turn back the clock and change how she'd felt in the years since Arthur had died, she could change how she felt now.

Slowly, she reached out and wiped away the younger

Thomasina's tears. The little girl kept crying. Thomasina didn't know what else to do, so she encircled the girl in her arms, feeling her sob more than ever.

Eventually, the girl's shudders subsided, and she detached herself from Thomasina, rubbing her knuckles into her eyes. She must be so tired, Thomasina realized. I'm so tired of carrying this guilt around with me all the time, after all.

"Look at me," she said. The girl looked up, tears still dripping down her cheeks. "This guilt has eaten up your life for years now. All the shame that you've—that we've—felt . . . it's destroying us."

The girl blinked, wiping snot from her nose. Thomasina knew then that, although Arthur's death would never be something she'd completely heal from, her soothing words had been a comfort and calmed the girl down.

"You're not a bad person," she whispered. "You didn't cause Arthur's death. No one did. It was just bad luck. You know that now, don't you?"

The girl didn't say anything, but looked at her, mouth puckered.

"You might not know that yet," Thomasina said. "But I do. And I'll keep telling you if you forget."

Her younger self looked up at her, and Thomasina realized the face staring at hers was Arthur's. There was so much about the girl's features that reminded her of her brother.

They both had red-robin cheeks and their mouths were shaped the same, and while Arthur had inherited Mother's cheekbones and eyes and Thomasina hadn't, their chins were almost identical.

Perhaps that's why Father didn't want to look at me or talk to me much, Thomasina realized. Arthur and I look so similar. Father couldn't bear being reminded of him.

"You take care of yourself now," Thomasina said. She wanted to hug the girl again, but, without a word, her younger self turned and trudged off through the snow. Thomasina felt something clear in her head, and all she saw was white mist surrounding her.

When she opened her eyes, she was alone. Inigo had vanished. She somehow knew that, like her, he'd forgiven himself at last, and this meant he was no longer tied to this world.

Thomasina bent down to Arthur's headstone, smoothed away a patch of ice creeping over the mottled gray, and kissed it.

"I love you, Arthur," she whispered. "I'm going to start living for both of us now. I owe it to you to do that."

The patch of ground in front of Arthur's headstone was bare. Thomasina resolved to plant snowdrops there the next chance she had. She got up, turned, and walked out of the churchyard, closing the gate behind her. She'd never be afraid of visiting Arthur again. He still needed her, even if he was dead, and she needed him, too. She'd talk to Henry as well about making a proper grave for Inigo, which she resolved she'd visit as often as Arthur's.

"Thank you, Inigo," she whispered as she made her way back home. She walked down Montgomery Street, pausing at the spot where she and Arthur had last been together in life.

I was there for him at the very end, she thought. *He knew I loved him.* Somewhere amid the sadness, something inside her heart shifted, as if the shards of ice resting dormant within her had melted into smaller pieces. She looked up at the vast black sky above and thought of all the people, generations before her time, who'd seen the same sky as she had, had loved and lost like she had, and had felt the bitter cold as she did now, biting against her cheeks. She wondered when the next frost like this would come, and who'd be there to see it.

33

Burgess & Hawke's

FIVE MONTHS LATER

The summer heat! It brought a flush to every face, made beads of sweat slick down every spine, and transformed the capital's colors from startling silver and piercing white to tawny brown and faded brick.

Southwark's roads teemed with every street seller imaginable. Butchers, bakers, and candlestick makers carried on their businesses as usual, beaming at the surging crowd around them, while weavers, palm readers, hatters, and needle makers called out to passersby, advertising their wares, and musicians played loudly, grinning whenever people tossed coins into their caps.

Several streets away from Raven Lane, in an up-and-coming neighborhood, there was a new shop, bearing a brightly painted sign that read:

BURGESS & HAWKE'S: THE MIRACULOUS SWEETMAKERS

Now that the ice had melted away, more visitors than ever were pouring into London, and the crowd surrounding this shop was so dense it almost blocked the whole street—worlds away from how things had been just five months ago. Nothing, however, compared to the transformation that had taken place inside.

Burgess & Hawke's was crammed full to bursting with appetizing confections. Trays upon trays of sugared flower petals and herbs were stacked in front of the counter, and a smoking cauldron of gooseberry porridge cast out spirals of steam in a corner. Strawberry and rose sponges were piled high at one end (being bought at a very fast rate), while a nearby tray of elderflower cakes proved popular as well and was nearly down to just crumbs. Lining the walls were sweet herbal tonics in brown bottles, and bunches of dried lavender and roses hung from all the beams and shelves, giving the shop's interior a sweet, musky scent.

Thomasina and Anne stood behind the counter, chatting eagerly to customers. Anne wore a sweeping apricot dress, and Thomasina was dressed in sky-blue breeches and a waistcoat. While Anne gave medical advice to a customer, Thomasina laughed with another as she twirled some tasty sweets around in a paper bag, twisting it closed and licking syrup off her thumb.

Meanwhile, a very sleepy Shadow sprawled on a shelf

nearby, watching the customers and giving lazy flicks of his tail to the mice he imagined scuttling behind the paneling. Miss Maplethorpe, who now worked at Burgess & Hawke's as a street seller, bellowed to the passing crowds, enticing them inside. And any minute Henry would arrive to help, having finished his studying for the day.

Standing a little farther up the street, and unknown to Thomasina and Anne, Mother and Father, together with Anne's uncle, Elijah Hawke, and Anne's parents, Samuel and Agatha Hawke, had traveled to watch them trade that day. All five of them beamed with pride as they took in the popularity of the new shop. Having helped the girls find loans across London to start up their business together, they could never have dreamed Thomasina and Anne would be so successful so early.

The bells of St. Bartholomew's Church sang out, and Thomasina looked up, knowing that somewhere, somehow, Arthur, too, was watching everything that was happening in the shop, and rejoicing in all that his sister and her friend had created together. Anne sensed Thomasina's pause, and she lifted her head to listen for a moment, too. The girls grinned at each other before resuming their work, a world sparkling with promise laid out before them.

Acknowledgments

Chloe Seager, my wonderful agent: I feel so lucky to work with you! Thanks also to Vanessa, Georgia, and the Madeleine Milburn Agency.

My editors at HarperCollins: the brilliant Alice Jerman in the US and the incredible Michelle Misra in the UK. I owe you both so much. Thanks also to the superb Clare Vaughn, Caitlin Lonning, Jessie Gang, Catherine Lee, and Renee Harleston in the US, and to Maxine Vee for your enchanting, beautiful cover illustration. Thanks also to the fantastic Tina Mories, Sarah Lough, Sam Stewart, Laure Gysemans, Kate Clarke, Hannah Marshall, and Val Brathwaite in the UK, and to Alex T. Smith for your stunning, magical illustrations.

Booksellers, bloggers, teachers, and readers, for all that you do.

Write Club: Clare, Clive, Emily, Geoffrey, Jenni, Jenny, Kate, Maggie, Max, Richard, and Zoe. LLEWP: Mandy, Mónica, Laura, Lucy, and Sian. Thanks also to my 2022 Author Group for their warmth and support.

Kirsten Stewart-Knight, Catherine Snelson, and Bill Foster for believing in me. Jess, Nancy, and the EH team.

The hospital staff who have helped manage my asthma over the years. Also: Remy, Holly, Luigi, Billie, Ozzy, Rocky.

Family & friends, including: Jonny, Rebekah, Hamish, my school friends, Peter, Alexander, Lawrence, and Duck. Mum and Grandma, for teaching me how to be brave.